Echoes of Appalachia

Denvil Mullins

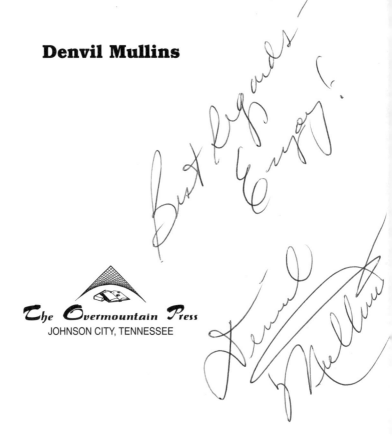

The Overmountain Press
JOHNSON CITY, TENNESSEE

ISBN 1-57072-021-5

1 2 3 4 5 6 7 8 9 0

To my wife, Connie,
for her love, patience, and support.

All of the characters' names and the names of the towns, rivers, creeks, hollows, schools, and churches included in this book are my own fictitious creations.

Introduction

As I go back once more to visit Coaley Creek, the home of my childhood, events of long ago come out to greet me. I can see the many people, and even the animals, who lived in that little community—as vividly today as if it were only yesterday. If I can't go back there in person to reminisce, I can let my mind flow back to that other place and time to select another humorous story to write for you to enjoy.

Humor is always around when I get ready to write about my fond memories, and when I search hard enough I can also find humor in the memories I would just as soon forget. But that is one of the joys of writing: being able to search and choose something funny to write about. If I make someone laugh, I have done one of the greatest things possible. But if I make that person sad, I have done nothing but make him sad. So I try to write what I think will cheer people up.

The Cornfields and their kinfolks, friends, and neighbors of Coaley Creek had fun without half trying. Fun and humor followed them wherever they went. Work could be a lot of fun, as shown in "The Joe-lot Ghost." Bean stringings were work, yet a lot of fun could be had. Many stories were shared by all. Ghost, haint, and witch stories were often the favorites of all stories told.

People may tell you that they don't believe in witches, haints, and ghosts. But if one of those people happens to pass a lonely cemetery on a moonlit night alone, or an abandoned house set back in the shadows with a porch falling down and the windowpanes broken, I'm sure his spine will tingle and the hair on his head will move just a little before his whole body breaks out with a rash of goose pimples. That person's feet will want to move on without an order from the brain, and usually the mind won't reprimand the feet for acting on their own.

Clem and Bart Cornfield and Seldom Seedy could attest to the fact that the Joe-lot Cemetery was a scary, creepy place after they roused the ghosts one night. Tavis Trent was scared by "The Ghost Lights at Isome Gap." The entire population was scared when "The He-witch of Coaley Creek came for a visit.

The Cornfield boys had aspirations to become celebrities like those they saw in the movies. You will enjoy their efforts to perfect bull riding and trapeze acts.

There are many more incidents which I would like to mention, but I would rather you read them for your own enjoyment.

I hope you enjoy this book as much as I have enjoyed writing it.

Table of Contents

Glossary

bait—a huge meal
banty—small breed of chicken
boogers—ghosts or scary things
blackguardin'—using vile language
Brahma—Brahman, a breed of cattle
brattice—material used to ventilate a mine
brud—brother
chickey-diddle—a baby chicken
chop sack—a bag or sack for packing hog or cow feed
chuck—to throw
chuckerhead—copperhead
consumption—tuberculosis
dander—dandruff
dog hole—a coal mine
doty—decaying, as decaying wood
drap—drop
drift mouth—a mine entrance
fer-field—far-field, field at the farthest distance from the
    farmhouse
fox fire—the phosphorescent light given off by rotting wood,
    caused by fungi
fly flit—poison used to kill houseflies
geetherd—numbskull
gimp—to limp around showing pain
gnyammed—chewed noisily with the mouth open
haint—a haunt or ghost
head chuckings—rubbing the head with the knuckles
hen granny—one who gathers eggs and feeds the hens
hog-dollar—silver dollar
hootsie—to give a boost
lunker—a huge fish
milk-gap—a place in a fence, usually in a corner, to milk
    cows
monkeyshine—a mischievous trick
mumble-peg—mumblety-peg; a game of flipping a knife from
    various positions to stick it in the ground; the loser has to

pull a peg out of the ground with his teeth
pert-near—nearly; almost
p'like—play like
poke—a paper bag
pokey dot—polka dot
pokeweed—a tall weed of North America with purple berries and poisonous roots
'rasslers—wrestlers
ragged out—tired; worn out
'sang—ginseng
scuzzing—chiding; tongue-lashing
sea grass—burlap sacking
shag—to move deliberately
shagging around with—hanging out with
signin' a fox—trailing a fox
slurp—to suck food into the mouth noisily
sluve—to laze around; to be sloven
snuffin'—kissing
som'ers—somewheres
sprag—a wooden scotch
sticking beans—pushing beans into the ground with the fingers
'still—a distillery
tater—potato
thunderation—an exclamation of surprise
Toby dreads—laziness
thrash—a childhood disease that affects the teeth
whoopie hide—hide-and-go-seek
yarn—an unbelievable tale

The Dead-horse Jitters

Marn Cornfield hurried along the rough Coaley Creek road, returning from Jenkins, Kentucky, where he had worked five days in the coal mines for Consolidated Coal Company. He had spent five days away from home, boarding with his first cousin Cletus Cornfield. The days and nights had been long and hard for him while he waited to return home to visit with his wife and brood of young 'uns. Unable to buy a car or truck, which would be very handy to drive to and from work, Marn hoped for a time when he could own an automobile or have a job much closer to home. Fifteen miles were a few too many to hoof every single day. He had on occasion walked that distance—for a day at a time, maybe—because there was no one on Coaley Creek who owned an automobile and worked at the mines where he was employed.

That particular night, Marn was wrapped tightly in his Mackinaw coat, heavy wool pants, and long underwear to keep out the biting cold. December had come in blustery and rainy. The weather had grown increasingly colder as the short days and long nights passed.

Christmas was approaching fast, and there would be a white one this year, most likely, for snow had fallen often throughout the month—snow covered the frozen ground right then, creating a white blanket over the countryside, smoothing out the rough places with its softness.

The night was dark and still; a fine dusting of snow fell, nipping and biting at Marn's chilled face. His boots made a crunching sound in the dry snow as he walked briskly along to keep the blood pumping through his body. Although the ground was white, Marn could hardly see anything in front of him. The heavy cloud cover held the darkness close to the ground. Since he had walked that lonely stretch of road so many times after dark, he could almost follow it with his eyes closed—he could have done as well with his eyes closed right then, for he could hardly see where he stepped.

The rapid movement of the man's moving feet sang a frosty song into the night.

A great horned owl called its bass "Who? Who? Who?" into the stillness, echoing from ridgetop to ridgetop, causing chills to run up and then back down Marn's spine, causing goose pimples to pop out over his entire body. Such a lonely sound could not be copied by any other animal on earth.

An answering "Who? Who? Who?" from the opposite ridgetop disturbed the quiet around the walking man. A small animal ran in front of Marn into the rhododendron bushes beside the road—a rabbit, he figured—causing his heart to leap up into his throat where it almost collided with his dried-out epiglottis. He could hear the little animal's hopping fade deeper into the woods while his own rapidly beating heart settled back down to a normal pulsation.

The five-mile trip from Big Onion Gap to the head of Coaley Creek took Marn about an hour and forty-five minutes to two hours to walk on an ordinary trip to or from town, but the cold night air put the man's body into a faster mode—he was cutting the trip, at that rapid pace, to only an hour and a half at the most. He was really picking them up and putting them back down.

Marn walked up the road, approaching the Joe-lot. The place was suspected of being hainted. He thought of the tales told about the boogers and other ghostly things that had been seen there by different people—some very trustworthy, others questionable. He was a very strong-willed man, but the eeriness of the place made him give the little clearing in the woods a close scrutiny. He had never seen anything out of the ordinary there before, but there was always a first time for everything, and tonight could be the first time for him to see something boogerish. He almost skipped along the road to get out of the Joe-lot, finally making it out without seeing or hearing anything.

The Joe-lot Cemetery lay just ahead, posing the next possibility of a vision of some kind.

Marn was unable to put scary thoughts out of his mind as he tried to sneak unnoticed past the rows of silent headstones gracing the white-blanketed final resting place of the dead. The crunch of the snow beneath his heavy work boots seemed to scream to the quietness about him as he tried to tiptoe along. "So far so good," he breathed, letting his breath filter slowly through his teeth.

Just as Marn thought he had it made—had the haints at the Joe-lot Cemetery licked—an apparition seemed to loom right in front of him in the shape of a tall man in the darkness. On approaching the man's position in the road, Marn spoke in a strained but friendly manner.

"Howdy, neighbor," he greeted. "It's a rough night to be out, for man or beast."

A muffled, grunting snort came from the stranger. And where a man once stood, a horse took its place, scaring Marn beyond any fears that he had ever had in his life. He hurried away from the scene—toward the head of the hollow—moving much faster than before he met the apparition in the road.

To make the situation even worse, as Marn hurried up the road, looking back over his shoulder to see if he was being followed, he reached the rail fence marking his property line—sooner than he expected—and fell forward, draping his tall frame over the fence. A pint of peach brandy that had once snuggled deep down in his hip overalls pocket for protection suddenly shot out of its resting place and struck a rock, shattering the glass container into smithereens, the alcoholic liquid melting the fluffy snow on the rock upon contact.

"Bust it all to hog snot!" Marn griped, pushing his hands on the cold ground to try to lift himself up from his precarious position on the fence. "I lost the only courage that I had in that little bottle of brandy."

After several slips of his hands on the damp earth, Marn finally raised to a standing position, letting the blood run back down from the top of his head. Finally gaining control of himself, he sped on home.

At the foot of the hill—just below the henhouse—Marn was met by a sudden movement. Old Bowser had heard the man long before his arrival at the chicken roost and had waited for the arrival of his master.

Marn almost lost his composure when the dog bounded out of nowhere and jumped up to try to lick his master's cold face, striking him square in the chest, knocking him off balance.

"Bust-take-it all to thunderations," Marn yelled, then hugged the frantic dog to his chest, happy that it was only his pet instead of another booger of some sort. "Ol' buddy, you scared the plain ol' tar out of me. But I'm sure glad to see you. I can't see you but I sure can feel you, and you feel real good to me out here in the dark of night. This has been some strange night," he told the faithful hound. "First I seen something back there, and now, you scared the living daylights out of me. I don't know if I can stand anything else or not. I hope things are pleasanter in the house than they are out here—no surprises, I hope."

The presence of the hound soothed the man's disturbed nerves as he walked to the house and mounted the steps to the high front porch.

The light from the smoke-blackened globe of an oil lamp winked at the darkness engulfing the house. The light rays were reflected by the windowpanes on the front porch. Marn could see Vann sitting in front of the big fireplace, reading her King James Version of the Holy Bible. The sight made Marn's heart bubble with happiness to be home at last. He gently tapped once on the door and entered.

Vann looked up, undisturbed by the opening of the door so late at night; she was expecting her man home.

"Howdy, Hon," Marn greeted, whispering to keep from waking the children, who were already in bed, asleep. He took his wife in his arms and kissed her on top of the head. "I ain't snuffed you in so long that I've almost forgot how pleasing it can be. It's real wonderful, I tell you, Hon."

"Thank you for saying that, and snuffing me, too," Vann returned. "It was nice, and it's nice to have you home." She returned the loving hug, gently squeezing Marn's slender waist. She felt a tenseness in that caress.

"It's good to be home," he replied.

"What's wrong with you?" she asked. Then went on. "You act real nervous—like you seen a ghost or something."

"Hon, I believe I did," Marn told her. "And to make things a whole lot worse, Ol' Bowser jumped upon me out there in the dark and scared me half to death."

"What did you see that scared you so bad?" Vann asked.

"You ain't gonna believe this, but I'm telling it for the Gospel truth, Hon," Marn began. "I was coming along the road lickety-split, walking fast to keep my blood pumping good, when I met a feller down there at the Joe-lot Cemetery. I was just this side of the gate leading into the graveyard when I met the stranger standing by the edge of the road. When I come up abreast of him and spoke to him real friendly, he suddenly changed into a horse, standing right there in front of me as big as you please. Hon, that liked to've scared me to death right there in the middle of the road. I thought sure I was gonna meet my Maker—ship out of here in a hurry. I ain't never seen anything like that in my life. I know that I laugh and poke fun at else folks that say that they see such things as that, but, Hon, what happened just down the road from here has made a believer out of me. I'm sure that there's haints and ghosts out there in the night."

Marn sat down in a chair in front of the fireplace and began to unlace his high-top boots, which reached to his knees.

"Are you sure that you really saw something and didn't just 'vision it?" Vann questioned. "Are you sure that you didn't stop som'ers and get something to drink and nip on it real heavy as you come home?"

"'Pon my honor, Hon!" Marn exclaimed, "I ain't touched a drap tonight. Yeah, I stopped and got a pint of peach brandy at the Man Hole Restaurant as I come through Big Onion Gap, but I didn't take the first nip from the bottle. I dropped it and broke it when I stumbled into the rail fence down at the road and draped myself over the top rail. The bottle slid out of my pocket just as slick as could be when my head was down and my feet was up in the air. Honest! I didn't take the first nip. There was a whole bottle wasted on nothing. It didn't do nothing but melt the snow off of that rock that it hit on. What a waste!"

"I wouldn't say that it was a waste," Vann replied. "You must have seen a vision or dreamed a dream, one. You might be at one of them ages. You know what it says in the Bible about what I just quoted. I was reading that when you come in the house. I'll read it to you," she offered, opening the Bible to the place that she had been reading, marked by a purple ribbon place marker attached to the book.

"I've read it a thousand times if I've read it once," Marn told her. "But go on and read it if it'll make you feel better."

"It ain't that it'll make me feel better. I'm hoping that it'll make you feel a little better," Vann said.

Vann read from Acts 2:17: "'And it shall come to pass in the last days, saith God, I will pour out of my Spirit upon all flesh: and your sons and your daughters shall prophesy, and your young men shall see visions, and your old men shall dream dreams:' That must have been what you were doing as you come along the road," she explained.

"Hon, I'm not in the category that they're writing about," Marn said. "I'm more than a young man, and less than an old man. So I wasn't seeing a vision or dreaming a dream like the Bible is speaking about."

"Marn, you were imagining that it was a man that you seen out there in the night," Vann said, pondering the report that Marn had made about seeing the man turn into a horse right before his eyes. It was very dark, she realized. Things looked differently in the dark—if one could see anything in the dark—she knew.

Marn placed his cold, bare feet as close to the open-hearth fire as he could to let them thaw out before time to go to bed. He continued to think about his experience at the Joe-lot Cemetery as Vann bustled about the kitchen, preparing a snack for Marn to eat. "I've not been drinking, Hon," he called to his wife. "I ain't had a drap to drink all week. I just seen a spook is all, and I've been a real good person. I've tried to be, anyway."

"It can happen to anybody. Come on and eat your snack before it gets cold," she told Marn, placing a plate on the table, along with two pots with warmed-over vegetables and a pot of cooked pork backbone and ribs.

* * * *

"That was a good meal," Marn said, capping the supper off with a glass of cold, sweet milk. "I wish I could have a meal like that ever' night for supper. Cletus' wife, Nervestie, sure don't set a table like you do, Hon. Sometimes I just about have to leave the table before I finish my meal. She ain't as clean with her cooking as she should be."

"Maybe you won't have to put up with that kind of cooking forever," Vann said, patting his shoulder while clearing the dirty dishes from the table. She placed the drinking glass, dinner plate, and flatware in a dishpan sitting ready on the back of the warm cookstove and began to wash them. She would not let the dishes sit dirty overnight. "People don't have to be nasty just to prove that they're poor" was her motto.

"Well, Hon," Marn spoke after several minutes in front of the warm fireplace, letting his supper settle, "I guess we ought to hit the hay and get some rest. I just don't know if I can rest much after my brush with the ghosts and boogers, but I'll try. You can help to protect me against them."

"I'll try. But I don't know how I'll do 'cause I ain't had much experience at fighting boogers and haints," Vann smiled.

"You'll do just fine, I'm sure," Marn told her.

* * * *

The weekend passed more quickly than Marn had

expected. There were so many chores that needed attention that the man could not get all of them done.

"I hate to leave all this work on you, Hon," Marn told his wife as he prepared to leave that Sunday afternoon to go back to work in the mines. "I'd like to stay with you and the young 'uns, but I have to get out there and grind to make a living."

"I know. But me and the young 'uns will make it all right," she sighed. "We know that you've got to work to make a living for us."

Marn hugged each child and snuffed it on top of the head, his way of showing affection, then gripped the doorknob, prepared to leave.

"Don't let the haints get you as you go by the Joe-lot graveyard," Vann joked.

"I'll keep my good eye out for them," Marn laughed. "I can see in the daytime all right. Maybe I can see how that man changed into a horse if he shows up today."

"I believe that it was just your imagination," Vann reminded him.

"Imagination or not, it seemed real to me," Marn shot back. "I'm gonna check that place out real good as I go past it." With that remark he waved good-bye and opened the door, where he was met by a blast of cold air. Pulling his Mackinaw collar up and his cap bill down, he faced the onslaught of the whipping wind.

Marn walked along at a brisk pace to keep as warm as possible. As he approached the Joe-lot Cemetery, he paused to look around the spot where he had seen the apparition two nights before. A thin layer of new snow covered the road, obliterating any evidence of the presence of a horse or man that Friday night.

Marn scraped the snow away, using his boot, searching for tracks in the frozen earth underneath. Faint imprints of a worn horseshoe were there in front of the man, pointing in the direction of the road's edge. Broken twigs and small sprouts bent over gave evidence of the movement of a large animal as it had left the roadway. Checking closer, Marn saw the carcass of a bony horse, covered with a dusting of snow.

"So you're the booger that I saw the other night," Marn chuckled, a little jittery still, remembering his meeting with the horse. "You were standing, looking at me, and that way you looked like a man. And when I come alongside of you, you looked like a horse. Bust-take-it all, that's what happened. You're Charlie Jackson's poor ol' starved nag. You just couldn't take the cold in your starved condition, could you? You just up and expired right on the spot and rolled over the hill to your final resting place. That's a shame, too. I just got the dead-horse jitters, I guess. What's wrong with me? Here I am, talking to a dead horse," he chuckled.

Shaking his head in disbelief, and with his mystery finally solved, Marn went on down the road toward Big Onion Gap.

Ghost Lights at Isome Gap

"That light is still up there on the hill in Barn Holler, just below Isome Gap." Tavis Trent told his wife, Martha, while they sat at the breakfast table that morning. Steaming cathead biscuits and homemade sausage on his plate gave off an appetizing aroma. The man dipped red-eye gravy onto the biscuits and sausages and set the gravy bowl back on a worn crocheted pot holder. He took a sip of hot black coffee and began to talk again. "I've seen that blue-looking light ever' night this week, since I've been walking from the gap where Hurley Watters lets me out of his car."

"What sort of a light is it that you saw?" Martha asked, placing a bowl of fried apples on the stained tablecloth with the rest of the breakfast meal.

"It's just a scary kind of light—a ghostly kind of light, I guess," Tavis mumbled through a mouthful of food. He took another bite of food, then continued, "The thing moves right along with you as you move along."

"Does it follow you all the way home?" Martha asked, curious.

Tavis coughed, then answered, "No. Ever'time I get right at a certain tree, it goes completely out, like blowing out a lamp. Poof! Then it's gone, and I don't see another thing the rest of the way home," Tavis told her.

"That is scary," Martha shivered. She shook her head in wonder. "Do you reckon it's somebody with a light searching for something or going hunting?"

"No, Martha," Tavis stated, coughing again. "If somebody was there, he wasn't very friendly. I spoke to whatever it was and didn't get spoke back to. That's why I believe it's ghost lights. Old people used to see a lot of strange lights in these hollers around here. Your maw used to see 'em all the time, you know."

"Yeah, bless her heart. She used to see a lot of things that other folks couldn't see," Martha remembered. "I've often wondered about that. Why was she doomed to see all them things when she was such a good ol' soul? It's a mystery to me why good folks sees things and the devil-may-care bunch don't ever get pestered by the mysteries of the hainting things out there in the night."

"I can't figure it out, either," Tavis grunted between bites of food. "There's one thing for certain, though. I'm gonna get to the bottom of them mysterious lights up there at Isome Gap."

"It's been dark and rainy ever' night this week," Martha remembered. "Why would anyone be out there in the night, walking in the rain, unless he was hunting."

"I didn't hear any dogs barking or anything like that, and it don't look like a person would hunt in the same spot night after night," Tavis said, "and then poof out of sight like a lamp blowed out. Looks to me like he'd look some'ers else if he couldn't find game there the first night. It's real spooky when you stop and think about it."

"Did you look for tracks where the light poofed out?" Tolley, the eldest son of the Trent family, asked, unable to control his curiosity any longer. "If you just guess about something, you'll never be able to figure it out. You've got to get out there and search for clues like a murder investigator."

"No, Son, I never thought about going to look for tracks. All I thought about was making tracks home," Tavis smiled. "That's a good idea, though."

"After all this rain we've been having, we ought to see tracks if somebody was on the hill with a light," Tolley stated. "I'll go up there and look for you if you want me to. If I don't find any tracks, I'll know that you saw a ghost, Dad."

"We can go up there Saturday morning," Tavis said. "I don't have to work Saturday, and you don't have to go to school. Us working together, we should be able to figure it out."

"I'm all for that, Pap," Tolley agreed. "We can solve this

light mystery once and for all."

"I want to go with you all," Claude said, hoping to go search for clues with his father and brother. "Can I go, Pap? Can I go?"

"Yeah, if you want to," Tavis told him. "We can take the whole family and make an outing of it."

"No, don't let ever'body go along, Pap," Tolley returned. "The whole family will make too much of a mess, walking around where we're to look for clues, mostly tracks. Me and you and Claude will be enough to go the first time. If we can't solve the case, then we'll let the rest have a go at figuring it out."

"Okay, fellers, you all had better get ready to head out of here to school," Martha told the boys, rising. She immediately began clearing the table of its dirty dishes.

"I wish I didn't have to go to school today," Tolley grumbled, rising slowly from the long bench behind the table. "I could go up to Isome Gap and check on them tracks. I don't see why I have to go to school when something so important as the Isome Gap mystery is out there waiting to be solved. If I could solve the case, then I could become a detective and solve big cases. That way I wouldn't have to go to school and get an education. I'd have my career started already."

"You need to go to school anyway," Martha encouraged the boy, smiling pleasantly.

Tolley left the room, grumbling as he went.

"Let's run up to Isome Gap after school today, if we have time, and see if there's any tracks where Pap said he saw that light ever' night this week," Tolley suggested as he and Claude walked along the road to school. "Me and you can figure out what's going on up there. Pap could be telling us about them lights to keep us out of there 'cause somebody's trying to hide a 'still and don't want us young 'uns to know about it. You know how grown-ups are when it comes to making liquor and home brew and stuff like that. They think that children don't know what's going on when they're told that a bear or pant'er or something is running loose at a certain place in the woods. When they start that, I know what's going on and smack-dab where it's going on at. They can't fool me." He kicked a rock and watched it skip into the bushes beside the road.

"Yeah, me too," Claude said. "I know what's going on, too. They must think we're dumb or something." He kicked a rock out of the road, aping his big brother. The rock skipped into the bushes, flushing a sleepy chickadee from its cover in a stunted pine tree.

* * * *

The day passed slowly for Tolley and Claude, but it finally ended, and the boys hurried toward home.

"Do you know exactly where Pap was talking about seeing them lights, Tolley?" Claude asked, hurrying to keep abreast of his brother. "I've been up through there, but I ain't too familiar with that stretch of woods. It's spooky in the daytime, and I'm sure it's spookier at night."

"Yeah, I know that neck of the woods like the back of my hand," Tolley assured Claude. "I've been there a lot. I really don't think he's telling us about them lights just to scare us out of there. That place is as dry as a bowl of popcorn. Nobody could make liquor there without piping the water from the head of the holler. The revenuers wouldn't think about looking there for a 'still, but nobody could afford to run a pipe that far."

A half hour of brisk walking brought the boys to the designated spot—where Tolley thought it was—and after a thorough search of the place, the boys drew the conclusion that their father had wanted them to stay out of the woods. Or maybe there was really a spook loose after all.

Tolley leaned against a dead stub of a beech tree by the path to rest. A piece of bark fell, striking his right foot. He picked the piece of wood up and threw it away. "I don't see any tracks around here. Let's go home."

The brothers hurried home to finish their late chores and to do their homework before dark.

"Mom, we went up to Isome Gap to check out Pap's ghost

lights and couldn't find hide nor hair of any tracks or anything out of the ordinary. We're gonna go back after it gets dark. We want to see them lights and figure out what's causing them to appear," Tolley told his mother excitedly.

"They ain't no *we* in this expedition," Claude stated flatly. "I don't want nothing to do with scary lights after dark. You can go if you want to, Tolley. I'm staying here where it's safe."

"Chicken," Tolley laughed. "You're chicken if you don't go with me."

"You're chicken if you don't go by yourself," Claude challenged. "I want to see the brave man go out in the dark alone and solve the big mystery."

"But you said you'd go with me," Tolley complained. "What changed your mind? Are you afraid to go?"

"Fact of the matter is yeah," Claude admitted. "And I know that you are, too—just as scared as I am."

"I'm not scared to go up there by myself, and I'll prove it," Tolley snapped, irritated with his brother's cowardice. "Right about dark, I'm leaving here. I'll show you that I'm not scared to go alone. And another thing, I won't even take a light. Now stick that in your nose and snort it back out."

"The sun's already gone down behind Isome Gap," Claude told Tolley. "By the time you get up there, if you start right now, it'll be about time for the boogers to start stirring good. Maybe you'll get there in time to see 'em come out of their day hiding places. That should be a first for anybody to see."

"Okay, smarty, I'll start right now," Tolley declared. "It's Friday night, and I don't have to go to school tomorrow. I'll have all the time I need to wait for the booger lights. I'll stay all night if I have to. I can wait for Pap to come in from work and walk back with him. I'll have the mystery solved and can explain it all to him."

"I doubt if it'll take you that long to get up to Isome Gap and back to the house," Claude laughed, rubbing it in on Tolley. "It'll take you about a half hour to walk up there, and about five minutes to run back."

Claude laughed so hard that he almost lost his breath.

"Laugh if you want to," Tolley shot back. "I'll get the last laugh when I solve a mystery that ever'body else is afraid to tackle."

"Brag all you want to," Claude laughed.

"I'm leaving now and I'll see you later on tonight," Tolley said, putting on his light jacket and leaving the room.

Old Feisty bounded upon the porch and jumped up as high as he could, trying to lick Tolley's hand. The dog was ready to go hunting.

"Tie Ol' Feisty for me, Claude," Tolley said. "If he goes along, he might scare the ghost lights away. I want to solve this mystery."

Claude went to the dog and held him by the collar. "Stay with me, Feisty. You might get run over by Tolley when he gets scared and runs back to the house. We won't close the door completely," Claude continued to taunt. "You might run through it when you come racing back scared half to death."

Tolley refused to say anything else. He left the porch and hurried through the open paling-fence gate.

After thirty minutes of fast walking, the boy arrived at the edge of the woods leading up to Isome Gap. He stopped for a few minutes to rest before entering the dark forest. The shadows beneath the heavy-foliaged trees looked dark and grotesque, giving Tolley the chilly willies, causing him to look back toward home. He couldn't go back now. He had committed himself to solving the mystery.

Tolley stood there, the Toby dreads griping his throat and holding his feet to the ground. "What have I got myself into here," he mumbled. "I guess I should have waited till Saturday and let Pap come with me, for moral support."

A rabbit ran out of a thicket, causing the boy's heart to leap into his throat, almost choking him. Beads of sweat popped out on his forehead and slowly flowed into the corners of his eyes, bringing tears to mix with the sweat and then flow together down his face. He wiped his eyes with the backs of his hands and then wiped his hands on his pants legs.

He had tarried long enough—killed enough time—so reluctantly he entered the still forest. After about five minutes of deliberate, slow-paced walking, Tolley saw the ghostly lights straight ahead. "Should I go on or go back home?" he wondered. "I can't let Claude and the rest laugh at me. I can't go back."

The nervous boy walked slowly toward the light. As he moved forward, the light seemed to move toward him, as if it were passing behind trees and then appearing again. As Tolley stopped momentarily, the light followed suit, stopping, too.

"Man, that's spooky!" Tolley groaned, letting the air in his lungs filter through his teeth, making a low whistling sound, adding to his fears.

When Tolley moved—reluctantly—forward again, the light moved directly in front of him. Step by slow step the boy crept on, dreading the meeting with the light, but knowing that he had to finish what he had set out to do. The light no longer moved. It had become stationary, prepared for the showdown, evidently, Tolley figured.

"It's now or never," Tolley shuddered, forcing his feet to move. He crept forward. The light was directly in front of him now, about ten feet away, right against the dead beech stub he had leaned against earlier that evening. As the boy slowly closed the gap between the light and himself, and as he stopped in front of the stub, his feet suddenly slid in the damp earth. Tolley fell headlong into the light, which turned out to be the old beech stub.

Pieces of dead bark covered the boy's head and entire body, falling to the ground all around him, creating an eerie, glowing light.

"Fox fire!" he shouted, relieved, his heart pounding like a grouse drumming. "Nothing but plain ol' fox fire. Wait till Pap hears about this!"

Relieved, but still trembling, Tolley sighed deeply and headed for home in a hurry, but not from fear. He could hardly wait to gloat and brag to Claude about his solving the mystery of the ghost lights at Isome Gap.

* * * *

"I saw the lights again," Tavis told Martha as soon as he got home from work. He coughed a couple of times to clear his throat, spitting over the edge of the porch. "They were brighter than ever," he continued. "I lit my carbide light, and that caused them to vanish. I kept my carbide light burning so they wouldn't come back."

"Pap, I went up there just about dark and solved the mystery," Tolley said, grinning from ear to ear. It wasn't anything but fox fire on that ol' beech stub by the side of the path. I went up there, figured it out, and come on back in no time at all."

"And I let that ol' stub full of fox fire scare me half to death," Tavis chuckled. He shook his head and sat down. He coughed before he leaned over to untie his boots.

"Yeah, Pap, it was fox fire. It takes a little grit in your craw and courage in your spine to figure things out sometimes," Tolley bragged.

Creek Water'll Do

"Roosevelt sure had a good idea when he went and set up this new thing that he calls 'works projects,'" Marn Cornfield told his patient wife late one evening.

The Cornfield family had just finished a wholesome supper, and Marn and Vann were sitting at the table after most of the children had vacated their bench to do the evening chores.

"Yeah, we've been hearing about the creation of jobs for ever'body that ain't got a job," Vann replied, toying with a spoon, turning it around and around on the tabletop by placing her index finger in the bowl and turning it idly, deep thought wrinkles furrowing her brow. "When are these jobs coming to Coaley Creek?"

"I don't know, Hon," Marn spoke. "Soon, I hope, though," he continued. "If the jobs ain't here on Coaley Creek to fix up things here, I'll follow the work anywhere an ever'where it goes, just to make a dollar or two to help get us over the hump in the fight against this thing they call a 'panic.' We need some things other than something to eat—like clothes and shoes."

"Good!" Clem piped up, grinning happily. "I can change my underwear then."

"What are you talking about, Son?" Vann asked.

"Well, I've just got one suit of underwear, and it's got holes in it," Clem replied. "I'd like to get a new suit so I can change."

"I keep your clothes clean and mended," Vann stated flatly. "You don't have to go dirty."

"I know that, Mom," Clem came back. "But I have to go without underwear while you wash mine."

"Well, Son, this 'Hoover's Panic' has got ever'body in a real bad shape," Marn told Clem. "Go on and get your chores done before dark."

"The boy's right, you know," Vann said. "He sure doesn't have much to wear."

"I know it," Marn sighed. "We can't even dress up to go to meetin' on Sunday morning anymore. That don't matter much, though, I guess, since the Lord don't judge us by what we wear. If He judged us that way, I'd vouch to say that the Coaley Creek Old Regular Baptist Church would be pert-near empty ever' Sunday morning, since ever'body about it is out of work and their clothes have worn pretty thin. I just hope that I can be one of the first 'uns to hire onto a job." He stopped talking for a moment, thinking. Then he went on. "Then we can get the children some clothes and shoes. It's about time for school to start again, you know."

"It would be a real caution if you could get hired on to a job here so close to school time and all," Vann hoped. "We could use a few things to get 'em started out in the year. I ain't run out of patching rags yet. I can keep the clothes they have patched up, clean, and decent enough to wear, but it's a never-ending job just to keep their old clothes mended."

"Jobs sure are thin this day and time around here. But Roosevelt's gonna make a big dent in the jobless numbers. He's gonna make a big change real soon," Marn stated, a smile chasing the seriousness from his face.

"Yeah, jobs ain't the only thing that's thin around here," Vann replied, looking at her worn, faded gingham dress, rubbing the thin material. She could see the pink skin of her forearm where the cloth was cigarette-paper thin on the sleeve of her dress.

"That's gonna change soon, I tell you," Marn said, looking apologetically at his pretty wife.

Vann was still beautiful, even though she had borne seven children into the merciless hard times of the era leading up to, and now during, the Great Depression. That radiant beauty made Marn's heart skip a beat as he looked at his woman sitting on the opposite side of that long table.

"We've made it this far, and we can make it a little further, but it would be nice to have some new clothes for the children," Vann dreamed, still turning the spoon around on the table. "It doesn't matter whether I have any new clothes or not. I don't have to impress anybody. I have a husband and a growing family, and that's about all that matters to me. But I do have to admit, a new outfit of clothes would be nice right about now." She smiled a tired smile, raising her eyes to look at her husband. She saw the same tired glimmer of hope in Marn's strong face that haunted the both of them. She felt that maybe she and Marn working together could corner hope somehow and extract from it what they needed so desperately—the chance to strengthen their pride and then pass that same pride on to their children.

"I told you that would change," Marn reassured Vann, interrupting her dreaming. "I'm going down to Big Onion Gap tomorrow and signing up on the WPA. The money will come rolling in then."

"I hope so," Vann replied, still idly turning the spoon around on the table.

"I'm going out to see how the young 'uns are doing with their chores," Marn said, rising from the table, scooting his chair over the rough, uneven, oak floorboards. "They might like a little help from their ol' dad."

"Send Beauty in here to help me with the dishes," Vann called after her departing husband, who waved his hand, an indication that he had heard. "The boys can do the milking and the feeding of the stock on their own. I need Beauty's help with the dishes and things. Tell Dump to be sure to split dry kindling wood tonight. What I had this morning was real doty, and I couldn't get a fire started without pouring a little lamp oil on it to get it to light and burn."

"I'll do it, Hon," Marn responded, leaving the room, letting the screen door close behind him with a resounding bang.

"I heard that we're all gonna get new underwear when you get a payday," Jake said, coming up to the porch where Marn stood looking toward the steep hill behind the house, in deep thought. "Clem told us that we are."

I hope so, Son," Marn smiled, then rubbed Jake's tousled hair.

* * * *

Marn Cornfield walked along the rough road that ran across the mountain from Coaley Creek to Big Onion Gap. He walked with his hands crossed on his lower back, a habit he had formed while working in the mines at Jenkins, Kentucky. The seams of coal were too low to walk upright in the mines, causing the man to bend his tall body forward to keep from bumping his head. His hands on his back balanced his movement while walking deep underground. He carried that habit to the outside world and used it whenever he walked up a steep hill; his hands on his back balanced his bent-over body outside as well.

Marn's mind was far ahead of his body—at Big Onion Gap, in the sign-up office of the WPA. Marn had been instructed, in a letter, to appear at the Big Onion Gap Courthouse to sign up for work. The coal mines were working only a day or two a week, and some weeks no days at all—closed completely. Marn was pleased with the prospect of a chance to work for his family.

Where Coaley Creek and Blue Domer Creek meet to form Bass Creek River, Marn met a young man, also on his way to Big Onion Gap.

"Howdy, young feller," Marn spoke, greeting the stranger. "How's things going with you?" He looked at the young stranger, who had stopped in the road to look closely at Marn, a habit of people meeting for the first time on Coaley Creek.

"Pretty good, I reckon," the stranger replied. "How're you doing?"

"I'm doing about the best you ever saw, if you ain't seen much," Marn returned, chuckling.

"I'm sure you don't have much to complain about then," the fellow said, laughing out loud. "You don't see too many folks that happy this day and time."

"No, you don't," Marn agreed. "Nobody has anything to be

real happy about. Times are real bad with the Hoover's Panic still chewing on us, but Roosevelt's gonna solve all of that. By the way, I'm Marn Cornfield from up on Coaley Creek," Marn said, reaching out to shake hands with the man, changing hands with his lunch pail in order to clasp the young man's hand in greeting. "I ought to've introduced myself sooner but I got to talking on the Panic and how Roosevelt's gonna fix ever'thing so that we can live and I just forgot to. Sorry about that, friend."

"That's okay, Mr. Cornfield," the newcomer answered. "I understand, with your mind on finding work and all. I'm looking..."

"Call me 'Marn.'" He broke a twig from a tree to use as a toothpick and began to chew on it idly.

"Okay, Marn, my name's Dee-Bo Seedy, from down on Less-Than-Perfect Creek," Dee-Bo spoke, introducing himself.

"Which one of the Seedy bunches are you from?" Marn asked, continuing to pick his teeth as he walked along at a brisk pace. "There's three or four clans of the Seedys, and neither one will claim kin to the other. I guess that's the way of about all folks. There's a lot of different Cornfield clans that won't claim kin to one another, and if the truth is known, they're probably thick-blooded kin. Are you any kin to Talmage Seedy and his clan. Good people, Talmage and his bunch is. They can be a little sluvin' at times, but they're okay in the long run."

"I'm Olden Seedy's oldest boy," Dee-Bo said. "I've got one sister older than me," he continued, "and a whole passel of young 'uns under me. I'm old enough to work, so I'm on my way to Big Onion Gap to sign up for work with the other job-less people around here. Talmage Seedy is probably a distant cousin, or something like that, since most ever'body around these parts are kinfolks in some way or the other when you get to checking on your family tree."

"Yeah, I know Olden Seedy," Marn said. "He's a horse trader, ain't he? I've seen him down at the trade grounds at Horseshoe."

"Yeah, that's him to a tee," Dee-Bo chuckled. "He'd ruther trade for an old nag of a horse or mule, then have to feed it to fatten it up so's it can work, than eat when he's about to die of hunger. Mommy gets real aggravated with him, but that don't do much good; he goes ahead and trades when he takes a notion to anyway. He don't let anybody tell him what to do when it comes to horse trading. He's his own boss when it comes to that."

"My paw was the same way: trade without realizing that he was gettin' took all the way to the front door of the poorhouse," Marn remembered. "I guess we're all that way about it," he continued. "By the way, how's your paw doing, anyhow?"

"He's knocking around pretty good," Dee-Bo reported. "He's still trading horses and mules like they're going out of style. He's the one that sent me down to sign up on the WPA.

"Col Modut told us about it and told me to come down to Big Onion Gap, at the courthouse, and sign up to work for him," Dee-Bo said. "He's gonna be an overseer of some sorts on the road projects. He told me that we'd be working up on Big Bull Creek, grading roads, cleaning out ditch lines, and puttin' in drain pipes at the swags and low places. They say that there's more car and truck traffic up that road than any other road around. They figure that truck and car traffic is more important than horse traffic and plain walking is. I'll be driving a team of horses that'll pull a grading scoop. I sure like working with horses."

"I got a letter in the mailbox that told me to come down and sign up if I wanted to work," Marn said. He thought a minute, then continued, "Big Bull Creek? That's just over the hill from where I live. I can walk over there in just a few shakes, easy."

"I live in Happy Holler, over the hill from there in the other direction, on Less-Than-Perfect Creek. It'll be easy for me to get there, too," Dee-Bo said.

The two men talked incessantly, getting better acquainted with each other as they walked along the road to Big Onion Gap. They arrived at the courthouse and found a long line of men lounging around in the courtyard and on the street in front of the building. People sat on the steps to the building, leaving hardly enough room for anyone to walk up or down the steep walkway.

Marn took a seat beside Tavis Trent. "How're you doing, ol' buddy?" Marn asked.

"Just tol'able, I guess," Tavis answered, then coughed and spat in the grass beside the steps. "This coughing problem that I have is getting the best of me. I don't know whether it's something to do with working in the mines, or maybe I've got consumption. Whichever it is, it's awful hard to try to stand up to." He coughed and spat again, his lungs rattling with the congestion caused by the disease.

"Are the mines shut down over in West Virginia where you've been working?" Marn asked, then waited for Tavis to cough and spit again before receiving an answer.

"Naw. I ain't been working at all. They're almost shut down," Tavis came back after spitting into the grass once more. "They're down to a day or two a week, and some weeks they don't even work at all. If they don't pick back up pretty soon, I just don't know what I'll do, what with all my big family. We're about to where it's all I can do to make it from day to day. I don't feel like working with this lung problem." He coughed and spat again. "If things don't pick up pretty soon," he continued, "I'm gonna have to..."

The door to the courthouse opened, interrupting Tavis Trent in mid-sentence.

"Dee-Bo Seedy, Marn Cornfield, and Lilburn Leatherwood," Col Modut barked out in a loud, sharp voice. "I want you three to come with me. We'll head over to Big Bull Creek Junction and start grading that road through the pine flats. Dee-Bo, I want you to drive a team of horses and run the scoop. Marn, do you have any skills of any kind," he asked, turning to face the tall man.

"Whatever you need done, I've got the skills to do it with," Marn came back quickly. "I need a job, so I'm skilled to do anything you want me to do, my friend."

"Lilburn, what about you? What can you do?" Col Modut

asked, grinning, thinking of what Marn Cornfield had said. He knew that everyone needed to work and would be willing and able and skilled at any type of job that was to be done.

"I might not be as good as Marn says he is, but I guess I'll be able to do anything you need done," Lilburn Leatherwood drawled, his eyes darting to the ground, then back to Col Modut's amiable face. "I can use a shovel and pick right up with anybody else there is," he went on. "I'm healthy and hungry. The hungry part will make me work as hard as you want me to, sir."

"Sounds good to me," Col replied. "Well, let's mosey on over to Big Bull Creek and earn our keep, men."

"Mr. Modut," Marn spoke, "would you give Tavis Trent a chance? He needs work real bad. I believe he's hurting worse than I am. He's out of work, and that little place that he has up there on the ridge ain't hardly big enough to whip a cat on, much less raise a crop on for his big family. So he's really hurting. Could you use an extra man on your crew?" Marn watched the foreman's face, hoping to receive a positive reply. "I'll help him all I can on the job to help him pull his weight. He's really not able to do a lot of work, but I admire him for hanging in there and trying. Just give him a chance."

"Well, bring him on with you," the boss said, walking down the steps, trying not to step on anyone in his path. "I'll put him on my gang list in the morning. Hurry up. We need to get over to Big Bull Creek and get in a few hours of work before too late."

"Thanks," Tavis said, coughing harshly and then spitting on the sidewalk. "That was nice of you, Marn."

The four men followed the boss down the sidewalk to an old pickup truck parked near the curb.

"Jump in boys," Col Modut invited. "We'll have to stop by my house and get my team to use to do the grading with. Dee-Bo, you can harness them up and take them over to Big Bull Creek for me. We'll get ever'thing ready for you, and all you'll have to do is hitch them up to the scoop and start grading when you get there. The rest of us will already be working, cleaning the ditches and dressing the banks of the road down."

"Let's me and you and Lilburn ride back here in the back," Marn spoke to Dee-Bo. "Let Tavis ride up there in the front with the boss. He's pretty puny with a lung disease of some kind. Have you noticed how he hacks and spits all of the time? The man don't seem to be able to walk, much less go out and dig and shovel and do a day's work. The mines have just about got the best of the ol' boy."

Marn placed his lunch pail in the bed of the truck before attempting to climb in.

"Yeah, that's all right with me if he wants to ride up there in front. I noticed him hacking and spitting, like you said. How about you, Lilburn? Is it all right with you for Tavis to ride up front with the boss?" Dee-Bo asked.

"Yeah. It's all right with me," Lilburn drawled. "I don't much want to ride up there in front. I don't want to get too close to the boss," he added, stepping on the bumper of the old truck, causing it to squat under his weight. "I've never got very close to a boss before on any job that I've been on. I always stay in my place and let him stay in his."

Marn and Dee-Bo followed the big man into the truck bed, their added weight lowering the back end of the vehicle by at least six more inches. They settled themselves as comfortably as possible on a wooden toolbox, which contained the tools they would be working with that day, and sat there, waiting for Col Modut to put the truck in gear and pull onto the street.

"Is ever'body ready back there?" Col yelled out the open window of the truck cab.

"Ready and raring to go, Boss," Marn sang out. "Let's get to the job and earn some money."

"Here we go," Col Modut called out, then forced the grinding gears in place by giving the shifter lever an extra-forceful nudge. Away they went, the springs and shock absorbers squealing and crying for mercy under the heavy load in the back.

"What do you think about this WPA deal?" Dee-Bo asked, directing the question to Marn.

"I think it's about the greatest thing that has happened to this country in a long while," Marn responded, then moved about to find a better position to sit.

"I've been thinking about this thing a lot," Dee-Bo returned. "And the way I look at it, it's a big waste of money. How's it going to be funded—paid for? You know that ever'thing's supposed to be paid for with taxes, and with so many people out of work and all there ain't any taxes coming in. So where will the government get the money to pay for ever'thing? I know what they'll do. They'll just add what they can't pay for to the deficit. They sure won't do the country any good by plunging it deeper and deeper in debt with all these social programs."

"The government has a mint and a printing press," Marn began. "They can print up all the money that they need to pay for anything they want to do. The need for money for the government don't pose no problem. We're the ones that's hurting is all. Their need can be eliminated by just pushing a button to start that printing press to running and spitting out the paper money, and the mint to stamping out new change. That ain't gonna be any problem for Roosevelt and the government. He's got all the power he needs to make that kind of decision."

"That's our problem now; we've got too much money printed and no way to back it up," Dee-Bo argued. "Money's just like any other piece of paper, if you don't have something to back it up with. When these social programs go into effect, then the money that we have ain't worth diddly-squat, and printing more to try to help out will only make the money we have plain worthless."

"I don't worry about that," Marn said. "I'm just thankful that we have somebody in the White House at last that cares enough about the poor man to try to help him out, and I don't care how much it costs the government. I need work and some money now, not a month or a year later. If Roosevelt can get the ball rolling and get some money into the hands of the working man, then our problems will be solved. We can worry about paying for the programs later. When I pay my taxes, I want them spent for something like the WPA. What good would taxes be if they weren't spent when they got to Washington? When people get to working good, they'll pay their taxes, and then the government can pay off its debts and have a few dollars left over to boot. They'll balance the budget that way. But right now we have to think positive and look out for ourselves."

"I can't agree with you on that, Marn," Dee-Bo said, looking at the man sitting beside him. "I'll agree with you, though, on one thing. We need work and money to spend, but on how the government is to pay for it, I disagree with you. A quick fix never works. The problem will come back twenty-fold, making it harder to fix the next time."

"Dee-Bo, we have to start somewhere, and the way Roosevelt's trying to do it seems to me to be the best way to do it," Marn declared. "If things don't work out just right this time around, he can fix it on the next go-'round."

"There won't be a next go-'round, Marn," Dee-Bo came back. "We're riding free on nothing to nowhere."

"Maybe so, but we'll just have to go along with it for now," Marn said. "Let's work and get us some spending money right now. We'll just have to let Roosevelt and the government worry about the big problems. We can make a little money and worry about our problems while they worry about theirs. If you're so set against the WPA, you don't have to work for it. You can go back home and do without the work if you want. I'm jumping on the wagon."

Col Modut pulled the old truck off the main road and followed a narrow lane up to his barn, where he stopped. "Dee-Bo, harness the horses and bring them on up the road. We'll be ready for you when you get there," he directed.

"Sure thing," Dee-Bo replied, jumping over the side of the truck bed. "Will you watch my dinner bucket, Marn?"

"I'll sure do it," Marn promised. "Got anything good in there?" he asked, lifting the bucket with his right hand to weigh the contents. "You must have enough for two or three people in there, as heavy as it is. My bucket's lighter than yours, and I thought I had enough in it for two people."

"Mommy packed it," Dee-Bo smiled. "It's untellin' what she crammed in it. It's good, I'm sure."

Col Modut turned the truck and drove down the lane to the main road.

The work crew arrived at Big Bull Creek about ten o'clock; Dee-Bo Seedy arrived about an hour later, stopping the sweating horses at the edge of the road, where he tied them to a sourwood sapling to rest and cool off before hitching them to the grading scoop.

The men worked hard, busying themselves with the duties that the boss had assigned to each man, allowing the morning hours to pass rapidly.

"Toooooot! Toooooot," Marn Cornfield called out. His fist was clinched as if he held a pull cord to a steam-powered whistle to announce the lunch hour. "It's twelve o'clock on the dot according to my ticker." He held his dollar watch up for the rest to see. "I always eat at noon whenever I'm at home, or on the job. My tapeworms seem to know just exactly what time I'm supposed to eat. They've started to gnawing on my innards. I'm gonna have to eat pretty soon in order to feed them something before they swallow me whole."

"I'm hungrier than a field full of slopping hogs," Dee-Bo remarked, unhitching the sweating team from the grading scoop. He led the horses to a clear stream to let the team quench their thirst before feeding them ten big ears of white corn each.

"I've got your dinner here in the shade, Dee-Bo," Marn called out as Dee-Bo went to the truck in search of his lunch pail.

"Thanks!" Dee-Bo said, taking a seat on a rock in the shade of a big beech tree near the edge of the road.

"I didn't know that I was so hungry till I sat down here," Marn told his young friend. "When you eat about four o'clock of a morning, your food don't last so long, no matter if it is the stick-to-your-ribs kind like Vann fixes," he chuckled, taking a big cat-head biscuit filled with fried pork shoulder meat from his bucket. He bit into it and smiled contentedly. "Real good," he said, chewing loudly, letting everyone know that he was enjoying his food.

"Mommy filled my bucket full of biscuits bulging with meat and stuff," Dee-Bo announced, then took a big bite.

Everyone gnyammed loudly as he devoured the contents of his bucket.

Lilburn Leatherwood ate slowly, making his food last as long as possible, while Tavis Trent sat alone on a flat rock, neither eating nor talking.

"Ain't you got anything to eat, Tavis?" Marn asked, noticing that the sickly man wasn't eating anything. "If you ain't got anything, I'll share mine with you, although I need it to stoke up pretty heavy to try to keep up with Dee-Bo and them horses of Col's. Here, Tavis, have a biscuit and jelly. That'll make you feel like working this evening." He handed the emaciated man the food and watched as Tavis tore into it with a vengeance, appreciation overflowing his thin, pale face.

"I didn't have anything to bring, and, too, I never thought that I'd get to work today," Tavis answered, bowing his head timidly.

"You should have said something about not having anything to eat. I've got some extra here," Dee-Bo said. "I've got a biscuit with apple butter in it. The biscuit is sorta soggy, but it's tasty and belly filling anyway. You're welcome to it." He handed the food to Tavis, who took it and nodded his head in thanks, unable to speak.

"I've got a biscuit filled with 'lasses and good ol' cow butter," Lilburn offered.

Tavis took the offered food, without voicing thanks. His mouth was too full as he gulped the food down.

"I never saw a little man eat so much food before," Col Modut commented as he watched Tavis devour the free food. "I've got a baked sweet tater if you'd like to have it," he told Tavis.

Tavis blinked his little beady eyes and motioned for Col to bring the yam to him. How he could eat so much—eat it without a drink of water or anything? The little fellow had finished all the filled biscuits and was down to his last bite of the big, baked sweet potato when he lost his breath and began to choke. His eyes bugged out and his face turned a beet red.

"Looks like the little feller is choking on that sweet tater," Marn said, rising to assist the choking man. He began to beat Tavis on the back, between the shoulder blades.

"Get him a drink of water, Marn," Col ordered. "If he don't choke to death on that sweet tater, you're gonna beat the daylights out of him with your big fist. That's gonna kill him. He can stand just so much, you know."

Tavis finally coughed—after Marn had given him a good beating. A cud of sweet potato shot out of his mouth and went about halfway across the road, where it hit in the dust with a plop, stirring up a dust ring.

Marn ran toward the truck to get a water jug to give Tavis a drink. He had to jump the creek to get to the truck.

Just as Marn reached the little stream, Tavis called out, barely above a whisper, "Creek water'll do."

When he heard Tavis' plaintive plea for water—even creek water—Marn began to laugh so hard that he almost fell in the creek.

"Let that be a lesson to you, Tavis," Marn laughed, handing the choking man a cup of water. "You may be hungrier than a starving dog, but you shouldn't try to eat ever'thing that you can get your hands on."

"Yeah," Tavis grunted, sighing, relieved by the drink.

Three Votes in One

The party nominating conventions were over. The candidates to carry the banner for each political party had been chosen. Each party was satisfied with its choice and was working hard to win the election, just a little over two months away.

Finley Pannell had received the nod for the Republicans. Conley Starnes had received the blessings of the Democrats. Independent, Mayo Coalfield chose to run on his own.

Mayo had garnered the required number of signatures on a petition to qualify him for a place on the November ballot. Since he had won a seat on the town council of the little town of Mullinsville, as a write-in Independent, and had done an exceptional job in serving the people in that capacity, he figured it was time to run for a higher, more powerful office—the state legislature. He had the experience needed to work with and for his constituents.

The campaigning for a special election to choose a state senator to fill the recently vacated seat held by Sherd Bratton, who had died in early June, had begun in earnest. Almost every telephone pole and electric power line pole in the district was disfigured with campaign posters and pictures of the leading candidates.

Mayo Coalfield could not afford campaign posters, so he could not compete with the other candidates on the light poles and telephone poles. He could only ride around the district on his saddle horse, going from door to door, talking directly to the voters. He was doing his best with what he had to work with, and so far he had done exceptionally well in getting his message to the people.

Tavis Trent walked along the narrow, dusty, snake-shaped

road that ran through the beautiful Cumberland Mountains, which separate Southwest Virginia and eastern Kentucky.

Honeybees buzzed as they worked the dry dandelion blossoms which grew abundantly in the little mountain meadow bordering the narrow road. A trace of white dust lay on each flower. The bees' moving wings, as they flitted from flower to flower, stirred up the dust, causing it to float on the early morning air like flour around a grist mill.

Tavis was on his way to Big Onion Gap to get his weekly supply of groceries. A sea grass sack bulged his right rear overalls pocket. The sack was his constant companion—used to carry his groceries home each week, and often used to carry bartering items to the store to trade on the groceries, like a couple of chickens, a turkey, a box of fresh brown eggs, or just maybe a jug of prime 'shine. If it weren't for the trade items, times would have been pretty hard for the Trents during the depression of the early '30s and its aftermath, World War II.

The sputtering rumble of a 1934 Chevrolet pickup truck carried on the still air as the little machine bounced along over the rough surface of the unpaved road. The rusted, loose fenders of the truck flapped with uneven motions, resembling a huge buzzard attempting to get airborne.

Tavis moved to the edge of the road, pushing branches of the scrub oak and sassafras bushes, along with numerous blackberry briars, out of his way to make room for him to get further out of the oncoming automobile's line of movement.

As the truck came abreast of the pedestrian, the driver applied the brakes, causing the worn brake shoes to cry pitifully for something to cling to as they tried to grip the turning drums. With extra pressure from a huge brogan shoe, the truck was brought to a frog-hopping stop, stirring up a cloud of dirty-yellow dust which dissipated among the dry leaves of the hardwood trees beside the mountainous road.

Tavis coughed, hacked, and spat on the ground. The dirt stirred up by the moving automobile added to the discomforts of the accumulation of coal dust in his lungs. He worked in the coal mines—had for the biggest part of his life, since he was a very young boy. After his throat was finally clear, he stepped out of the bushes into the road and waved his right hand, a greeting to the driver of the old truck, Perry Hall.

"How're you doing, Tavis?" Perry greeted the dust-covered pedestrian, his longtime friend.

Tavis hacked to clear his throat once more, spat in the dust, watched the spittle roll into a ball, picking up the sandy dirt and making a marble-like pellet that stopped in the middle of the road.

Before Tavis could come back with an answer to his friend's greeting, Perry, now out of the truck, began talking once more, almost making a campaign speech.

"I'm out campaigning and electioneering for Finley Pannell, the Republican nominee for state senator for our district, the best man for the job, and you well know it. I'm sure that you'll vote for him. But the fact is, I have to canvass the whole district and talk to each and every one of the voters in order to get out the *big* vote. We need a man like Finley Pannell in the state legislature to represent us. We want a man that will watch over our tax money and see that it is spent for just what we need it for—no wasting of it just to spend it 'cause it's there. We had enough of that when Sherd Bratton was in there for thirty-some-odd years, spending our tax money like it grew on trees here on Coaley Creek and then jumped right off in his pocket to be spent ever' which way." Perry Hall then began slinging a thick layer of mud at his party's opponent. "I just can't understand why," he continued, "ever'body has always voted for him ever'time he's run for office. Looks to me like they would've got tired of seeing their taxes raised ever' year the legislature meets. Sherd always voted right down the line on raising taxes and then spending the money they collect. I'm glad he's out of there, rest his soul. Dying was the only way to get him out of office. That's real harsh to say, but it's the living truth. If he hadn't died, he'd be in the legislature forever. It was unlucky for the man that he died, but we're lucky that he did. What do you think about it, Tavis—about his taxing us so much and then spending the money all the time he was in office? He let our roads deteriorate so bad that it's hard to drive a car over them. You know, if people have good roads they're real happy. We'll have to get some good roads in these hollers so people will be happy again. You know they ain't happy with the roads that they have right now."

Tavis cleared his throat, kicked a low tire on the old pickup truck, and spat in the dusty road, near the wet spot where he had spat before. Now there were two wet balls of muddy spit lying about two inches apart near the middle of the road.

But before Tavis could reply, Perry Hall continued his campaigning. "We've got to elect Finley Pannell to that high office of state senator," he said. "If we don't elect him now, and Conley Starnes is elected, we'll have that same tax and spend scenario that we've had for over a quarter of a century. We can't stand that anymore, and you know it. You know that Conley Starnes is just like Sherd Bratton. I believe they cloned him from Sherd when they saw that Sherd's health was going downhill fast. What do you think about it? You ain't said much one way or the other. What's your political philosophy and party affiliation? The way you live and save your money, I'd have to guess that you vote like I do. Maybe I shouldn't have asked you that, Tavis. But since I've asked, would you tell me?"

Tavis cleared his throat and spat in the road, causing a third spitball, coated with dust, to roll over the rough highway, stopping near the other spitballs.

"I hope that you ain't gonna vote for Conley Starnes. And I sure hope that you ain't gonna vote for Mayo Coalfield, either. Poor ol' Mayo. You know as well as I do that Mayo Coalfield don't stand the chance of a snowball on a red-hot pot-bellied stove, running against a strong Democrat and a stronger Republican, like Conley and Finley," Perry Hall said before Tavis could respond to his questioning. "I talked to Mayo the other day, and he told me that he couldn't pay for campaign literature and posters. He told me that his young 'uns have been drawing pictures of him—showing him on a big stump out in a field making a speech—and tacking the posters on fence posts, trees, and gates way out in the country. You know as well as I do that that kind of campaigning won't amount to a hill of beans on a flat rock during a dry spell. But poor ol' Mayo is doing the best he can—using his kids to draw up his campaign posters—with no money to run a strong campaign on. You would have to admire the ol' boy, though. There's many a person that wouldn't even think about running for any kind of office without a big wheelbar' full of money. But ol' Mayo is out there beating a path to ever' door in these hollers—just a waste of time and shoe leather, if you ask me. You have to have good literature and attractive posters with good slogans on them this day and time to get people's attention and cause them to vote for you. What Mayo's doing in his poor-funded campaigning won't hold shucks when it comes to a race like we're putting on the line this year."

Tavis scuffed his shoe sole on the road, stirring up a swirl of dust that quickly dissipated in the still morning air. He then kicked a rear tire of the old truck to clear his shoe of the lingering dust, then waited for Perry to continue the lambasting of Mayo Coalfield and Conley Starnes. He was a little disappointed when Perry turned to his truck to leave. He was enjoying himself—talking to a friend that he hadn't seen for a while.

"Well, I'd better be moseying on down the pike," Perry said, opening the door to his old truck, the rust-covered hinges squeaking loudly, and getting in. He slammed the door shut and was on his way, waving a calloused hand from the open window.

A wet line in the dust followed the old truck as it bumped along over the rough, rocky road. The radiator had boiled over while they talked.

Tavis watched the departing truck pass from view around a bend in the road, then started walking on toward Big Onion Gap—in the opposite direction from which Perry Hall had gone. He had walked only a few yards when he heard the drone of the engine of another automobile coming up behind him. He stepped over to the left side of the road and fought his way into the thick wall of bushes to let the vehicle pass.

Price Bolton applied the brakes to his 1937 Ford truck and stopped in the middle of the road. "Where are you headed, Tavis?" he asked the man standing in the swirling dust stirred up by the movement of the truck.

"Big Onion Gap," Tavis answered, trying to wave the choking dust out of his face. He coughed, almost losing his breath. Black lung had a strong hold on him, and it didn't take much of anything foreign entering his weak lungs to start him to coughing. He spat the coughed-up mucus from his mouth, which rolled into a ball and stopped by the side of the road.

"I won't take up much of your time," Price told Tavis. "I'm out canvassing the district in search of votes for Conley Starnes. He's the Democratic candidate for state senator, you know. I hope you can help our party put another good man in office to carry on the work that was already being done by Sherd Bratton, who passed away back in June. I sure hated to see that happen. I'm almost certain we can never have his equal in that office again in our lifetime. But we've chosen a mighty fine feller to carry the banner for us in this fall's election, though. He'll be close to being as good as Sherd, someday, 'cause Conley knew Sherd Bratton real well. Fact of the matter is he knew him personally, well enough to have long talks with him on how to vote in the legislature and how to talk other senators into voting his way on certain bills—the ones that would help our district. With Conley knowing all of what Sherd told him, he's got a good running start on any other person who might think he can beat him. Forgive me for just sitting here gabbing so much. I'm too excited about this election, I guess. Jump in the truck and let me take you on down the pike. Are you going to Big Onion Gap? If you are, I can take you right along with me, since I'm on my way over there anyhow to see Luke Watters. I need to get his vote for sure. He does a big business up there at Big Onion Gap, and he can be a lot of help to me and the party this go-'round. Have you made up your mind on who you'll vote for this time,

Tavis? I'm almost sure that you'll vote for a good man like Conley Starnes. I can just about tell that you vote Democratic by the way you're able to carry home a big poke of groceries ever' week. You're working at a job, and I know that you appreciate that job. If the Republicans get in office, you can bet a dollar against a big fat dog tick that you won't be working regular long. They'll cut spending and cause people to lose their jobs right off. That won't happen if we get our man in there. Conley's gonna run on Sherd's record. Poor ol' Finley Pannell and Mayo Coalfield don't have a record to run on—in the legislature, that is. Finley has never run for office before—just run that hardware store of his all of his life—and Mayo was a town councilman once, in office for about ten years, but what can you do as a councilman? A councilman don't have the power to persuade like a state senator. What kind of a record could Mayo have to run on when he runs for the big office of senator?"

Tavis cleared his throat and spat in the road before climbing into the old truck.

"If you ain't decided yet, I highly recommend that you make up your mind by voting for Conley Starnes," Price Bolton said before Tavis could reply. "I'm sure that we can depend on your help this fall. If I wasn't, I wouldn't have stopped to talk to you."

Tavis settled himself in a butt-shaped depression of the worn seat of the old truck. The springs had worked their way through the upholstery, making a lumpy, uneven surface to sit on.

"You know that if we let the Republicans in, which is highly unlikely—they ain't been in there for about thirty years—we're in for some lean times in our district. You know how that bunch of Republicans is. They talk about us taxing the people, but they won't turn down any taxes that come in when they're in office. Have you ever noticed that they complain about taxes but they never cut them out while they're in office. They just like to talk about us, then go and do the same thing as we do—take your taxes. But they don't want to spend any of the money when they get it. They just want to hold onto it and let the public suffer. That ain't fair, and it ain't our way of doing things. We've got to stop anything like that before it happens by electing Conley Starnes. He won't let any money in tax revenues accumulate and pile up in that way. He won't let mold grow on it and ruin it; he'll spend it for us and make life a lot better and easier for us here in the district. Do you agree with me or disagree with me on what I just told you about the Republicans holding on to our tax dollars and letting us suffer for their dolessness?"

Tavis cleared his throat and spat out the window of the moving truck, but before he could comment, Price continued his electioneering—slapping his opponents in the face with a big bucket of mud.

"I know," Price went on, "that a little saving is all right, but the people's needs come first, the way I look at it. You agree, don't you?"

Tavis just blinked his eyes and said nothing. He knew that the loquacious gentleman sitting behind the wheel of the old truck would cut him off if he were to say something, so he just sat there and waited for Price to continue his harangue about the upcoming election.

"I'll let you out at Luke Watters' store while I go on over to speak to Col Modut. I see him over there at the hardware store," Price said upon arrival at Big Onion Gap. "I'll talk to Luke after you get your trading done. See you around, Tavis," he said as Tavis closed the truck door and walked toward the grocery store.

* * * *

His shopping done, Tavis Trent shouldered his sack of groceries and started his long walk home. He had gone about a half mile when he saw Mayo Coalfield riding up the road on his saddle horse, Old Pacer. The horse racked along as smooth as water over a slick rock, giving Mayo a relaxing ride.

"Howdy, friend," Mayo greeted as he came abreast of Tavis, standing beside the road, waiting for the rider to pass on by or stop, one.

Tavis set his sack of groceries on the ground, straightened up, removed his old slouch felt hat, and wiped the sweat from his brow with a red bandanna-type handkerchief. He then waited for the smooth stepping horse to bear its rider along the highway.

"How're you doing, Tavis?" Mayo Coalfield called out in a booming, oratorical voice, one well practiced for the campaign trail. "What're you doing out in this sweltering heat? I'd say it's nigh on to ninety degrees in the deep shade. This is one of the hottest days of the summer—hot like the campaign amongst me and my most worthy opponents. I saw Perry Hall going up the road, campaigning for Finley Pannell, and Price Bolton going down the road, campaigning for Conley Starnes. Both of 'em stopped to ask me to change my mind to run as an Independent and join forces with their respective candidate and help elect him. I politely spurned their request. I told them that I am doing right well the way that I'm working to get votes. They'll just have to campaign the way they want to. Those two are burning up good gas and wearing out good rubber going around the country campaigning for somebody else. I can't see doing something like that myself. I don't have a campaign manager to help me out. I don't have any contribution money to run on—just my own personal funds. I loaned myself some money to run this campaign with. I figure that it's a good investment, since I know the borrower and the lender and I can trust them both." Mayo grinned when he saw a smile spring to Tavis' dry lips. "Did they beat your ear off with their gabbling garbage?" he asked.

Tavis cleared his throat to speak but was stopped short of saying anything by the continuation of Mayo's talking about his opponents.

"It ain't too long till election day," Mayo Coalfield went on. "I'm trying to see and talk to ever'body in the district before that day. If Ol' Pacer here can hold out that long—and he's doing a good job at it—I'll probably make it. I'm meeting some dyed-in-the-wool Democrats and Republicans on my rounds through these hills. I bet they've voted the same way all their life. When I first start talking to those people, they look at me sort of leery like, like they don't trust me. I don't let that stop me, though. I hit 'em with my platform—what I stand for and what I'm running on. By the time they hear all that I have to say, they become more friendly, and even talk some before I leave. I think that I'm getting to them pretty good. I believe I can convert some of them. Along with the rest of the Independent voters in the district, which I think I have all locked up in my corner, I believe I can sway enough Republicans and Democrats to my way of thinking to win the election. There's nothing like confidence when you're running for office. Well, I don't have a lot of money to spend like the Democrats, or to hold on to like the Republicans, so ever'- body should be able to trust me and support me for election. They realize that if I don't have any money, I can't spend any, nor hold onto it, either. What do you think, Tavis?"

Tavis spat in the road to get ready to reply, but he was interrupted before he got started.

"I know that I can count on you for you and your family's vote this year," Mayo said. "Well, I guess that I ought to move on down the road and call on some more people before the day's out. I can't let Perry Hall and Price Bolton get too far ahead of me. If I do, I'll never catch up with them. Take care of yourself, Tavis. And tell your wife and young 'uns howdy for me. I'll be seeing you again pretty soon, I hope."

Mayo goaded Old Pacer with his heels and shook the reins, making a clucking sound with his mouth to get the resting horse to move on up the road toward his destination, Big Onion Gap.

Tavis Trent waved a hand and picked up his grocery sack. He placed the sack on his shoulder and moved on down the road toward home.

The sun was slowly sinking below the western horizon as Tavis arrived at his house on Coaley Creek.

"Did you have a good trip to the store, Tavis?" Martha asked as her husband entered the kitchen and set the grocery sack on the table.

Martha bustled about the room, preparing the evening

meal for her family.

"Yeah, I had a pretty good trip, considering," Tavis answered, removing the groceries from the soiled sack and placing them in the rickety cupboard standing in the corner of the room.

"Considering what?" Martha asked, stopping her work to look at her husband.

"Considering that I was held up along the way by political campaigners for the Democrats and Republicans, and then Mayo Coalfield, the Independent, campaigning for himself 'cause he don't have no money to hire anybody to help him get out the vote," Tavis answered, placing a package of sugar in the cupboard. He covered his mouth to stifle a cough, then closed the cupboard door. He folded his grocery sack and laid it on top of the cupboard, where he would know where to find it when the time came to go shopping for groceries again. "I listened to all of them, and do you know what? Each one of them thinks that I'm gonna vote for him. That would be three votes in one, wouldn't it? Two of them's got another thing coming, I tell you. They're gonna be surprised when they find out that I didn't vote for them."

The man coughed loudly, cleared his throat, then went outside to spit.

"How're they gonna find out which way you voted?" Martha asked. "The vote is secret, ain't it?" she went on. "Nobody is gonna know how you voted unless you tell it."

"I may up and tell them, just for the fun of it," Tavis said, returning to the kitchen.

"I'm glad that you enjoyed your trip," Martha said. "I could have used your help here at the house, though. I've had my hands plum' full, what with the children and all, and the summer canning and all. I've got a cannin' of beans on the outdoor furnace right now that'll be ready to come off in about fifteen minutes. Would you have Tolley and Claude pull the fire from under the tub to let the jars cool off? I want to be able to get the cans to seal good before bedtime tonight. You know that I'll have to peck the lids to get them to seal down on the rubbers."

Tavis went out on the porch without saying whether he would or wouldn't tell Tolley and Claude to carry out Martha's order. He would, though, and Martha knew it. He cleared his throat and spat in the dusty yard. The spit rolled up in a ball and came to rest near a meager clump of grass. He had really enjoyed his grocery-shopping day, especially all that good conversation with the campaigners.

A Snake in Each Hand

The mixture of aromas from the supper meal lingered long after the Cornfield family had finished stuffing their bellies full of good, energy-filled food.

Marn Cornfield sat in front of the cold, empty fireplace, occasionally spitting tobacco ambeer spittle into the faint trace of wood and coal ashes on the hearthstone. The thick spittle dripped slowly, sluggishly from the curved bars of the aged, stained grate. The man took the poker from its resting place against the mantle and scraped the slug-slow streams of spittle from the grate, then knocked it from the poker onto the hearth—as far back in the fireplace as he could. He rattled the poker—from force of habit—in the grate to dislodge the ashes and coal clinkers, which weren't there; it was summer and there was no need for a fire. Marn Cornfield liked his fireplace, no matter what season it was. He usually sat in front of the empty fireplace for a little while each day.

Vann, Marn's wife, and Beauty, the couple's eldest daughter, stood in front of the wood-burning range—the heat in the kitchen was almost oppressive. The clatter of dishes in the big dishpans and the chatter of conversation—woman talk— was an indication that the womenfolk were getting their after-supper chore behind them. Soon they would be able to go out on the front porch to cool off in the early evening breeze.

The rest of the children were out doing the evening chores: milking the cows, cutting stove wood, carrying up water from the spring in a little cove down below the house, gathering eggs, and feeding the chickens, turkeys, geese, ducks, and hogs.

"Does anyone want to go down to see the Holy Rollers with

me tonight?" Beauty asked. "I heard that they put on a pretty good show jerking, twitching, and handling rattlers and copperhead snakes. I wonder if they'll talk in their unknown tongues? I probably won't understand a word that they're saying if they do. Probably won't understand a word of the sermon, either. Do they preach in the unknown tongue?"

"Beauty!" Vann exclaimed. "Girl, you ain't s'posed to talk bad that way about people, 'specially church-going folks."

"Well, Mommy! I'm not talking bad about anyone. I'm just repeating what I've heard other people say about them," Beauty came back defensively. "Why don't you and Daddy go down there with me and take in the Holy Roller services tonight?" She wiped a squeaky-clean flowered plate twice, waiting for her mother's answer.

"I've been to the Holy Roller church before," Vann admitted. "They're good people that go down there to the Jestus Branch Pennycostal Church. I don't want to hear you say anything that's blackguardin' toward them. Do you hear me now? You know that me and your daddy have Pennycostals in our families, too. I ain't ashamed of it, either. Actually, I'm proud of it. They're good folks. They're trying to go to the same Heaven that we are. Maybe their way is just as close as ours is. They're probably just as right as us. We can't fault their faith and beliefs just 'cause we don't go to their church and believe exactly the same way that they do."

"You're probably right, Mommy," Beauty came back, smiling to herself. Then she spoke again. "We have everything else in our family tree—from preachers to moonshiners to chicken stealers to pig rustlers...so I guess we have some Holy Rollers mixed in there, too. I know that some of the other folks that I mentioned are pure hellions, if I have to say it, but the preachers and Holy Rollers are all right, I'm sure."

The Cornfield family—a God-fearing family—lived up the hollow from the Coaley Creek Pentecostal Church. Marn and Vann were Regulars, as the members of the Old Regular Baptist Church were called. Although the family lived near the Holiness Church, they had never taken services with that particular congregation.

Marn and Vann, out of curiosity—the same curiosity that Beauty had—had attended services in years past to feed and quench their wonderings about the handling of snakes and talking in tongues.

Marn Cornfield would not pretend to be better than anyone else, pertaining to a religious belief, and Vann would never think, much less feel, that she was better than anyone else. Marn would in no way attempt to stop his daughter, or any member of his huge family, from attending services at that church, although he did not follow the Holiness belief. He had always said that his children would have to make up their own minds in selecting a church to attend in their efforts and hopes of getting to the same Heaven that everybody else was hoping to go to. He didn't believe in telling somebody else, even his children, that his way was the only way to reach eternal rest with Jesus. Maybe he felt that his belief was the *right* belief, and the *only* belief, but his children would have to make up their minds on their own—without any prodding from him. If they should happen to ask his opinion as to how to worship God, he would gladly guide them. But if they didn't ask him, they would have to decide on their own.

"'They shall take up serpents; and if they drink any deadly thing, it shall not hurt them; they shall lay hands on the sick, and they shall recover,'" Marn spoke aloud—to no one in particular. He quoted Mark 16:18 from the King James Version of the Holy Bible.

"What did you say, Daddy," Beauty asked, turning to her father, who continued to putter with the fireplace grate and talk to himself—a habit.

"Just thinking out loud, I s'pose," was Marn's only reply.

"Just wondered," Beauty said, returning to her dish-wiping chore.

With the dishes safe in the cupboard, the womenfolk retired to the front porch, where they sat and fanned their flushed, red faces with their aprons, flipping the bottoms upward to stir the air, their movements in unison.

Marn left the cold fireplace—none the cleaner—to join Vann and Beauty on the four-foot-high front porch. "Hello, neighbor," he called to a passerby as he emerged from the living room onto the porch, letting the screen door close behind him with a bang. "Come on over and sit a spell. I've got a good plug of 'backer I'd like for you to try out with me—Day's Work, it is. Come on over and sit a spell with me and we'll talk and chew, Conley."

"Got to be shagging it on down the road," Conley Steel returned, waving his left hand while gripping his lunch bucket in his right, which swung in time with his moving left foot. "Got to catch my ride with Talmage Seedy at the mouth of the holler and go to work over at Jenkins. Got me a good-paying job with Consol," Conley called over his shoulder, continuing to walk at a brisk pace on toward the mouth of the hollow to meet his ride.

"Good company to work for. Worked for 'em for many a day, myself. Well, be careful on the job tonight. Work safe, 'cause we don't want you to be a mining statistic. Stop by and visit when you've got a little spare time to," Marn called after the departing man. He bit a big hunk off the new plug to freshen up the chew already between his cheek and gums. After a few attempts to mix and blend the new chew with the old cud, Marn spat toward the edge of the porch. Part of the ambeer spittle splattered on the edge of the porch floorboards; the rest dripped on his chin and the front of his bibbed overalls. He wiped his chin with the back of his hand and then wiped his hand on his overalls' leg.

"I guess I ought to get inside and take me a sponge bath before church time," Beauty mentioned, then looked at her mother, knowing that there would be a quick response from her.

The response was not long in coming, and it was a short, brassy retort.

"Yes, you'll take a bath 'fore you go out in public with church folks," Vann returned, peering over her wire-rimmed glasses. "You'll take a bath, girl, or stay here. Make your choice right now." She caught her breath, wheezing the air through her almost-closed nostrils. The heavy glasses pressed hard on her narrow-bridged nose. They were not fitted to her facial contour. She had bought them at the five-and-dime store down at Big Onion Gap, and they were very uncomfortable. She could see through them, and that was all the comfort she needed.

"Mommy, you know that I'll take a bath—just wanted to hear you say what you did," Beauty laughed, then rose to prepare her bath. "What should I wear, Mommy?" she asked, knowing which dress her mother would select.

"That black 'un that covers you up good," Vann suggested. "You're filling out like a woman, you know, and ever'body else will notice it, too, especially them young whipper-snapper boys that go to church just to eyeball the girls. If you wear anything tight and revealing, you'll sure be looked at, so stay covered up, girl."

"I thought that I might wear that short, red pokey-dotted 'un," Beauty replied, smiling impishly.

"You'll not, neither, Beauty!" Vann snapped, rising from her straight-back chair, letting the legs of the chair smack the floor with a thump. "I'll help you pick out what you're to wear tonight," she said, opening the screen door to enter the house behind her daughter.

"Mommy, I don't need help in picking out my meetin' clothes," Beauty protested. "I was just joshin' you about wearing that pokey-dotted dress. I'm sixteen years old—big enough to pick out my own meetin' clothes. Furthermore, I don't have that many clothes to need help in deciding on what to pick out of my wardrobe. That decision won't be so difficult."

"I agree that you ain't got a whole lot to wear, but you've got more clothes than I ever had," Vann came back, stopping in the open door. "I just want you to wear a decent type of dress to church is all. I don't want you to give people any reason to talk by wearing revealing clothes."

"I'm almost a grown woman, Mommy. Don't you think I'm capable of selecting something that's decent? I don't have anything that's revealing. You've made sure of that," Beauty complained. "You always help pick out my clothes when I get the chance to buy new 'uns."

"You can go on and make your decision, as long as I agree with that decision," Vann said. "Do you want to go down there with Beauty, Marn?" she asked her husband, who sat on the porch chewing his tobacco, spitting only once in a while. "I think I'll go along with her. I ain't been to a good Holiness preaching in the longest time—years, to be exact."

"I guess I could go, too, Hon," Marn answered, wiping his chin with the back of his hand.

"Well, get up and get ready," Vann ordered. "You need to clean up and change your clothes so you'll look decent amongst the rest. You could shave, too, while you're at it. Your face looks like a chestnut bur, all scraggly with that week-old growth."

"I'm going just like I am, woman," Marn came back. "I'm as decent as any of that bunch of church folks. My dirty overalls might keep them snakes from biting on me. If I ain't dressed to suit them, they can tell me to leave, you know. You girls get ready. I'll walk you all down there—keep you out of trouble as you go along the road." He smiled at his fussy wife.

"Your clothes ain't very clean, Marn. You should change like the rest of us. Hurry up. Me and Beauty will be ready in a few shakes," Vann promised, entering the house, allowing the screen door to close behind her, banging once, then again, but with less snap than the first.

"I'm already as ready as I'm ever gonna be," Marn called after Vann. "It don't take me long to get ready to go anywheres," he said to himself. He could hear his wife and daughter bustling about the house, getting ready to go to church.

* * * *

Marn walked a few paces ahead of his wife and daughter—normal for him. He told them that he would watch out for them, protect them by knocking snakes out of the road for them, if any snakes happened to be in the road soaking up the early evening heat on the roadbed.

"I ain't seen a sign of a snake," Marn said, breaking a long silence. "Ain't even seen a zigzag track of one that's crossed the road anywheres."

"We'll see plenty of them when we get to the church-house," Vann said, looking over the top of her glasses, searching for snakes by the side of the narrow dirt road. She was afraid of snakes—any type of snake—poisonous or non-poisonous. It didn't matter; they were all poisonous to her.

"I hope they have some big 'uns tonight," Beauty giggled, showing a bogus bravery for the benefit of her mother.

"Hush that nonsense, girl," Vann said, startled by a mysterious movement in the weeds at the edge of the road. She picked up the pace a notch or two, looking over her shoulder into the approaching darkness, trying to catch up with her husband for protection.

The twanging of guitars and the jingle of tambourines burst upon the evening stillness as the front door to the church-house was opened to accommodate the arrival of a devout member. An up-tempo rendition of a favored hymn accompanied the avid playing of the musical instruments. The happy voices were lifted up to the heavens in their worship.

"We're late, and I don't like to go in a church-house when I'm late," Vann complained. "Seems like ever'body's neck's on a swivel when you walk in the building late and disturb the sermon or the singing, one."

"The way they're singin' and playin' them guitars and things, we won't even be noticed," Marn said.

"I don't know about that," Vann snapped. "I don't know why I let you all talk me into coming down here to church in the first place. I come along to hear the preaching and singing, and you all come to see a show of snake handling and hear the unknown tongue talked. I don't think we should've come for that alone. The Lord will make us pay for doing that."

"The Lord ain't gonna fault us none just for coming down here to see what's going on. He might think that we've come down here to listen to the services to decide on whether or not to join up with the church membership," Marn said, smiling to himself, knowing well that his wife would respond quickly to his statement.

"We've come to just snoop on these people, and you know it, Marn," Vann replied, stumbling on the first step to the high front porch of the church-house. She gained her balance by leaning on the handrail to her right.

"I come to hear the preaching and watch them handle snakes, if they handle them," Marn said, reaching the top of the steps. "What did you come for, Vann?"

"We're just plain intruding on these good people. We'll have to pray hard about this tonight," Vann replied, ignoring Marn's question.

Marn was already at the top of the steps, his hand on the doorknob, ready to open the door to enter. He didn't hear his wife's last statement.

The singing and playing ended just as Marn, his wife, and his daughter entered the crowded sanctuary of the quaint church-house.

The room became very quiet and heads turned—as Vann said they would—when the congregation felt the draft from the open door.

Vann felt like crawling under a pew to hide. She didn't like having people stare at her, even in her own church, and since she was in a church as a visitor, she felt more uncomfortable than ever.

"Brothers and Sisters...," Brother Hamp Thomps, a tall, thin man, said, then stopped and looked toward the back of the room—looked straight at Marn, standing in the aisle between the two rows of pews, blocking Vann's and Beauty's way. "Brothers and Sisters," the preacher continued, "we have Brother Marn Cornfield and part of his family with us tonight. Come on in Brother Marn and have a seat, right here on the front pew. You won't miss a thing if you sit here, Brother Marn."

Brother Hamp pointed to the front pew, then reached out to shake hands with Marn. "Come on in. It's awful good to see my good friends and neighbors come to take services with us. I know that you're Reg'lars and attend the Coaley Creek Old Reg'lar Baptist Church, but you're welcome at our church anytime. Come on in and take part in the services if you want to, or just sit back and enjoy yourselves," the preacher invited.

"I'm gonna be honest with you Brother Hamp," Marn said, shaking hands with the preacher. "I come to see what you do at one of your services. Mainly I want to see you handle them rattlers and chuckerheads. You're gonna handle them, ain't you?"

"We will if the Spirit directs us to do so," Brother Hamp told him. "Have a seat, all of you." He pointed once more to the front pew, still almost empty.

Vann and Beauty shook hands with the preacher and took a seat beside Marn.

"Let's have another good song," Brother Hamp directed.

Jacob Wesley strummed his guitar a few times, humming to get the right key and pitch for the next hymn. He started a song and was joined by the entire congregation. The church-house resounded with the voices of at least a hundred joyous people, each trying to sing louder than the rest.

"Amen! Hallyluyer! Amen! Hallyluyer! Praise the Lord! The singing alone is enough to fill your heart with a great blessing," Brother Hamp Thomps responded when the enlightening hymn ended and the congregation quieted to a low whisper, discussing the arrival of the visitors from the head of Coaley Creek, of course.

An occasional cough and a loud sniff from a spiritually touched church member broke the near-silence.

Beauty looked around the big room, eye-searching the place for rattlesnakes and copperheads. She had the eerie feeling that there would be a handling of the poisonous serpents. After thinking the situation over thoroughly, she became leery of the chance she was taking. What if the Lord should take exception to her curiosity and let the snakes get loose in the church-house. She knew that very thing could happen, and it would be her fault, most likely, since she had

— 52 —

come for the show, although it wasn't a show on the part of the church. The Lord would chastise her, she was sure. "Daddy and Mommy will have to pay for their wonderment, too," she reasoned to herself.

Soon Brother Hamp Thomps was into a spirit-filled sermon. How he got into such a spirited way, Beauty could not understand. He didn't even grunt and thumb through the Bible, waiting for the *real* Preacher to come in, as she had seen ministers in her church do so often—waiting for the Lord to touch them and give them a message for the flock.

Brother Thomps began chewing the sinners up and spitting them out on the floor with his words of warning to the "lost and dying world," as he repeated that phrase so often in the delivery of his sermon.

People began to freeze up and fall on the floor and between the pews, scaring Beauty to no end. She thought that the people were having heart attacks or something by the way they were falling down. "Mommy, can't we help these sick people? They're dying off like a bunch of flies that have been sprayed with fly flit, it looks to me like. What can we do?" she whispered.

"They're all right, Beauty," Vann smiled. "They're just in the Spirit."

"It looks to me like they're all dying right where they fall on the floor," Beauty whined. "Ain't the others gonna help them up?"

"No, Honey. They're real close to Jesus right now," Vann explained. "They don't need any help from mankind at the moment. Don't worry about them. You need help worse than they do."

Beauty glanced over her shoulder at the congregation, then returned her attention to the preacher. Her eyes went beyond the preacher and congregation, searching for the dreaded snakes. She had not seen anything that indicated that there were snakes anywhere in the building, but she had that uncomfortable feeling that they were there somewhere. She wanted to know just where they were so she could run for her life if necessary.

Brother Thomps lost his breath a time or two but was able to suck in enough air to keep from toppling over, and to continue his anointing sermon.

"And as Moses lifted up the serpent in the wilderness...." Brother Thomps vanished from sight as he bent over and took something from beneath the lectern. He rose—a snake in each hand—still quoting from John 3:14 of the Holy Bible, King James Version.

Beauty didn't realize that she was so close to the pit vipers, hidden beneath the lectern.

People approached the preacher, throwing caution to the wind, and took the snakes and moved among the crowd, the serpents under complete control. There was not the slightest hint that they would attack their handlers. They seemed to be hypnotized by the worshiping congregation.

Beauty was certainly not hypnotized; she was scared nearly to death. There was nothing to do but sit as still as she could, hoping that the snakes, which were being passed from one person to the next, would by-pass her. She wasn't that lucky, though.

As Brother Thomps took possession of the snakes once more, Beauty noticed that the preacher was approaching her pew, making an offering of the two poisonous snakes.

In her terrible fright, Beauty dropped to the floor, almost passing out in a fainting moment.

"Praise the Lord! Hallyluyer! Praise the sweet name of Jesus!" Brother Thomps shouted, waving the snakes about above his head, then lowering them. "This young sister has got in the Spirit, folks."

Beauty tried to crawl under the low front pew, but to no avail. She just lay there, scared stiff.

"Take up the serpent and prove your faith, Sister," Brother Thomps preached, lowering the snakes for Beauty to take them up.

"I'm showing my faith right now," Beauty croaked from a fear-dried throat, her words squeaking, almost inaudible due to her paralyzing fright. She held her hands up, palms forward, and indication that she was trying to ward off the approach of the snakes, trying to protect herself. Her face was as white as a sheet.

"She's trying to get away from the snakes, Brother Hamp," Marn said, a hint of a smile playing around his wrinkled mouth. He spoke to the preacher, but kept his eyes on the snakes. "I think she got a lot out of your sermon tonight, Preacher," Marn explained, "but not enough to take up the serpents."

"I hope she got some good out of it," Brother Thomps said, turning away to approach another entranced worshiper.

* * * *

"That was as good a sermon as I've ever heard preached by any preacher in my life," Marn commented as the trio walked along the road on their way home from the Coaley Creek Pentecostal Church that night. A bright moon lighted their way, making the night light enough for them to walk along without stumbling over raised rocks in the road.

"I agree with you, Marn," Vann said, checking each shadow in the road for hidden boogers and snakes.

"I agree with you, too, Dad," Beauty added. "The next time I go to that church, it'll be for the sermon instead of the show. They have to be good people in that church. Those snakes would have eaten them up alive if they weren't right with the Lord."

"I told you that before we went down there," Vann replied.

"They shall take up serpents...," Marn said aloud, thinking of the sermon.

"What was that you said, Daddy?" Beauty asked, taking her father by the arm for protection.

"I was just thinking out loud, I guess," Marn answered, breaking a twig from a low limb on a bush growing beside the road.

The sudden noise startled Vann, but she said nothing as she walked along in total silence.

Tater Jelly

"I'm sure glad you wanted to go in halvers growing these taters," Olden Seedy told Marn Cornfield as the two men stood at the edge of the potato patch that day. "We ought to harvest at least a hundred and fifty bushels off of this field."

"Yeah, we ought to," Marn agreed. "I had my oldest boy, Dump, dig a hill or two the other day to see just how they looked and all. He found four big 'uns 'bout the size of a coffee saucer and six smaller 'uns—teacup-size—in one hill. Now, this'll be a harvest to brag about."

"I believe we'll be able to do a heap of bragging this year,' Olden came back, bending over to scratch in a hill where the earth had cracked open and a potato was showing, forcing the clay soil under his fingernails. He lifted his hand, gripping a huge potato. "I believe that's the biggest tater I ever saw in my borned days, and I was borned a long time ago," he bragged. "Man, we've got a gold mine right in this field, Marn! We'll take 'em and load 'em in my two-horse wagon and go over to Jenkins, to the coal camps, and peddle 'em out to the miners. In the coal camps they don't have enough room to scold a cat in without getting hair in their mouths, much less make a garden patch. Them people will be ready to buy taters. We can sell 'em enough taters at one time to do 'em all winter long. I can just hear 'em now. 'I'll take two or three bushels of 'em pretty spuds you've got there, buddy,' they'll say."

"We should do good," Marn agreed. "We'll load taters on the wagon till they start rolling off, and then cram another 'un or two on it for good measure. We can harness up my Ol' Jock and your Ol' Dock and head out bright and early this coming Saturday morning to peddle taters."

"We'll probably sell all of these taters out before dinner," Olden predicted. "We can take another load next Saturday and do the same thing. We can sell ever'one we have in about a month and divvy up the profits in time for a good Christmas."

"We ought to make enough profit to pay our taxes and give the young 'uns a good Christmas to boot," Marn said, dreaming of the good times to come, brought on by a big crop of Irish potatoes. "My oldest boys and girls are on their way right now to help dig the taters."

"Dee-Bo and the rest of my brood's on the way with the wagon to load the taters in," Olden said, taking a look down the road to see if they were in sight, hoping they would arrive soon, itching to get started harvesting the big field of potatoes. "I hear 'em coming now. Listen to the trace chains jangling around the bend of the road."

The fine, sleek team of horses soon appeared, stepping lively in the harness, prancing along in perfect step. The Seedys were singing a happy tune—each trying to sing louder than the rest.

Dee-Bo brought the horses to a stop with a loud "Whoa there, Dock. Whoa there, Henry."

Seedys of all ages and sizes bounded out of the wagon bed and began chasing each other around the field, jumping potato ridges and stumps, playing a game of follow-the-leader. Little Teddy Seedy stumbled and fell on each row, his short legs unable to step over the potato ridges. Falling didn't bother him. Each time he fell, he laughed and bounded right back up, eager to try again. He was little but was having big fun.

The Cornfield clan could be heard long before their arrival at the tater patch. Singing, laughing, and yelling carried clearly on the crisp October morning air as they hurried down the steep hill-path to Happy Hollow on Less-Than-Perfect Creek. Each Cornfield boy and girl carried a hoe and a ten-quart pail.

After everyone greeted everyone else, the younger boys and girls—Cornfields and Seedys—formed a line that almost spanned the entire potato field. The long line of young people continued to play follow-the-leader through the rows of potatoes—Bart Cornfield leading the way—like a long train on a short track.

Dump Cornfield helped Dee-Bo Seedy tether the horses to the rail fence, where they could reach the maple, sassafras, and poplar leaves on the scrubby sprouts growing in the fence row. They could browse on the leaves while waiting for the potato diggers to fill the wagon for the long, hard trip back home.

Beauty Cornfield and Jaley May Seedy stood around and talked girl-talk while they waited for the men to decide on when to commence work.

"Grab a hoe and find a row," Olden Seedy sang out, calling the line of players to work. "I want ever'body to watch what you're doing, too. Don't cut the taters as you dig 'em. Me and Marn want to take good taters to Jenkins to peddle in the coal camps. Cut taters don't sell too good."

Potato digging commenced in earnest. Hoes striking the dirt and the numerous rocks in the newground field made a clanking sound as the harvesters searched for the potatoes.

"Bart, I saw you cut that big tater and try to press the cut piece back in place," Marn said, reprimanding the boy for his error.

"I thought sure I was gonna get that by him," Bart whispered to Clem, who worked in the row just below him.

"There ain't no way you can get anything by him," Clem whispered back. "He's got eyes like a hawk. He don't miss a trick, and you should know that by now."

"I know it well enough, but I had to try to sneak it by him anyhow," Bart said. "I was hoping to be able to put that tater in one of the Seedys' buckets and let him or her take the blame for doing it. I almost made it work. I tell you for a fact, these taters are so big that you can't help but cut a few. I'll bet that else folks will cut some, too, before the day's over."

"That ain't acceptable with Dad, and I believe that Olden Seedy is just about as cantankerous about how well you do your work as Dad is, don't you think?" Clem said.

"Yeah," Bart agreed, "I'd say he is at that."

Only the clanking of hoes on rocks and the thump of potatoes being dropped into buckets could be heard for a long while.

Suddenly the quiet was broken by the shrill scream of Jaley May Seedy. "Somebody chucked a tater and hit me with it," she said, stopping and looking hard at the boys—at her brothers and the Cornfield boys. "Someone hit me with a tater and it ain't a bit funny. Wait till I find out who done it, then I'm gonna scalp him with this hoe."

Everyone had a good laugh at Jaley May's expense, with Bart Cornfield laughing the loudest of all, an indication that he could have been the one who hit the girl with the potato.

"Bart done it," Clem laughed, tattling on his mischievous brother. "He's in love with Jaley May and he hit her just to prove it and get her attention."

"I did not!" Bart denied, quickly coming to his own defense since no one else would defend him. "She's real pretty and all that, but I wasn't flirting with her. I've been too busy digging these blasted taters to notice if there was a pretty girl amongst us."

"You flung that tater anyway," Clem continued to tease and tattle.

"Bart, did you hit me with that tater?" Jaley May asked, raising her hoe in a threatening pose, ready to attack the rowdy boy.

"It was Bart all right," Jake Cornfield added. "I saw him with my own eyes."

"What are you all trying to do to me—get me killed?" Bart asked, looking as innocent as he could under the circumstances. "If I was flirting with her, I sure wouldn't knock her in the head with something just to prove to her that I like her."

Jaley May still held the hoe at the ready, waiting for the right moment to attack. "Did you do it, Bart?"

"Jaley May, why would I hit you in the head with a tater?" Bart asked. "You're too pretty, and your hair's so neat and clean looking to mess up with a dirty tater."

"I don't know why, but I do know you did it," the girl said. "I didn't say where you hit me. I just said that you hit me. You told on yourself, boy," she stated flatly, judging the boy guilty where he stood. "Did anyone hear me say that he hit me in the head?" she asked, then waited for an answer.

"Yeah!" all the boys sang out in unison, hoping to add a little fuel to the girl's fiery anger.

"No, she did not!" the girls answered, coming to Jaley May's aid, Beauty Cornfield leading the defense.

"See what I told you, Bart," Jaley May charged, continuing to hold the hoe in the air, poised, ready to strike the boy at any time.

"Wait a minute now," Bart said, preparing to argue further. "You found me guilty and condemned me without a trial by jury," he protested.

"The girls are the jury," Jaley May shot back. "You heard what they said. They said that you done it."

"The boys said that I didn't do it," Bart argued. "So that leaves us with a hung jury. We can throw the case out the winder."

"We'll vote again," Dump said. "We vote like the girls voted. Right, fellers?"

"Right!" everyone yelled together.

"Wait a minute! That ain't one bit fair," Bart said. "You're just a bunch of turncoats—a bunch of Arnold Benidicts. That's what you are."

"Who in the cat hair is Arnold Benidict?" Judge L. Cornfield wanted to know.

"He means, 'Benidict Arnold,' the turncoat during the Revolutionary War," Dump laughed, slapping his legs, tickled almost to the point of hiccuping.

"All of you all are a bunch of turncoats," Bart said again.

"See what I told you, Bart," Jaley May said, running toward Bart with the hoe as a weapon. "Ever'body knows that you're the guilty bird."

Bart ran across the potato patch with the girl in hot pursuit.

"Come back here, Jaley May," Olden called after the irate

girl.

"You get back here, too, Bart," Marn called out. "You ain't got time to fall in love in the tater patch. We've got these taters to dig before dark."

Bart stood at the edge of the field, watching Jaley May turn and walk back to her row of potatoes and commence digging with a fervor, pretending to vent her anger, a pleasant smile playing around her pretty mouth.

The field resounded with hearty laughter.

Bart crept quietly back to work, keeping an eye on the pretty girl in the third row above him.

Soon the diggers settled back into a routine of work, stopping only at noon to eat a snack of lunch that each family had brought along, then back to digging potatoes. At four o'clock the job was finished.

The two-horse wagon was filled with big, beautiful, well-proportioned Irish potatoes, and Dee-Bo clucked to the horses and shook the check lines to get the horses to move, and soon he was on his way home.

"Get them shovels and picks over by the fence, boys," Marn Cornfield ordered. "We'll dig some holes and put these taters in the ground to protect them till we can hall them home."

Soon, three huge holes, resembling graves, had been dug on a sloping part of the potato field, steep enough for water to flow away from the protected potatoes in the event that rain should fall before they could be transported to the protection of the cellar under the Cornfield's house.

The sun was setting behind the steep mountains in the west, its soft rays an orange glow on the big fluffy clouds hovering above the horizon, when the last of the potatoes were poured out of a bucket into a hole and covered by leaves and dirt—the leaves first, and then the dirt on top of the leaves.

The potato field became a quiet, lonely place, left that way when the avid potato diggers went home.

* * * *

Marn Cornfield rode Old Jock to the top of the mountain and out the ridge on his way to Happy Hollow to meet Olden Seedy to go potato peddling in Kentucky. The trace chains and the check line rings on the hames jingled in the early morning quiet. A bright October moon filtered its rays through the many colored leaves on the hardwood trees on the mountain's nearly flat top. Crickets chirped sleepily, while a screech owl called out to the night, disturbed by the intruding horse and rider, its quavery, chilling cry echoing from the Buzzard Cliffs on the opposite side of the deep hollow. A hoot owl hooted in response to his smaller cousin's calling, as if to tell him to quiet down, that he was making too much noise for such a small bird. The small nocturnal animals were in hiding, afraid of the predatory birds calling out to the dark world.

Marn rode with his hand out in front of his face to ward off the whipping tree branches, disturbed by the horse's movements. He did not carry a light. Old Jock could see for both himself and his rider, leaving Marn free to hold the reins in one hand and cover his face with his other hand.

Dee-Bo Seedy had just hooked Old Dock's trace chains to the double trees on the foreside of the wagon tongue when Marn rode up and dismounted.

After friendly greetings to Dee-Bo and Olden, who was already seated on the wagon, Marn helped Dee-Bo lift the wagon tongue and lace the breast chains through the rings on the tongue yoke. He then hooked Old Jock's trace chains to the singletree on the off-side of the wagon tongue. He patted the horse on the rump and climbed into the wagon bed.

"Do you think that we have enough taters to take on our first trip to Jenkins?" Olden Seedy asked as Marn Cornfield searched in the moonlit early morning for a seat somewhere on the potato pile.

"Looks like we ought to have enough," Marn said, taking a seat on a bucket turned upside down in a corner of the wagon bed. "We'll find out pretty soon, won't we?"

"Yep. We sure will," Olden replied. "Dee-Bo will do the driving for us, and me and you'll have to do the peddling."

Dee-Bo sat on the right side of the long wooden seat, behind Old Dock. He picked up the leather check lines and clucked to the horses, slapping them gently with a flip of the lines. Obediently the horses settled into their collars and moved the loaded wagon from its parked position. With the big wheels cutting into the soft earth and the horses snorting to blow dust out of their nostrils, the trip to Kentucky began.

The two-horse team walked along the narrow, winding road from Happy Hollow to Big Onion Gap. At the bustling little town, Dee-Bo stopped the team at a watering trough in front of the feed store. The horses drank the cool, clear liquid, sucking air in around the bridle bits as they took the water into their lathered mouths, causing the water level to drop at least three inches.

While the horses drank their fill, Olden and Marn went into the Much-And-A-Plenty Grocery to buy a lunch of potted meat, cheese, sardines, and crackers, with three big Nehi orange drinks to wash their food down, without first asking Dee-Bo what he would like for lunch.

The two men climbed back on the wagon, and with the trace chains jingling, and the wagon wheels squeaking from the lack of lubrication, the peddlers went through the busy street, stopping often to let pedestrians cross in front of the horses.

The town was finally behind and Cumberland Mountain stood majestically in front, posing a problem for the poor horses. The winding road went up, up, and on up some more.

Dee-bo clucked often to the tireless team and shook the check lines to remind the horses that he was still in command of their destiny.

"Guide them over to the side of the road in this wide space and let them wind a few minutes before we hit the steepest grade," Olden said. "We'll have to get off of the wagon and walk along beside it on the steepest parts, until we get through the gap and into Kentucky. After we get on through the gap, it'll be nothing but clear sailin' on down to Jenkins."

"Whoa!" Dee-Bo called out, pulling back on the check lines

to stop the horses, the trace chains and the squeaking wheels becoming silent.

"Did you grease them axles like I told you to?" Olden asked, directing the question to Dee-Bo.

"Sure did, Poppy," Dee-Bo told him.

"I noticed that they still squeaked pretty bad as we come through town at a snail's pace," Olden said. "If you greased them, they shouldn't sound that loud."

"I greased them, but it takes a while for the grease to soak into the axles and stop the squeaking," Dee-Bo replied, winking at Marn to let him know that he was trying to pull one over on his dad.

Marn grinned and nodded, indicating that he understood that Dee-Bo was joshing his father.

"We ought to get out right here and walk on ahead," Marn suggested, rising from his water bucket seat and jumping to the ground. He stretched his stiff body and yawned. "You get awful stiff sitting all scrunched up on a bucket," he complained. "Walking will be good for us, Olden."

"I say it will," Olden grunted. "I'd ruther walk anyway." He fell in beside Marn and the two men walked on, talking about working in the mines at Jenkins. "Bring 'em on in about five minutes, Dee-Bo," he called over his shoulder.

"Okay, Poppy," Dee-Bo promised, leaning back in his seat, closing his eyes to shade them against the sun just then peeping above the eastern horizon.

After the designated five minutes of extra rest for the sweating horses, Dee-Bo started the team with a sharp command of "Git up, you two."

The climb to the top of the mountain grew steeper with every curve of the winding road. Dee-Bo allowed the team to stop as often as it needed, starting it after about five or ten minutes of rest each time, finally reaching the top of the mountain. The cut through the mountain where Kentucky and Virginia are joined together was a welcome sight to the boy and the team.

On the Kentucky side of Cumberland Mountain, Dee-Bo stopped the team at a wide spot in the road, where Olden

Seedy and Marn Cornfield sat on a decaying oak tree that had fallen during a storm many years before. The two men sat there whittling and talking, their favorite pastime.

After a lengthy rest, travel was resumed—Olden and Marn riding again. The squeaking wagon wheels cried for more grease as they were forced to roll along the rough road.

"Dee-Bo, I say that you didn't grease them wheels yesterday like I told you to," Olden spoke after several minutes of listening to the wheels turning on two dry axles.

Dee-Bo grinned and said nothing. There was no use in arguing with his father—he had forgotten to carry out the chore Olden had given him Friday afternoon. He would do it when he got back home, he was sure.

The trip off the mountain was much easier and quicker than the climb to the top from the opposite side.

The trio of peddlers reached the foot of the mountain at about ten o'clock. By then the sun was up and the morning air had warmed considerably, melting the heavy frost that had covered everything. A few shaded roofs stood out like sore thumbs on otherwise-healthy hands in their vestments of white frost. Feathers of steamy fog rose slowly, hovering momentarily, then rising from the surface of a beautiful little lake at the edge of the busy town of Jenkins. Three white ducks stood at the edge of the water preening their feathers after an early morning bath in the clear, cold water, while another bunch of ducks bathed and swam around on the calm surface of the lake.

"Turn in here at the Lakeside Hotel, Dee-Bo," Olden said, straightening up from his slouched position. "We might sell the whole load to the head cook. I always make a good sale here, no matter what I'm peddlin'."

Dee-Bo pulled hard on the right-hand check line, saying, "Gee, Dock. Gee, Jock. Turn on in here and you can rest a spell while we unload this pile of taters."

The two horses did as the boy commanded, turning as ordered.

Olden Seedy hit the ground with a loud groan, rubbing his back to get the circulation going in it once more. He then walked up the steps to the porch of the hotel and went to the back door, to the kitchen area. At his knock the door opened.

"Howdy," the low, friendly voice of the hotel's head cook greeted the peddler. "Can I help you?"

"Howdy, ol' Cuz," Olden returned the greeting. "You sure can," he went on. "How many taters do you need today? I've got the prettiest Arsh taters that you ever laid your peepers on—cheap, too."

"How cheap?" the cook asked, wiping his wet hands on a white apron, well-worn and stained by bits of food.

"I'll let you have them for forty cents a bushel today," Olden told him. "That's as cheap as I can let you have them, Cuz. I have to make a little on 'em or I'll go in the hole on 'em, and that would put me out of business, just like that," he said, snapping his fingers.

"Sure wish you had come by yesterday real early," the cook said, pushing the big chef's hat farther back on his balding head. "I bought a whole wagon load of taters yester-day morning. I had to give fifty cents a bushel for them, and they weren't too pretty at that. Come back the next time you're through here. Maybe I can buy something then."

The cook backed out of the doorway and let the screen door shut with a bang.

"Can't you take another load today?" Olden asked, yelling through the door. "They'll keep till you need 'em."

The cook had gone back to his work and ignored Olden's plea to buy the potatoes.

"We're a day late here, Marn," Olden reported as he climbed into the wagon. "That cook told me that he bought a whole wagonload yesterday, and they weren't as good as ours are. What do you think of that?"

"That's about normal," Marn said. "It's always like that. When you've got a lot of something, ever'body else has a lot of it, too."

The peddlers went through the town, stopping at each house to try their luck at selling. No one needed potatoes. Everyone had bought from another peddler on the previous day.

"Did you do any good?" Olden asked as Marn came back to the wagon after a climb up a long flight of steps to reach a house clinging precariously to the steep hillside.

"That woman up there had the gall to ask me to sell her a nickel's worth of taters. We ain't sold any taters to anybody yet, so I'm gonna give her a peck of taters for a nickel," Marn announced.

"Here, let me have them taters," Olden said, smiling to himself. "You fellers ain't seen a peddler before. I know that that woman ain't seen anything like me before, either. She don't know it yet, but I'm gonna sell her a bunch of taters, instead of a nickel's worth. Watch me."

With that threat, Olden took the peck of potatoes out of Marn's hand and started to climb the long flight of steps to the house on the hill.

"Howdy, ma'am," Olden greeted the heavyset woman sitting in a swing at the end of the porch. "I've got taters for sale."

"Howdy, and taters is all I've heard for the last two or three days," the lady replied, looking hard at Olden.

"Yeah, but you ain't seen taters like the ones that I've got in this bucket," Olden began. "I brought you a nickel's worth, which happens to a peck in this case. I don't always give that big of a measure to anyone, but I want you to know that I'm concerned about you all here in the coal camps of Kentucky. I want you to have good taters to feed to your family."

"I only have a husband and one son, and we don't eat a lot of taters," the woman began to explain the reason for buying a small amount of potatoes.

"Buy a bunch while they're cheap like they are. They'll keep for you," Olden said, arguing his case.

"I told you, I don't need any taters," the lady snapped. "I don't want your nickel's worth now. I don't like to be pressure-sold, and that's what you're trying to do to me."

"I'm not trying to pressure-sell to you," Olden said. "I want you to get you a bunch of taters while they're real cheap."

"I wouldn't buy them now, no matter how cheap they are,"

the lady snapped.

"Buy them while they're cheap and make tater jelly out of 'em," Olden said, using another ploy to make a sale.

"Who ever heard of tater jelly?" the woman asked. "I've heard ever'thing now."

"Ma'am, taters make the best jelly you ever tasted, and it's so easy to fix," Olden began. "My wife makes it all of the time—ever' year for the last ten years now. You don't even have to cook the taters and stand over a hot stove to make tater jelly. All you have to do is peel the taters and slice them as thin as you can. Then you put a layer of taters in the bottom of a big crock—a big picklin' crock is the best size to use—and then spread a light coating of sugar over the tater slices. Then you put more layers of taters and sprinkle them with sugar till you get the crock full. You cap it off and wait for a week or two. Then you scoop you out a plateful and eat to your heart's content. We love it at our house. I had a samige of tater jelly this morning as I come along peddlin'. I should've saved some and give you a good taste of it."

"How many taters does it take to make that jelly?" the woman asked, showing interest. "And how much sugar? You know sugar is expensive."

"It takes about ten bushels of taters and about ten pounds of sugar. You can get by with about five pounds, since sugar is so expensive right now," Olden told her. "My wife has used 'lasses before, but 'lasses gives tater jelly too tart of a taste to suit me. You can make it whichever way you'd ruther. It's good either way you make it."

"How much are your taters, sir?" the lady asked.

"They're fifty cents a bushel today," Olden replied. "How many do you want?"

"I'll take ten bushels for me and ten bushels for my sister. I know she'll want to make some tater jelly, too," the woman said, rising. "You can pile them up there in the yard, and I'll get John to cover them up till I can find time to make jelly."

"That's a good idea, ma'am," Olden agreed. "We'll carry them up here while you get your money ready."

Seven trips up the steps by each man made a big pile of

potatoes in the woman's yard.

"How did you get that woman to take that big pile of spuds?" Dee-Bo asked his father as the peddlers climbed onto the wagon.

"I just told her how to make tater jelly was all," Olden laughed.

"Oh, no, Poppy, not that ploy again," Dee-Bo whined. "You've ruined it for us if we ever want to come back over to Kentucky to peddle again. You've ruined Marn's chance to come back, too."

"You never know, boy," Olden smiled. "It could work. That woman might have the best tater jelly you ever tasted."

"I hope so," Dee-Bo said, shaking his head and flipping the check lines to start the team moving again.

The Cob Fight

"You know what? We've never beat Big Bull Creek Elementary School in baseball," Bart Cornfield said while talking with his brothers and friends at Coaley Creek Elementary School after having received a good shellacking at the hands of the team.

"We should have won one game at least," Shag Moss spoke. "We've been going over there twice a year for the last six years now, and we ain't won a game yet. That's got to end sometime. We may not be able to beat them in baseball, but looks like we could beat them at something."

"That's the only game that anybody on Coaley Creek and Big Bull Creek knows how to play," Dump Cornfield said. "What other games can we play?"

"We could play follow-the-leader or something like that," Seldom Seedy suggested. "But I believe Bart and Shag could beat that whole bunch by themselves. We could have a good ol' fashioned 'rasslin' match with 'em. But I think we'd have a big advantage on them there, too. Clem's about the best 'rassler for his size of anybody in the country."

Clem only grinned, not saying a word. He was much quieter than the other boys. But when someone got him started clowning around and acting funny, he could talk right up with anybody.

"He's the best around, ain't he, boys?" Dump said, lauding his brother for his strength and agility as a wrestler.

"What do you say about it, Clem?" Shag asked. "Can you prove that you're the best 'rassler there ever was?"

"Get a 'rassling match going, and I'll show you what I can do," Clem boasted. "I don't have much to say about what I can or can't do. So I just let my 'rassling do my talking for me."

"This boy sure has a lot of confidence, don't he fellers?" Shag said, punching Clem playfully on the shoulder.

"He sure does have confidence, and good reason to, too," Seldom Seedy quipped. "I've seen him back up his brag. I've seen him, and you all have, too, throw three or four boys at once and 'rassle the whole bunch all over the place, even sweep the ground clean with their hides." Seldom grinned, showing big, yellow buckteeth.

"That bunch knows that they can't beat us playing follow-the-leader, and they won't even think about playing that game against us," Dump added. "They're afraid that they'll get beat and don't want to break the trend of winning against us. Bart can beat them by hisself. He can jump like a kangaroo and climb like a monkey."

"Yeah, and he looks like the kangaroo and smells like the monkey," Seldom Seedy joked, then ran around the corner of the schoolhouse, chased by Bart.

The rest of the boys ran around the corner of the building, joined by a group of girls, curious as to what was going on between the two scrapping boys, arriving just in time to see Bart make a flying tackle and grab Seldom Seedy around the waist.

The two rambunctious boys fell to the ground, thrashing and wrestling around on the dirt and grass on the basketball court. First one was on the top, and then the other. There was a sea of elbows and kneecaps humping and thumping in the boys' efforts to best each other.

Bart came out on top of the heap and gave Seldom a thump with his fist, causing a frog to pop up on a shoulder. When Seldom began to moan and groan from the pain caused by the frog's trying to jump off his arm, Bart rose slowly and helped his friend, who was still gimping and groaning, rise.

"Whew, Bart!" Seldom winced, sucking air in through his buckteeth. "You broke my arm, you overgrowed horse!"

"Aw, it'll heal up and hair over in no time at all, Seldom," Bart laughed. "Now, who smells like a monkey?"

"I sure don't," Seldom smiled, ready to run for cover in case Bart wanted to thump his shoulder again.

After the rest of the boys, and the girls, had a good laugh, Dump asked seriously, "What game can we play, and how can we get in contact with that bunch on Big Bull Creek?"

"I'll see Red Bolten at the show Saturday," Bart said. "He's always there, and I can challenge him to whatever game we're gonna play. Does anybody have a suggestion of what kind of game I can challenge him to?"

"Follow-the-leader is out," Dump declared, "'cause Bart and Shag would win that game, hands down. "'Rassling is out of the question, too, 'cause Clem could whup them all at once, pile them in a heap in the middle of the road—no challenge at all. What else is left to do? We know that baseball is out, 'cause we don't stand a chance with them in that game. They would thrash us in a hurry."

"What about a good old-fashioned cob fight?" Bart asked excitedly.

"Miss Wills won't let us have a cob fight here at school, and Mr. Tedder won't let us do it over there on Big Bull Creek," Dump replied. "Somebody could get hurt—get an eye knocked out or something. You'll have to come up with something else, Bart."

"We wouldn't have to have it at either one of the schools," Bart said. "We could meet at somebody's house on a Sunday after church and have an all-out cob war amongst ourselves."

"Who's house would we meet at?" Shag asked. "We could use a big laurel thicket near my house to search and destroy the enemy. That way it would be just like a war, where you couldn't see anyone. Then you'd have to hunt for one another. That sounds good to me."

"No, we can't do it that way," Bart came back. "That would take too long to fight a fight to the end. Somebody could hide in a thicket all day. That won't work at all."

"Does anybody have a suggestion?" Dump asked, then waited for someone to speak. When no one said anything, he went on. "Let's meet up at our milk-gap. The fence runs right along with the top of the ridge. The land slopes away from the top of the ridge in both directions—a real good place for a cob fight."

"That sounds like a good idea, Dump," Seldom Seedy said, agreeing.

"Yeah," Dump continued. "We can defend one side of the gap, and they can defend the other. That way we can work our way up the hill and meet on top and fight it out."

"We'll have to save up a bunch of cobs and be ready to go to battle," Bart grinned, thinking of the fun that they were sure to have. "Fellers, I have a plan."

"What is it?" Shag asked, then waited impatiently for Bart's revelation.

"I can't tell you right now," Bart went on. "I'm afraid that somebody might let my plan slip to the enemy. A good-laid plan must never be revealed. It ain't good war strategy to let else folks know what's going on. I'll tell ever'body before we get into the heat of the battle, though."

"Does ever'body agree that a cob fight is the best challenge that we have?" Dump asked. "Clem? Shag? Seldom? Jake? Judge L.? Cousin Jubal? Tarncie? Bertsie? Does ever'body agree? A cob fight? Is that what ever'body wants?"

Everyone agreed that a cob fight would be the perfect challenge.

"We'll have to make sure that no little fellers get into the fracas, 'cause our dads would thump us good if we got the little 'uns hurt."

"I'm big enough to fight with the biggest and best," Esker Seedy spoke up. "Me and Teed and Gillis and Tester and Satch Hood can hold our own right along with the rest of you big fellers," he bragged.

"We'll see," Dump told the boy, chuckling. "We'll wait till that bunch from Big Bull Creek arrives," he continued. "Then we'll know where to make our cut in the size of the participants."

"You can cut below us," Teed Cornfield spoke up. "We're big enough to stand any thumping that any of you can do with a cob. The enemy's problem is going to be that of hitting us. We're faster than greased lightning."

"We don't want help that runs all the time. We want people that can stand and throw cobs," Bart said.

"Just give us the chance and we'll show you some real fighting," Esker Seedy promised.

"Are you going to let any of the girls in the fight?" Beauty Cornfield asked her brother. "Me and Jaley May could dress up like boys. That bunch would never know that we weren't boys. They'll be getting thumped with cobs so hard that they won't notice that we're girls beating the tar out of 'em."

"That's right," Jaley May Seedy said, agreeing with Beauty.

"I don't know about that," Dump said, gripping his chin in thought. "Girls can get hurt pretty easy."

"You know just how tough I am, Dump," Beauty smiled, baiting the boy into letting her into the action. "I can hold my own against you most of the time."

"That's right," Dump admitted. "But we'll have to talk to Red Bolten at the show Saturday and make plans for the set-to. If you and Jaley May join us, you'll have to dress up like boys. And you'll have to promise not to whine and cry if you get hit real hard."

"That's a promise, ain't it, Jaley May?" Beauty giggled.

"Yep, sure is," Jaley May agreed.

"It'll take about two weeks to get together on this," Bart said, getting back into the discussion. "I'll have to set ever'thing up since it's my idea. I'll discuss our plan with Red on Saturday and try to strike up an agreement to my plan. Then maybe we can get on with it the next Sunday after that. It's gonna take longer to discuss it with Red and his bunch and then get it all set up than you might think."

"Yeah, ever'body's gonna have to do a lot of corn shucking and shelling to get a good supply of cobs laid in for the fight," Judge L. Cornfield said, finally getting his two cents worth into the planning.

"This weekend is turn day at our house," Dump announced, referring to the taking of corn to the gristmill to have it ground into meal for bread.

"It's turn day for the rest of us, too," Seldom Seedy added.

"We should have plenty of cobs," Dump said.

Everyone agreed on Bart's plan of action, hoping that he could organize the anticipated cob fight with their archenemy, the Big Bull Creek gang.

* * * *

"Red assured me that they'd be here," Bart told his small army as they waited at the milk-gap that Sunday afternoon. "And I want to make them suffer defeat one time, at my hands. Our hands," he corrected.

"What time did you tell them to be here, Bart?" Jake asked. "I was there when you all came to your agreement, but I didn't hear a whole lot of what you fellers was talking about."

"If you'd been listening to what was going on you'd know what time they said they'd be here," Bart said. "Your mind was some'ers else, most likely."

"I had my mind, and eyes, on a pretty little sweet tater," Jake said, grinning. "You should have seen what a beautiful little syrup-soppin' sugar-booger she was."

"Anybody'd know that you were trying to impress a girl," Dump chuckled. "You've always got your mind on the pretty little girls."

"Not a bad thing to have your mind on," Jake grinned.

"I hear them coming," Beauty said, rising from her seat on a chestnut stump, where she had been sitting while talking with Jaley May Seedy.

"Now that they're arriving, and we're ready to choose up and go into battle, what's that secret that you told us you had up your sleeve?" Dump asked. "You've sure kept it to yourself for the last two weeks, and wouldn't even tell us about it. Now what's your plan?"

"Look under that brash over there in the fence corner and you'll see?" Bart said, grinning broadly.

Everyone ran to the milk-gap corner of the fence and had a look under the pile of brush, pushing and shoving to get a better look.

There it was, a two-bushel washtub filled with water-soaked cobs, many of them taken from the swampy, manure-covered barnyard. The rest were clean cobs that had been soaking in the tub of water for two weeks. They were just as soggy as the water-soaked barnyard variety, good ammunition to force their enemy to surrender quickly. It was an advantage, of course, but the type of cob had not been discussed before the cob fight.

Bart grinned all over himself. "What do you think? Do we have a chance to win one game against that bunch?"

"Yep, I believe so," Dump laughed. "That bunch is in for a rude awakening. After this fight's over, that bunch will be so gun-shy that they won't ever want to play us at anything."

"That's fine with me," Bart chuckled.

"Boys, I know that you're real excited about your secret weapon," Clem drawled. "Did you ever think that that bunch might just have a secret weapon, too? They might have some water-soaked cobs, too."

"They might," Dump agreed. "We'll find out soon enough, though. Man! Look what a crowd they've got!" he said as the army came into view from around a curve in the narrow road. "Now, I know that they don't have that many students in their whole school enrollment. They must have recruited some help along the way."

"They've got a bunch of little 'uns with 'em. Look how little they are," Seldom Seedy exclaimed. "We can beat the britches right off their bodies, with that bunch of shavers tagging along after them."

"Great!" Bart shouted, stumbling over a bushel of broken-up cobs, falling flat on the hard-packed earth near the milk-gap where the cows and calves had trampled it. "This fight ain't gonna last any longer than Pat stayed in the Army."

Red Bolten led his troops up to the milk-gap, where the Coaley Creek combatants stood waiting.

"Howdy, ever'body," Red Bolten spoke, looking all around at the silent faces staring back at him. "Did I come to a funeral or a cob fight?" he asked. "Man! I ain't never seen a bunch as solemn-looking as you all."

"I guess you're right, Red," Bart spoke up. "We're preparing for your all's funeral. We're gonna lambast you bunch of geetherds all the way home. Ain't we fellers?"

"We sure are!" a chorus of replies came from the once quiet bunch. "And we're ready to do it now."

"You'd better get your cheering section out of the way before we start," Dump told Red.

"We ain't got a cheering section," Red replied. "These," he pointed to the smaller boys, "are fighters for our team."

"If they get hurt, it's gonna be your fault, Red," Bart told the Big Bull Creek leader. "We ain't letting Teed and Esker and the other little 'uns participate. They're gonna watch, and as a little friendly advice, it would be a good idea to set your young 'uns down to watch."

"We need ever'body we brought to even up with you," Red shot back, looking all around the group. "Who's them two big fellers sitting on that stump there?" He pointed to Beauty and Jaley May.

"Them two?" Bart asked, nodding his head in the direction of the two girls dressed as boys.

"Yeah, them two," Red said. "They're bigger than anybody on my team. That's cheating."

"It's not cheating, either," Bart shot back defensively. "They go to our school—just moved into the neighborhood. We're gonna use them. You brought about a million little 'uns, so we can use two big 'uns to off-set the odds and make it even."

"I still don't think it's fair to use them two big gawkers against us," Red complained.

"Let me at him," Beauty said, preparing to attack Red before the start of the game. "I'll wring your scrawny neck for calling me a gawker. You'll wish you never seen me before, feller."

"With a squeaky voice like that, I don't think there's much fight in you, boy," Red laughed. "Squeak. Squeak. Squeak," he bantered.

"Hold on there, Barney," Dump said, taking Beauty by the arm to stop her from lambasting Red on the spot. "You, too, Herb," he continued as Jaley May Seedy prepared to come to Beauty's aid. "We can settle this with cobs at thirty paces if you wish, but we must do it by the rules. What's the rules, Bart?"

"I'll settle this with you later, Dump," Beauty whispered. "I'm not Barney, you know."

"Red, you take your army about twenty paces on that side of the fence," Bart said, pointing to where Red was to take his stand. "Me and my team will take this side of the fence, twenty paces toward the barn. When I give the signal, we'll commence to chuck cobs at each other. When somebody has had as much pelting as he can take, he'll have to sit down and watch. We'll do it that way till ever'body is sitting down or has given up. The team that don't have anybody standing and fighting is the loser. Okay?"

"Okay," Red replied.

"We're gonna drive you all the way back to Big Bull Creek with your tails tucked between your legs like whipped dogs," Bart threatened. "Take your places and the game will begin."

"I can whup that bunch of wimps by myself," Beauty boasted. "Let me at 'em."

"I'll help bash 'em and batter 'em all the way home," Jaley May threatened.

After each team was in place, Bart gave the signal to commence.

Cobs, red and white, rained down on each team as everyone threw without aiming.

The level of the cobs in Bart's team's baskets began to shrink as everyone hurried to fill his or her hands to continue the fight at a rapid pace.

The sacks in which Red Bolten and his team had brought their ammunition shrank to wilted masses on the ground. Each combatant began retrieving the Coaley Creek team's cobs to fight back.

The teams fought back and forth—one team winning—then the other team winning. The action went on and on like that for some time, with neither team holding the upper hand. Soon, though, the little ones began to cry and run out of range of the cobs to sit in a huddle, thinking that there was safety in numbers.

"Geeeoo!" Jaley May Seedy screamed. "Somebody knocked my eye out, it feels like."

Blood streamed down the girl's face, dropping onto her bibbed overalls. She sat down on a stump and began to wipe the blood from her face with the tail of her shirt.

A cob had struck the girl over her right eye, cutting a small gash in the eyebrow. The cut was merely a scratch, but the blood streaming from it gave it the appearance of a large laceration.

The sight of blood made Bart and his team fight harder, driving their enemy down the hill.

"This has gone on long enough," Seldom Seedy said, racing for the tub of soaked cobs. The rest followed suit, and soon heavy, wet cobs filled the air, causing screams to come from the opposite side of the fence.

Dump jumped the fence, followed by Clem, Bart, Jake, and all of the other boys, throwing cobs as fast as they could, forcing the enemy farther down the hill.

"Come on, little fellers," Red Bolten called to the smaller boys, "I'd better get you home. This bunch has gone plum' loony-crazy. We'll come back and get them the next time, though."

"You might come back and get them, but you won't have us to help you," Gordie Bowin yelled as he herded several of the smaller boys ahead of him, headed for Big Bull Creek. Everyone else agreed with Gordie, leaving Red Bolten to face the onslaught of the Coaley Creek avengers, and soon his side of the fence was vacant and quiet.

"What did you think of my secret weapon, boys?" Bart asked, strutting around like a boss rooster. "How's your eye, Jaley May?" he asked, checking on the injured girl.

"It's okay," she answered, wiping a little bloody ooze from the scratch.

"I'm proud of you and Beauty," Dump said. "You all can be on our team anytime you want to."

"Thanks, Dump," Beauty said, sitting down on the stump beside Jaley May, breathing a tired sigh. "I wouldn't want to be in a scrap like that very often."

"The wet cobs were our only hope," Clem commented. "That bunch had us outnumbered two to one, but we persevered and sent them shagging it on out of here."

"It don't matter how you play the game, it's the win that matters," Bart laughed. "A win's a win, no matter how you get it. Now we can hold our heads up and face that bunch any ol' time."

The Joe-lot Ghost

The long, slender White Hastings cornfield beans were bountiful that year on the Cornfield's farm up there at the head of Coaley Creek.

Marn and Vann Cornfield had sent the boys and girls to "stick" beans in the richest part of the field—on the north side of the hill. Each year, after the second hoeing of the corn, beans were planted next to the hills of corn—pushed into the ground by hand, called "sticking" beans—to grow and climb the corn stalks for support. The vines often grew all the way to the tops of the tall corn, bending the stalks over from the weight of the growing green bean pods. And almost every year there came at least one damaging thunderstorm with high winds which blew the corn-and-bean field hard enough that the crop was laid on the ground. The children dreaded and despised having to go into the fields to fight the mangled mess to search for and pick the many bushels of beans.

There were too many beans grown for one family—no matter how large that family of near-grown-ups to little ankle-biters still in diapers was—to pick, string, and can all by itself. Therefore, there were several bean stringings at the Cornfields' house to get help from friends and neighbors to prepare the green vegetables for canning. The Cornfields had to pick the beans on their own, of course. No one offered to help do that. Stringing the beans and preparing them for canning was the exciting part of the work. People could visit, play games, and just plain have a good ol' time while doing it.

One August weekend, about the last of the month, the beans were picked and piled in the middle of the big living room floor—a pile big enough to hide an army behind.

The word had been sent around the neighborhood and

across the hill to Big Bull Creek—to the town of Big Onion Gap, even—to invite everyone, adults and children alike, to be at the Cornfields' house about dark that Friday evening to help string beans and have a lot of fun.

The Seedys were sure to be at the bean stringing. They enjoyed having fun—the work may not be as exciting as the fun, but they *would* work. They also hoped for a snort of 'shine and a big helping of food.

Talmage Seedy led his brood and wife, Sadie, up the hollow to Marn Cornfield's house, set back against the hill.

Esker and Tester Seedy walked along, far ahead of the slow-paced Talmage and Sadie. Little Seedys were strung along the road, some behind their parents, and some far ahead.

Seldom Seedy, the eldest of the Seedy clan, walked along by himself, his mind on a pretty Cornfield girl—Beauty. He hoped to do a lot of courting and very little bean stringing that night.

Lemon Eskers (Talmage Seedy's nephew) and his wife, Dusty, and their gang of young 'uns walked over from Bass Creek River, joining Talmage and his family down near the Joe-lot Cemetery, the huge community cemetery where everyone was buried as each lived out his or her life and passed on to that final, everlasting sleep.

The Joe-lot Cemetery was known by everyone to be hainted. Moving lights, with no origin or destination, had been seen in that old resting place of the dead. Spooky moans and groans, like the wind blowing over the open mouth of a fruit jar or syrup bottle, often emanated among the silent grave markers. Stories had been told that the huge oak trees which grew in the four corners of the fenced-in burial place often bent in silent prayer as the voices of the haints sent out their pleas of mercy on the moaning, groaning wind that continuously stirred the leaves on the bowing branches, asking to be freed from their eternal bondage in haint land there on Coaley Creek.

Each member of the passing families eyed the rows of silent graves as they hurried just a little to leave it behind in the growing dust of the approaching evening.

Everyone stepped up the pace just a notch or two—everyone except Seldom Seedy. His mind wasn't on the dead or the memory of the dead; his mind was on a very-much-alive girl. There weren't enough haints or ghosts in the world to worry him when his mind was on Beauty Cornfield. Maybe she was just a wee bit on the chubby side, but those sparkling brown eyes and that long, flowing, dark brown hair with a hint of natural curl in it offset any chubbiness that might show. Seldom Seedy could see the inner beauty of that Coaley Creek lass, and that was enough beauty for him.

Seldom walked along the narrow road, looking into the approaching darkness, his eyes almost crossed and his tongue lolling to one side of his mouth, giving him a moon-struck appearance. The dark freckles on his ruddy face stood out like the shot pattern on a white cardboard at a Saturday-morning shooting match. Seldom's mind was agog with love thoughts.

Twenty feet back, Esker chased his younger brother, Tester, up the rocky road in a playful threat of annihilation for something that Tester had done to him. As the two playing boys came abreast of lovelorn Seldom, Esker slowed down and thumped his big brother a frog-popper lick on the shoulder, which brought the boy out of his love stupor. His eyes uncrossed, and his lolling tongue shot back into his open mouth like a spring-loaded measuring tape.

"Gosh take it all to whang-dang!" Seldom yelled. He humped and gimped around in the road, rubbing his aching arm, trying to shoo the humped-up frog off his arm and make the pain go away.

Esker and Tester ran on up the road, Esker trying to catch Tester to give him a dose of the same kind of pain he had given Seldom.

"If I wasn't all growed-up and all, I'd give you two little heathens a good thumpin'!" Seldom called after the fleeing boys. "A man can't walk along and think to hisself in peace," he grumbled. He continued to pet the frog on his arm, trying to get it to go away and not bother him. It had done enough damage already.

"What's your complaint there, boy?" Talmage asked as he caught up with Seldom. "You're doin' a lot of moanin' and groanin' there like you'd been scuzzed right hard by somethin'."

"Them two little worms running up the road's got my dander up just a tad," Seldom reported. "Esker was trying to show off or something, 'cause he lambasted me a good 'un on the shoulder as he chased Tester up the holler. I was just trying to talk that frog that popped up on my arm into hoppin' on its merry way and letting my arm get better. It must be deaf or something, 'cause it sure ain't listening none at all."

Seldom continued to rub his arm and hump and gimp along the road.

"It'll get better when you see that little Cornfield gal that you've gone goo-goo over," Sadie laughed. "Love can always make you forget your hurts and pains."

"Yeah, when you get your little lovin' gal all cuddled up in your arms, the only pain you'll have is from trying to squeeze the tar out of her to prove that you care a lot for her," Talmage laughed, then continued. "I always done your mommy like that when we was a-sparkin' back a few years ago." Talmage grinned, thinking of his courting days and trying to woo Sadie.

"I don't want to hurt her by hugging her up too tight," Seldom said, then went into that eye-crossed, tongue-lolled look, thinking once more of his beloved Beauty Cornfield.

"You can't help but squeeze a little too tight sometimes when you're so desperately in love," Talmage said, dreaming of the past. "You just can't help it sometimes is all."

"I say you can," Sadie butted in. "A man don't have to bust his woman's ribs up just to prove to her that he cares for her."

"Aw, what's a few broke ribs when you're being loved?" Talmage asked, grinning amiably at his plump, pudgy, homely wife.

"Love sure ain't that exciting for me to get all busted up during a fit of your way of loving," Sadie came back. "I guess that you've noticed that I sorta dodge your advances here of late."

"Yeah, I have, woman," Talmage chuckled. "But that don't worry me as much at my age as it would have a few years back. Things was a whole lot different back there in my heydays. I was strong as an ox and smelt a whole lot worse, some folks said."

* * * *

A number of people joined the Seedys, and soon there was an army of friends and neighbors parading the Coaley Creek highway on its way to the Cornfields' house and the anticipated bean stringing.

"Ever'body come on in the house if you can get in," Vann greeted the crowd, inviting everyone to join the huge crowd filling all the chairs in the house, with children lined up on the edge of the hearthstone, sitting like a flock of turkeys on a roost.

Several people stood on the porch and peeped into the dimly lit room, where two oil lamps, one on a table on each side of the room, sent out their rays to meet in the middle of the floor.

"Yeah, come on in," Marn invited. "Here, you young 'uns get off the hearth there and go outside on the porch," he said, pointing, and the children scattered at his blunt order.

"Where's Beauty?" Seldom Seedy asked, entering the crowded room, almost stumbling into the big pile of green beans in the middle of the floor.

A giggle in a dark corner gave the girl's location. If her whereabouts were to be a secret, that little twittery giggle gave her away.

"Aw, there you are," Seldom said, trying to walk around the beans without crushing some of them under his big brogan-clad feet. "I'd know that sweet voice, even amongst a drove of slopping hogs."

Beauty giggled again as the crowd roared, laughing at Seldom Seedy.

"I should've brought my guitar and serenaded you while ever'one else strung that pile of beans," Seldom said, pointing toward the bean pile as he came closer to Beauty and sat down beside her.

"You don't need a guitar to make music to her," Bart Cornfield said. "You can make a little bean-string music. You'll have to work tonight, boy. Anyway, Ol' Bowser will probably have a possum treed pretty soon, and his barking will be better music than you can get out of a guitar. His barking is better than your singing, too."

"I'll string as many beans as you will, Bart," Seldom challenged.

"I doubt that," Bart laughed. "If you google-eye at Beauty all night, like you are now, you won't even be able to find the bean pile, much less do any stringing."

"Has anyone seen Cousin Jubal?" Teed Cornfield asked, entering the room. "We're playing whoopie-hide, and nobody can find him. I thought maybe that he had snuck in here to mingle amongst you while we looked for him outside."

"We ain't seen him anywhere," Clem told Teed.

"No, I don't guess he's in here," Teed said. "If he was, we could hear him sniffing. We'll have to look outside for him, I guess."

"Just let him stay hid," Allamander Skinner said. "The haints'll find him and bring him out in the open."

"No they won't!" Cousin Jubal shouted, running from behind the quilt stack in the corner of the big room, where he had been hiding.

"I figured that would find him if he was in here," Allamander grinned.

"Has anyone seen Brother Trankle Cornfield?" Marn asked the laughing crowd, still tickled at Cousin Jubal.

No one spoke.

"Well, I guess the Joe-lot ghost must've got him as he come by," Marn went on. "It's getting about late enough for the ghost to come out to haint people going by."

"Don't fret none about Trankle getting caught by the Joe-lot ghost," Allamander chuckled. "It'll turn him loose when it gets a good look at him. He's so ugly that he'd scare the ghost."

The house roared with hearty laughter. Before it had time to subside, Brother Trankle elbowed his way through the crowd.

"We figured that the Joe-lot ghost had got you, you being so late and all," Marn said, shaking hands with the preacher.

"I could've got caught by it," Brother Trankle said. "I saw something as I waltzed by the graveyard down there. I saw a dim light hovering over Grenade Shores' grave-rock. I couldn't see anybody around the grave—just the moving light. I got up real close to it, to investigate the goings on. When I got about ten foot from the tomb-rock, all at once the light went away, and I couldn't tell where it went. Do you know what I figured it was when I first seen it? I figured that it might've been Ram Bolton come over from his resting place on Big Bull Creek to get Grenade to go fox hunting with him. They used to fox hunt together all the time, you know."

"Yeah, them two was a real close-knit pair in real life," Talmage Seedy spoke. "I've seen some eerie things down there at the graveyard, too. Did you see or hear their dogs signin' a fox?"

"No. Come to think of it, I didn't," the old preacher answered, smiling broadly but trying to be serious. "Them dogs could've been up in the woods or som'ers looking around for fresh fox sign, though."

"Well, since Brother Trankle's here, safe and sound as a hog-dollar, I guess that we ought to get started into our bean stringing," Marn announced. "We can talk about haints and ghosts while we work."

Vann handed each person an empty chop sack to lay across his lap to hold beans in while he strung them. Empty bushel baskets were placed about the room in places where several people could use the same basket to get rid of the strings after having removed them from the beans.

Soon the bean stringing was under way, and the telling of stories began.

Seldom Seedy and Beauty talked in whispers, stringing

the beans and dropping the strings back with the other beans in the chop sack on Beauty's lap, making a mess of things. They didn't care, though. They were thinking of love, not beans.

"The other night," Colter Skinner began, "since ever'body's telling ghost stories, I was coming up the road toward home, down there at the lower end of the Joe-lot, when I saw this little baby toddle across the road in front of me and start up into the woods beside the road. It had a glowing light around it, like an oil lamp globe. I ran up to the edge of the woods to pick it up, when all at once it just plain disappeared into thin air. I didn't know what to think of that. I thought about it all the way home, though. Since that happened, I've tried not to get caught out near that graveyard after dark."

"I saw something one night that would make your toenails curl up, it was so scary," Ferd Skinner said, turning ashy-white just thinking about what he had seen.

"You ain't gonna tell that 'un are you, Ferd?" Meg asked, looking at her husband and then at the growing darkness outside.

"Yeah, I sure am, Hon," Ferd said. "That's bothered me a whole lot, and I need to tell it to ever'body to get it off my chest and out of my mind for good maybe. I don't know if I can ever forget about it, though, since it was so scary and all. You folks may not believe this, but it's the Gospel truth if ever I told the truth before."

"If you have to tell it, go ahead and do it," Meg said, shivering. "Tell it, but don't let the young 'uns hear it. If they hear it tonight, they'll have nightmares for the next solid month. Where are the young 'uns, anyhow?"

Meg, along with the rest of the mothers present, looked around the room, searching for the children.

All the children and several of the bigger boys and girls had gone outside to play whoopie-hide, after Teed came into the room in search of Cousin Jubal.

"I guess it'll be safe enough to tell it to the grown-ups and big boys and girls then," Meg told her husband, returning to her lapful of beans.

Ferd went on with his story. "I was coming in home late that Friday night after working over in Kentucky all week in the mines. I was tired as usual. And my body was sore from that long week of hard labor underground in them dog holes. I had just took a good drink of whisky to take the stiffness out of my joints. You know your knees and other joints will stiffen up on you after you've worked all week in the mines. Well, anyway, I had took a nip or two and could feel the stiffness leaving my sore joints when all at once I bumped into something in the road—just a little ways below the graveyard. It was so dark that I couldn't hardly see my hand when I held it up in front of my face. I could see a dark outline of something almost as big as a barn against the skyline. It must've been a big animal of some kind. It was as broad as the road was. I couldn't go around it 'cause it reached from the woods on one side of the road to the woods on the other side of the road. I couldn't see what it was. I got up enough courage, which lasted only a second or two, and reached out and touched that thing. It felt hairy—felt like a goat's beard to me—and the dew had fell on it, making it wet to the touch. I don't know what happened next. I do remember that I heard a snorting sound, and that was all she wrote. I must've fainted from the fright, 'cause when I come to it was morning and daylight. Whatever it was, it was gone then. I looked for tracks but couldn't find any. It must've been a spook of some kind that didn't leave tracks in the dusty road. I ain't seen it since, and don't want to see it again, ever!"

"I don't believe that malarkey," Seldom Seedy spoke up, doubting that there was any truth in Ferd Skinner's tale. "I've been up and down the Coaley Creek road all my life, and I ain't seen or heard anything down there at the Joe-lot Cemetery like what you all are telling that you seen. You all are just making up all your stories just for entertainment, ain't you?"

"No. I'm not making up any stories," Colter Skinner spoke seriously. "I saw that glowing baby just as I told you I did. I wouldn't lie about something that serious."

"I don't believe you," Seldom continued to argue. "Looks

to me like else folks would've seen the thing that you saw, Colter. And the thing that you saw, Ferd, ought to be big enough to see anytime, night *or* day. I don't believe that stuff, and I'll go to my grave not believing in stuff like that."

"I seen, and even felt, that hairy thing down there," Ferd replied. "I can't prove it, but at least you could take my word for it."

"I ain't taking anybody's word for it 'cause I just don't believe you," Seldom continued to argue.

"Just give it time and it'll be there for you to see some night when you're waltzing back down the holler from Marn's house after coming up here to court Beauty," Ferd chuckled, although he was serious about what he alleged to have seen.

"Seldom, you're too much of a fraidy cat to be caught out after dark," Bart laughed.

"No he's not," Beauty butted in, coming to Seldom's defense. "He's here in this house courting me, ain't he, and Daddy and Mommy are right here in the same room with us. That's brave, ain't it? You'd have to say that he's a brave man. You may not think so, but I sure as the world do."

"Courtin' in front of me and Vann could change in the twinkle of an eye," Marn responded.

The room became ghostly quiet. Beauty's half-hearted giggle was the only sound in the room.

Seldom said nothing at all.

The spinning of ghost and haint yarns stopped abruptly, and the conversation turned to the weather, late crops, and the dreaded approach of winter.

The crowd began to disperse after most of the beans had been strung and broken—about eleven o'clock. They had to return to their homes to get some sleep and rest and to prepare for another day of work on the morrow.

"Are you going with us, Seldom?" Talmage Seedy asked. "Or are you gonna stay 'round here and court Beauty a little while longer? You ought to come on pretty soon. We've got a lot of work to do tomorrow, and it ain't long before gettin' up time."

"You all go on. I'll be along directly," Seldom told his father, then returned his attention to Beauty, causing the pretty girl to giggle at something he said, too low for anyone else to hear.

"Yeah, he'll be along pretty soon, too," Marn told Talmage. "Some of us have to work tomorrow."

"Don't let the Joe-lot ghost get you, boy," Talmage warned his son.

"It won't get me," Seldom bragged. "I ain't afraid of your ghosts and little baby crossing the road in the night all by itself, shining like a lamp globe. And, Ferd, I ain't scared of your big hairy beast that fills up the road and makes you faint in your tracks. I'd say that you took more snorts from that bottle than just one or two. You took enough to pass out on. And another thing, they ain't nothing to be scared of out there in the night, except maybe yourself when you're alone. Why, I'd stop and talk to anything that I met in the road—night or day."

"No, the ghosts and haints won't get ol' Seldom," Dump Cornfield surmised. "He'll be running too fast as he goes by the Joe-lot Cemetery for any ghost or haint to see him, much less take a hold onto him."

Everyone laughed at Dump's prediction.

"Let's hurry down to the Joe-lot before Seldom leaves," Bart whispered to Clem. "Let's get down there and climb up in a corner tree of the graveyard and scare the living day-lights out of that bragging boy as he goes by the graveyard on his way home."

"That sounds good to me," Clem chuckled. "We'll climb up in that big tree in the corner of the graveyard next to the road—in that big oak. He can't see us up there amongst the tree limbs and leaves, with us in the dark, too."

"Good idea," Bart agreed.

* * * *

"This 'un will be easier to climb than the others," Clem said as they arrived at their destination. "The first limbs are closer to the ground on this 'un than the others."

"Yeah, it'll be a lot easier to climb," Bart replied, looking the tree over, figuring on how best to scale it to the first limb, about eight feet from the ground. He gripped his chin with his left hand and pondered the situation. "I tell you what," he finally said. "You hoostie me up as high as you can, and maybe I can reach that bottom limb and snatch a hold of it. When I get up there on that limb, then I'll reach down and pull you up in the tree with me. What do you say?"

"Sounds good to me, Brud," Clem said, agreeing with Bart's plan. He bent slightly and gripped his hands, lacing his fingers together. "Here, step into my hands and I'll hoostie you right on up into the tree. You'll have to help me by jumping when I say to jump. We'll go on 'three.'"

"Okay. I'm ready," Bart announced.

"One," Clem counted, raising, then lowering his hands to give Bart the feel of a little pressure, preparing him to be ready to go at the right time. "Two," he counted, continuing to raise and lower his clasped hands. "Three," he grunted, quickly raising his whole body with all his strength, gripping Bart's foot to boost him into the tree.

Bart's movement was just a little out of sync with Clem's, and as Clem lifted his hands, Bart lifted his foot, losing his balance, falling backward on the ground at the base of the oak tree.

"Whew! That ground sure is hard," Bart groaned, rubbing the back of his head, wincing with pain. He raised up slowly, checking for cuts and bruises. Finding that he was okay and in one piece, he prepared for another attempt to jump to the limb overhead.

"We got to get it right this time," Clem said, bending over to permit Bart to step into his hands once more. "Seldom will be coming along here pretty soon. We've got to get up in that tree before he gets here."

"We'll do it," Bart assured him.

The second try was a success. Bart caught the limb, hung onto it momentarily, then scrambled up into the thick branches above. He gripped a limb with his legs and suspended his body over Clem, reaching a hand down for his brother to jump up and grab.

Clem jumped as high as he could and grabbed Bart's wrist with both hands. He then climbed, with Bart's help, to the safety of the tree's branches.

The boys made themselves as comfortable as possible and waited for the arrival of the unsuspecting Seldom Seedy. They did not have a long wait.

Seldom walked along the road, his mind still on his sweetheart, Beauty Cornfield. He whistled softly, an unrecognizable tune, then hummed happily—a love song, of course.

As happy Seldom came abreast of the big tree occupied by the ghost imposters, the two boys began their rehearsed routine.

"Ooooooh," Bart moaned. Then in a quavering, eerie voice he asked a question into the still night. "What did they hang you for, Rubin?"

"Ooooooh," Clem groaned. Then in the same quavering, eerie voice, he gave an answer. "I was a horse thief when I was alive. I got caught. They hung me high with a new rope. My neck still smarts from that scratchy plow line they used. What did they hang you for, Jonah?"

"I was just a petty chicken thief," Bart replied. "They was hard up to have a hanging when they strung me up. They could have let me go on that charge."

"Yeah, that ain't near as bad as a horse thief," Clem agreed.

Seldom Seedy froze in his tracks, fear gripping his inner soul, choking him like someone trying to choke a dog off a possum. Finally gaining his composure, he tore out of there at full throttle, running down the road as fast as he could. He was looking back at the Joe-lot Cemetery and didn't realize he was going into a stiff curve in the road. Seldom plowed into the brush and briars growing near the edge of the road. He thrashed around in the trees for a moment until he got a good foothold in the soft dirt, then tore out of there like a yearling bull running through a field of shoulder-high corn. He did not look back again during that mad dash home.

Bart and Clem laughed so hard that they almost fell out of the tree.

"Ooooooh," an eerie voice emanated from a tree in another corner of the graveyard.

The laughing stopped abruptly and everything grew deathly still.

"What was that?" Clem whispered.

"Don't know," Bart croaked, showing fear of the mysterious sound in the other tree.

"Ooooooh," the moan came again. "You fellers didn't do much to get hung for," the ghostly voice continued. "I went to court the wrong woman and got caught, and I was hung on the spot. Now that was a good reason to be hung. Your reasons for gettin' hung ain't worth snot, compared to mine."

The two boys almost fell from the tree. They landed on their feet, though, and hit the ground running at breakneck speed up the hollow road.

After about a half of a mile of hard running at a sprinter's speed, Bart slowed down. "Who do you think that was in that other tree."

"I'd bet that voice we heard was Dump," Clem said, breathing hard, like a wind-broke horse after a hard pull on a saw log. "It had to be Dump. He must have heard us planning this little caper. He was right there beside of us. Yeah, that's who it was. There ain't any reason for us to run anymore."

"That was him all right," Bart agreed, slowing to a walk.

"But that sure scared the tar out of me," Clem panted.

"I don't believe it was tar that he scared out of me," Bart allowed. "Didn't feel like tar anyway."

"Let's gang up on Dump when he gets back to the house and give him a good wallering—just for the fun of it," Clem suggested, laughing.

"Yeah, let's do it," Bart agreed. "We won't hurt him or anything like that, even though he deserves it. We'll just make him think we're going to tear him up like a sow's bed. He had no call to scare us like that. It wasn't funny to me."

The brothers continued to talk about the voice in the tree

at the Joe-lot Cemetery as they hurried on toward the house.

* * * *

"Where have you two fellers been?" Dump asked as Clem and Bart entered the living room, where Marn, Vann, and the rest of the family were cleaning up the mess made by the bean stringers.

"Whaaa—Howww—Whooo—Howww?" Bart stammered, turning as white as a sheet.

"Yeah, how did you get back here ahead of us so fast?" Clem asked, more composed than Bart. "You must have took a shortcut on the way back. We know that it was you at the cemetery, up in that big oak tree."

"They ain't no shortcut back here. It's a straight line back to here," Bart said, gaining control of his voice, shaking his head in wonder."

"Dump's been here all the time," Vann told the boys. "He's been helping clean up the house while you boys were out trying to scare somebody. I'd say you were trying to scare Seldom Seedy, most likely."

"Come on and help us finish the cleaning up so we can get to bed," Marn said. "We've got a long, hard day of work ahead of us tomorrow. We'll have to help your mommy wash and can these beans."

Clem and Bart looked at each other, bewildered by the mysterious voice at the cemetery.

"Did anyone else hear us plotting to scare Seldom?" Clem asked.

"Not that I know of," Bart told him.

"You know something, Bart?" Clem croaked out, swallowing against a big lump in his throat. "There *is* a Joe-lot ghost after all."

"There sure is," Bart agreed, his trembling legs giving way under him as he plopped down in a chair to keep from falling flat on his back on the floor.

Clem did likewise, while the rest of the family laughed—with Dump laughing harder than the rest.

A He-witch on Coaley Creek

When the stranger showed up on Coaley Creek, no one there knew him. No one knew where he came from. No one trusted him. He was just a nomad—no place to call home. Why he came into the little, quiet mountain community, no one knew. Maybe he was a slacker trying to elude the Army; maybe a fugitive trying to elude justice; maybe a revenuer! He wouldn't stay on Coaley Creek very long if he were a revenuer. The moonshiners would see to that. Maybe if everyone ignored him, he would go away. The people tried to ignore him but kept an eye on when he moved about the community, in the daytime, that is.

When the day turned into night, the stranger seemed to disappear—to where, no one knew, even though Ferd Skinner had volunteered to tail the stranger all the time.

The stranger must have known that Ferd was trying to keep him under surveillance, for he disappeared every night like a puff of smoke.

"We need to talk to all the folks in the neighborhood about that stranger that's been hanging around here for the last week or so," Marn Cornfield mentioned to his son Judge L. early one September morning as the two prepared to go to the upper cornfield to commence harvesting the corn crop on the steep slope. "Maybe we should have a get-together and have a discussion about this feller."

"We don't need to worry about that stranger," Judge L. said. "Why do we need to get excited about him? The only people who worry about strangers around here are the ones making moonshine."

"You know that the fellow's not here for no good at all. If he was a real friendly man, he'd come right out and tell us what he's doing, or speak to us—something like that. I believe he's a spy for the revenuers."

"Well, Dad, did you ever think about it? We've not given the man a chance to tell us what he's doing here," Judge L. declared. "I've not seen anyone talking to him, that I know of, 'cept Col Modut. Have you?"

"No. Come to think of it, I ain't. No, I sure ain't," Marn said, shaking his head.

"Well, why don't some of you grown-ups go find him and talk to him," Judge L. suggested. "You should introduce yourselves to him and have a good man-to-man talk with him. That way you might get to know him instead of wondering about him."

"That's a real good idea, Judge L.," Marn came back. "I'll tell you what I'll do. I need some help cutting the corn in that fer-field 'round yonder from the barn. I'll approach that feller and see if I can hire him to help out 'round the place while we're harvesting the crops. Maybe we can get acquainted with him and find out who he is and where he's from, and why he's hanging around here like he is."

"I'm all for that, Dad," Judge L. agreed. "We need a lot of help since you have to go back to work in the mines at Jenkins and can't be here to help the rest of us do the farming."

"Yeah, I know," Marn mused, thinking. "You know, I don't believe that I'll plant as big a crop next year as I did this 'un. Since all of you boys are growing up so fast, you'll probably be going in the mines next year to work and make your own way. Some of you will probably join the Army or go to Baltimore to make your fortunes, then I won't have much help left on the farm. It takes a lot of workers to plant, work, and harvest a crop as big as we grow. Yeah, I think I'll cut back on the size of my crops next year."

"I know better than that, Dad," Judge L. smiled. "You will start plowing just as soon as the weather changes in February and the sun begins to shine just a little warm. Then you'll plow as long as you can find land without trees on it. Ain't I right, Dad?"

"Yeah, I guess you are, Son," Marn said, smiling broadly. "But getting back to that stranger. I'll go see if I can hire him to help cut the corn. I need to finish corn cutting this week, and then get back to Jenkins. The super of the mines would only let me off for one week. I tried to get him to extend it to two weeks, but he wouldn't. Said he was shorthanded as it was."

"Yeah, it would be nice if you could be off for a couple of weeks," Judge L. agreed. "But me and the rest can handle the harvesting so you can work at your job. If we can't finish it this week while you're here helping, the rest of us can finish it next week sometime."

"If I can get that stranger to come and help us, I know we can finish up by this weekend. That is if the man knows anything about farming," Marn declared. "You know as well as I do," he continued, "that he could be someone scouting the area for coal," Marn reasoned. "I hope no coal company ever comes in and buys ever'body out and strips the land like they're beginning to do ever'where else. I'm getting too old to have to move around over the country like an Arab in the desert."

"I don't think that's what this feller's here for," Judge L. replied. "As I told you, I saw him with Col Modut the other day, and they were talking real friendly like. I know that Col Modut wouldn't be too friendly with a coal prospector. I'm sure that Col doesn't want to move around. He's dug in over in his holler like a big groundhog. He's gun-shy about moving away—just the way you are about moving, Dad. I guess the best thing for us to do is go visit Col and talk to him. You know how gossipy Col is. He knows ever'thing that's going on around here."

"Aw, Judge L., the gossiping that he does is good for his health," Marn chuckled. "Old people thrive on that. Grandpaw Dalker is getting up in years now, and if it wasn't for a good dose of gossip once in a while, I'd say he'd be a goner from here in no time at all. He'd probably just dry up and blow away on a strong puff of March wind in the springtime. So don't fault Col Modut for gossiping. That's the key to his long life."

"I guess you've got a point there, Dad," Judge L. said. "But we ought to give the stranger the benefit of the doubt, give him the chance to prove himself one way or the other—for good or for bad. We ain't supposed to judge others without being sure of what we're judging them for. You know what the Bible says about judging other folks."

"Yeah, I know what the Bible says about it," Marn returned. "You go down to Col Modut's house and see if he knows where that feller is. Tell the stranger, if he's there, to come and talk to me if he wants to earn a little pocket change. Me and your mommy and the rest of the young 'uns will be cutting corn. Hurry back," Marn ordered. "Dump's herdin' them up right now," he went on. "Get a move on now. I want you back in a hurry—quicker than you can say 'hog snot.'"

* * * *

Hooker Joe Moss slipped silently through the lush, green forest overlooking Marn and Vann Cornfield's farm, taking in every movement made by the nonstop, hardworking family members. The children were such a happy bunch, he could tell, even though he had not been very close to them. He had often heard them laughing boisterously down there in the viridescent valley between the steep, rocky hillsides. He wished he could be all laid-back like those kids. They worked hard, he noticed, and they romped all over the hills afterward, just like they had not worked at all during a long day in a cornfield or hayfield.

He watched the boy leave and go walking down the road toward Big Onion Gap while the father and the rest of the family entered the large cornfield behind the barn and commenced cutting the tall, ear-ladened stalks. They used large machete-type knives made from worn-out crosscut saws, with tough hickory handles. Evidently the boy had to run an errand before working in the field, or maybe he had gone to get more tools to work with. There were a bunch of people in that field. Maybe there were too many workers for the number of corn knives they had.

Hooker Joe finally stood up, slowly stretching the kinks out of his tall, thin body. His tousled black hair reached to his shirt collar and out over his ears, longer than usual. He needed a haircut. He wore dungarees and a faded denim shirt. The worn heels of his cowboy boots cut into the soft dirt as he left his look-out and stole quietly out the ridge. At a faint trace of a path that went off from the ridge, he turned with that trace, following it into a dark, damp hollow where a moonshine 'still stood beneath an overhang of rock that jutted out from the steep hill.

A healthy, clear stream of water spouted from a crack in the cliff and flowed into a ten-gallon natural basin eroded into a huge limestone rock at the base of the cliff. A rusty tin cup sat handily by the spring, waiting for anyone who needed a drink to take it up and dip it into the cool water to quench his thirst.

Hooker Joe picked the cup up from its resting place on the rock, rinsed it out, and threw the water into the bushes bordering the spring. Satisfied that the cup was clean enough, he walked over to the 'still, where he skimmed the top of the working mash away to reveal the whitish liquid beneath called "sour beer." He dipped out several yellow jackets and hornets that had drowned in the working mash, then drank a cupful down and dipped out another, unaware that he was being watched. He drank the second cupful, then sat down on a rock to rest and enjoy the effects of the raw-mash beer.

Judge L. Cornfield peered from behind a shagbark hickory tree beside the ridge path, observing the stranger stirring around in the contents of a fermenting box at Uncle Ferd's 'still. Was the man a revenuer or an FBI agent? The man was in plain clothes, but maybe he wanted to look like everyone else on Coaley Creek. Surely he wasn't a revenuer! A revenuer wouldn't be sipping a cupful of sour mash beer, and enjoying it, too. A revenuer would be chopping up the boiler and bursting up the fermenting barrels and boxes, not sipping sour mash beer.

Hooker Joe sipped another slurp from the cup, set it down, then rubbed his opened right palm over his left hand, closed into a fist. Suddenly something that looked like a biscuit appeared in the man's hand. It was something to eat, all right, for Hooker Joe popped it into his mouth and bit off a huge helping. He chewed a few times, then drank from the cup to wash the food down.

"A he-witch!" Judge L. exclaimed to himself. "He has to be a he-witch to be able to do magic like that—make a biscuit suddenly appear from nowhere."

Judge L. had heard and read about magicians who could do tricks like that, but what would a magician be doing on Coaley Creek? A magician would be on a stage in New York City somewhere, making money with his abilities to make magic. No, siree! No doubt about it; that strange man had to be a he-witch!

Judge L. left his hiding place behind the big shagbark hickory tree on the high ridge and ran at full speed toward home to report to his father what he had just discovered about the stranger at Uncle Ferd's 'still.

* * * *

"Dad!" Judge L. called, entering the cornfield. "I saw the stranger. I saw him over in the head of Barn Holler. He was messing around Uncle Ferd's 'still," he reported, panting, almost out of breath from his mad dash down the mountain.

"A revenuer," Marn surmised. "I knowed it the whole time. I knowed he was a revenuer."

"No, Dad," Judge L. gasped. "He ain't a revenuer, as you think. He's a he-witch!"

"What gives you the idea that he's a witch?" Marn asked. "I've heard about people with witchin' powers, but I ain't seen one around here. That don't mean that they ain't any witches around, though. Your Grandpaw Dalker has seen the results of their powers."

"Well, Dad," Judge L. began, "the feller made a biscuit appear from nowhere—actually out of his closed fist."

"Maybe he just had it gripped tight in his hand and you couldn't see it is all," Marn said.

"Gosh, no, Dad!" Judge L. exclaimed. "The biscuit was as big as his hand was. His hand wasn't big enough to hide anything that big. The bread was plucked right out of the air. I saw it with my own two eyes. He ate the biscuit and drank sour mash beer with it. I don't see how he could stand to drink from that barrel of fermenting mash, full of dead yeller jackets, hornets, and waspers. He had to stir the insects out of the way and make a quick dip to get some clean beer in his cup."

"How come you to see this feller at Ferd's 'still 'stead of you going on down to Col Modut's house and asking about him?" Marn asked.

"Well, Dad," Judge L. began, "I was going out the ridge above Barn Holler when I saw a glimpse of someone slipping along through the woods on the other side of the hill. I snuck in behind a tree—playing Indian—and watched till I saw that he wasn't anybody that I know. Then I saw that the person was the stranger that ever'body's been talking about. So, I stayed real still, hid there behind that hickory tree, and watched the man go on past me and drop over the hill toward Uncle Ferd's 'still. I believe that he knew where he was going. Been there plenty of times, I'd say. I snuck on out the ridge and looked in on him down there at the 'still. I watched him skim the scum off the top of the working barrels of beer. Then's when I saw it. He made that biscuit jump right out of the air, right into his hand—just like magic. I tell you, he has to have witching powers, Dad."

"No doubt about it, he does have them kinds of powers," Marn declared soberly. "We'll have to tell ever'body about this feller—what you seen him do. The folks around here need to be warned about this he-witch."

"Do you want me to ride Ol' Jock around to ever'body's house and tell them about what I saw him do?" Judge L. asked, ready to saddle the horse and ride through the neighborhood to announce to his friends and neighbors that the witch had come.

"No, Son," Marn chuckled, "We can get the word out soon enough. We've got corn to cut. So let's get to work."

Reluctantly Judge L. joined the rest of the family busy cutting the cornstalks and shocking the fodder in Indian tepee shocks to cure for winter feed for the livestock.

* * * *

The magic powers of Hooker Joe Moss were related to everyone in the Big Onion Gap community, and for many miles around. Odd things had happened lately, things that would have been ignored otherwise. Most of the odd happenings were just everyday things, but since there was someone handy to attribute them to, that cause was used often—more often than necessary. The powers of Hooker Joe had become so prevalent that people in other communities and adjoining counties were having unexplained happenings.

One day Dalker Skinner stomped into the Cornfields' kitchen, almost out of breath after the one-mile walk from his house around in the next hollow. Perspiration had run from his forehead, down his nose, and dropped onto his drooping gray mustache, where it stopped just under his nostrils. The man removed his sweat-stained handkerchief from his overalls pocket and wiped the sweat from his face, giving his mustache a good mopping.

"Marn," the old fellow said as he tossed his hat on the meal chest in the corner and slowly sat down in an empty chair at the end of the table, where the family was eating an early breakfast. "I need your help in the worst way. There's something wrong with my mare, Ol' Maude. This morning when I went out to feed her—I kept her in the barn last night so I'd be able to find her and catch her to haul some chestnut logs for stove wood—she was wringing wet with sweat. When I told Zonie about it, she said that it might be that witches have been riding her during the night."

"They'll do that," Vann spoke up. "I ain't heard of them doing that much around here lately, though. But since that stranger come onto Coaley Creek, and he has witching powers, I'll agree with Maw. Judge L. seen that stranger use his witching powers over there at Ferd's 'still to snatch bread right out of midair. Yeah, snatched it right out of the air—a biscuit bread. Now if that ain't witching powers, I don't know what is."

"That's what it sounds like to me," Dalker stated seriously. "That happened to Pap's mule one time. He had to send for Grandpap to come and witch doctor the mule. Took care of it just like that." Dalker snapped his fingers together. "I wish I could send for him to come and help me, but it's too late for his help. He's been dead nigh on to fifty years. I'm too late to call for his help. But my brother Corbitt learnt how to witch doctor animals to get them out from under a witch's spell, before Grandpap passed on."

"I'll look at her and see if I can do something for her," Marn offered. "She might've eaten something that made her sick. She could have eaten a big bait of acorns or something. That'll make 'em sick and will make 'em sweat real bad. You know, she could have got into Ferd's 'backer shed and eaten a bait of 'backer. He just got it cut, and it's still partly green. Horses will do that sometimes—eat 'backer. You know that a horse can't puke up anything that it eats, and it won't settle in its stomach. Now a dog will puke it guts out all over the place if it eats something that don't agree with it, but a horse can't puke at all. I'll run over there and walk Ol' Maude around the barn to try to get her to pass what she ate on through to the outside as quick as she can. We might have to walk her all day to get that to happen, but it's what we've got to do. If she gets down, we won't be able to get her back on her feet to walk her. Let's shake a leg and get on out to your barn and do something for that brute before it's too late to do anything at all."

Marn sipped the remaining drops of coffee from his cup, pushed his chair back, scrubbing the legs over the bare wood floor, and rose. He went to get his sweat-stained felt hat from a nail on the back of the kitchen door. "Let's go, Dalker," he said, hurrying his father-in-law. "Ol' Maude may already be down and dying."

"I should have time for a cup of good black coffee, shouldn't I?" Dalker asked.

"No, you won't have time to drink a cup of coffee, Dalker," Marn replied. "Come on. We can drink coffee later."

"By drabbs," Dalker said, "that coffee sure looks and smells delicious. Wish I could have just a sip of it. Surely Ol' Maude can last that long, looks to me like."

"Here," Vann said, "take my cup. You can drink it as you go along. Marn can bring the cup back when he returns from doctoring Ol' Maude."

"I believe we should send for Corbitt," Dalker said. "I sure believe that witches rode her all night last night. Why don't you send one of your boys over to get Corbitt to come and help us, Marn?"

"Come on. We can do that later if walking her don't help," Marn stated, growing impatient with Dalker's slowpoke gait.

"Can I go with you, Dad," Judge L. asked, then waited for an answer from his father, which was slow in coming. "I'll already be over there if I have to go on and get Uncle Corbitt."

"Yeah, come on," Marn said, leaving the room.

"Can I go, too?" Jake asked, rising from the table, ready to go if allowed. "I can go with Judge L. to get Uncle Corbitt. I ain't been to his house in a long time."

"Come on," Marn called over his shoulder. "But the rest of you will have to stay here," he told the other children before they could ask for permission to go along, too.

With Jake bringing up the rear, the two men and two boys left the house.

It turned out to be as Marn had suspected. The mare had eaten something that had disagreed with her. After several hours of walking the mare around and around the big log barn, she passed whatever was bothering her. She settled down in her stall and started munching on a bundle of fodder in her manger.

"Witches didn't ride her and make her sick," Marn reported. "It was just something she ate."

"Yeah, I guess you're right, Marn," Dalker said.

* * * *

"I still say that that feller's a witch," Marn declared early one morning as he and Vann sat at the table after breakfast, drinking an extra cup of hot, black coffee. The children had left the table and were doing their chores. "Even though Ol' Maude ate something to make her appear to have been rode all night by witches don't mean that the brute wasn't really witched in some way. What happened last night, and for the last four or five nights in a row, leads me to believe that there's really a witch in the neighborhood. Hooker Joe—that stranger—he's not a stranger anymore. I met the man and got acquainted with him. He ain't a real bad person—just odd-acting is all. I don't trust him at all, though. I could never trust a odd-acting person. He'll look at you with his odd-looking eyes. They're real pale looking—makes me think of a snake's eyes, and I can't trust anybody with snake eyes."

"Well, if you don't have any truck with him, there ain't any reason to distrust him," Vann said, getting into the conversation.

"Well, it ain't that I distrust him, Vann," Marn began to explain. "It's just that he makes me feel uneasy around him is all. You've seen people like that before, I'm sure."

"I understand what you're saying," Vann said.

"Have you heard that dog barking ever' night here lately?" Marn asked.

"No, I've not heard a thing," Vann told him. "I sleep like a log now that the baby has started sleeping all night without having to be changed and fed."

"Well, I've heard it enough for both of us. The thing sets over there near the barn and yaps all night long. What I think is causing it to do all that barking, at nothing, too, is that he's being witched by that Hooker Joe feller."

"Why in the world would you think that he's witching you?" Vann asked. "You've not given him any reason to witch you, have you?"

"No. But I noticed when me and him and Col Modut were talking the other day, he'd be grinning like a skinned skunk when I'd happen to look in his direction. I believe he was thinking about witching me. I sort of mentioned something about strangers with witching powers roaming around on Coaley Creek."

"You shouldn't have said anything like that, since you ain't sure that he's a witch," Vann said.

"I said it all right," Marn replied. "And I believe that he took it as a sort of slap in the face and decided to get even with me by making that dog bark all night long at nothing but maybe the moon."

"Well, he should," Vann declared.

"Anyway, ever' time I get up at night to try to shoot that blasted stray dog—it come on Coaley Creek about the same time that Hooker Joe did—it gets quiet. Then as soon as I get back in the bed and almost back to sleep, it starts that yapping again. It's witched, I tell you. I believe that the man has the dog witched just to bother people that he don't like much."

"Maybe he has got the dog witched to obey his command, and maybe you're just making things seem worse than they really are," Vann commented.

"No, I'm not exaggerating about this," Marn declared. "Ever' time I get up at night to try to sneak out and shoot that dog, it quietens down and runs away. Now if that ain't a dog that's controlled by a witch, I don't know what is. It's a mystery that's got to be solved, and soon! That could drive a man crazy in a hurry. That's probably what the man wants me to do. Go crazy."

"It sure is a mystery," Vann agreed.

"The next night that dog barks and disturbs my sleep, I'm gonna send one of the boys to get your Uncle Corbitt to come and witch doctor ever'body and maybe drive that feller off of Coaley Creek and back to where he come from."

"We need to do something about what he's doing to bother ever'body," Vann said.

"'Pon my honor," Marn began, "I'm gonna do something about it instead of just bumping my gums about it..."

Judge L. burst through the door, interrupting his father's

statement.

"Grandpaw's coming again," Judge L. reported, panting heavily from his mad dash for the house to announce the arrival of Dalker Skinner. "He's got some news to tell you about that witch, Hooker Joe."

"I guess he's been witching Paw," Vann said, rising from the table to watch the approach of her father.

Dalker shuffled along the yellow-clay-bank path leading from the milk gap over on the knoll above the barn to the Cornfields' house at the foot of the hill. The man walked along with his head bowed—smoking his pipe—in his normal posture. He entered the house, his head still bowed, his pipe puffing and smoking like a steam engine-powered freight train on a steep grade.

"Come in the house and have a cup of coffee," Marn invited. "Draw you up a chair and set down and rest a spell. Looks to me like you're about tuckered out, man."

"Plague-goned witches, no how," Dalker growled without greeting Marn and Vann.

"Here, Paw. Sit down and rest while I pour you a cup of coffee to help settle you down a tad," Vann said, rising while holding the baby, Koodank, on her hip with her left hand. She took a coffee mug and saucer from a cupboard in a corner of the room and placed them on the table in front of her father. She then proceeded to fill the mug with coffee, still holding Koodank on her hip.

Immediately Dalker poured the saucer full of the steaming coffee and slurped a huge gulp of the hot liquid. "Hot!" he shouted, fanning his mouth with both hands after having set the saucer on the oilcloth-covered table, spilling some of the coffee. "Plague-goned, that sure was hot!"

"Vann brews it strong and hot," Marn replied, smiling, enjoying the humor he saw in the incident.

Dalker wiped his mouth with his shirtsleeve, gently patting his scalded lips. He licked his lips and tried another sip of the coffee, more carefully, taking a smaller slurping gulp, swallowing loudly. "That was much better," he commented, grinning across the table at Vann.

"What have the witches done now, Paw?" Vann asked her disgruntled father. "You come in griping about witches."

"Well, now I know that Hooker Joe is a real witch," Dalker began. "I seen him up above the barn in the woods a while ago," he continued. "He had my hogs witched, and there he was, thinking that nobody could see him all hunkered down behind a big chestnut stump, grinnin' all over hisself at what them hogs were doing. He had them hogs doing about ever'thing you could think of. They was staggering around, sitting on their haunches, and my boar-hog was trying to stand on his head. Fat as that hog is, it's a wonder that he didn't break his neck. I tell you, I ain't never seen hogs act like that before in my whole life. We need to send for Corbitt to come and stop that feller from witching my hogs and horse."

"Yeah, Dalker, I agree with you," Marn spoke. "I can't sleep for that yapping dog that's witched, and I've got to get back to the mines to work. Without any sleep I can't work safe, and the mine super wants us to work safe on the job. We'll sure have to get Corbitt over here in a hurry."

"Dad, can me and Jake go and get Uncle Corbitt to come and do the witch doctoring?" Judge L. asked.

"Yeah, go ahead, and hurry along," Marn said.

"Can we ride Ol' Jock over there, Dad?" Judge L. asked.

"Yeah, you can," Marn told the boy. "Shake a leg now. You're wasting time standing there grinning."

Judge L. tore out of the house, shouting for Jake to come and go with him to get Uncle Corbitt.

* * * *

"They're witched all right," Corbitt Skinner said as he watched the hogs.

Most of the swine were lying down. Only the boar-hog was trying to root out a soft bed to lie down in. He almost fell forward on his fat-jowled head. His long nose stopped his forward movement. Finally satisfied that he had a good place to lie down, he plopped down with a snorting sigh.

"Yeah, they're witched," Corbitt continued to say. "They're plum' ragged out and need some rest. I'll go out here in the woods and take care of that witch. Judge L.," Corbitt said, turning to the boy, "you're son number seven, ain't you?"

"Sure am, Unc," Judge L. replied, curious as to why his great uncle wanted to know if he were the seventh son of Marn and Vann. Although he wasn't the seventh son, Uncle Corbitt wouldn't know the difference, Judge L. reasoned.

"Well, I'm a seventh son, and my paw was a seventh son," Corbitt began to explain to the boy. "I learnt how to witch doctor from Grandpap, now I can learn you how to witch doctor."

"Boy, this is great!" Judge L. beamed. "I'll be able to do something that the big boys can't do. I'll sure have something on them when I learn to witch doctor. But I thought that *you'd* have to have a child that was a seventh son to carry on any kind of a tradition, like witching and curing the thrash and things like that. I didn't know that you could skip around in the family to find a seventh son. I don't know if it will work on me that way, since I ain't *your* seventh son."

"Aw, that don't make no never mind, Judge L.," Corbitt told the boy. "I can pick whoever I want to carry on the tradition, as long as I don't have a seventh son. So you being someone that I can teach the powers to, it'll be just fine. Come on. Let's get this over with."

"Okay. That suits me just fine, Unc," Judge L. said, grinning all around at everyone present.

Corbitt and Judge L. went out into the wooded area behind the barn to commence the first lesson in witch doctoring.

"Now pay close attention to what I do," Corbitt instructed Judge L. "Watch closely what I do and how I do it."

The man took a stub of a pencil from his shirt pocket. He then searched in his hip overalls pocket and found a dirty, wrinkled piece of lined tablet paper and proceeded to draw a crude image of a man. He took a nail from his pocket, picked up a small rock, and nailed the picture to a smooth-barked poplar tree near a sluggish stream that meandered through the woods.

"Watch this," he told Judge L. Taking a thirty-eight caliber Smith & Wesson revolver from under his belt, he shot at the picture on the tree, after chanting an unintelligible incantation. He walked over to the tree and checked his marksmanship, then motioned for Judge L. to join him.

Judge L. hurried to the tree, excited.

"Now, boy," Corbitt spoke solomnly, "you'll have to pay close attention to my ever' move. I drawed this picture of the witch and shot at it. See where the bullet struck him in his right hand. If he's a real witch, a sore will come on his hand where I shot him. I'll learn you the words to what I said before I shot the witch. We've got plenty of time for that. Let's let this first lesson sink in real good before we go on. We don't want to go too fast. If you go too fast, you may not learn it good enough for it to work ever' time, and if you don't do it right the first time, the witch will leave without you ever getting the chance to break his spell and his will to carry on his evil deeds."

"This sure is interesting, Unc," Judge L. beamed. "I sure didn't know that you had such powers. I want to learn ever'thing that you know so I can get me a big pistol like that 'un you've got there and go around over the country shooting witches' pictures and making sores come on them so I can break their powers. Will people have to call me Dr. Judge L. then? Let me heft that big gun so I can get the feel of it."

"You can't go out and shoot pictures and find witches," Corbitt explained to the boy. "You have to be asked by someone that's being witched 'fore you can be a witch doctor. It ain't something that you do on your own. Furthermore, I don't like for other people to handle my gun. So I'll just keep it in my belt." He patted his hip and smiled at Judge L. "Let's go down and talk to Marn and Dalker about this. They'll have to look for a man with a hurt right hand to know who the real witch is."

Corbitt and Judge L. found Marn, Dalker, and Jake at the edge of the woods where the hogs lay sleeping in the shade of the trees.

"Well, they look like they are sleeping like little hog angels, don't they?" Corbitt commented. "You fellers will have to look for someone with a hurt right hand. When you find him, you'll have your witch for certain."

"Who's that feller coming out of the woods up yonder above the house?" Jake asked, pointing toward the approaching man.

"Why, that's Hooker Joe Moss, the he-witch that I've been telling ever'body about," Dalker said.

Hooker Joe walked cautiously and slowly toward the crowd standing near the sleeping hogs. The man held his right hand in a precarious position and rubbed it gently with his left hand.

"Looks like something is wrong with his hand," Corbitt commented. "Looks to me like he has a white rag tied around it. I'd say he's hurt, and I have a good idea what caused his hurt, don't you Judge L.?" He smiled at his protégé.

"Sure do," Judge L. replied, grinning. "Us doctors know what's going on around here."

"Some doctor you are," Jake stated sarcastically. "You ain't a witch doctor yet. Furthermore, you ain't the seventh son. Gillis is the seventh son in our family, so he should be the one that's learning how to break witch spells, not you."

"Uncle Corbitt said that that didn't matter at all," Judge L. came back. "He can teach me if I'm willing to learn and believe in witches like he does. I'll believe anything as long as I can become a doctor and know more than you and the rest. You all will have to call me Dr. Judge L. when I become a doctor."

"I'll call you Dr. Judge L. when you become a real doctor," Jake declared. "You can't a bit more learn how to break witches' hexes than I can fly to the top of the hill up there." Jake pointed toward the top of the hill above the barn, and everyone automatically looked in that direction.

"Howdy, fellows," Hooker Joe greeted as he came up to where the men and boys stood waiting. "You've got some nice hogs there, sir."

"Yeah, they're a pretty fair bunch of hogs," Dalker agreed.

"You ought to keep an eye on 'em and keep 'em fenced in," Hooker Joe told Dalker.

"I don't have to keep them up," Dalker shot back. "There ain't a stock law in force here on Coaley Creek. Stock can roam as it pleases, and they're roaming on my own property. I own this whole area here, from mountain top to mountain top. There's better'n five hundred acres in my tract. It's all laid out like that on the deed, too."

"I didn't mean it that way, Mr. Skinner," Hooker Joe said, smiling timidly. "I meant that you had better watch where they go to eat. They've been at that 'still up there on the hill all day. They've been eating out of the sour mash barrels. They came staggering into your hog-lot a while ago, drunker than skunks."

Dalker, Marn, and Corbitt looked up on the hill, in the direction of the 'still, and then looked at each other.

"One of your biggest hogs wasn't as lucky as these," Hooker Joe went on. "It's up there in a barrel of mash right now. I don't know how long it's been in there. He looked like he'd been in there long enough to pickle right good. I tried to get him out, but he was too big for me to do it by myself. I skinned my hand trying and wrapped it in my handkerchief to stop the bleeding. I bled like a stuck hog for a few minutes—till I wrapped it up real tight.

"Right hand, Uncle Corbitt," Judge L. whispered. "What do you think?"

"I really don't know," Corbitt replied, whispering, too low for anyone else to hear, Judge L. even.

"What did you say, Unc?" Judge L. asked out loud, forgetting to whisper.

"You must be hard of hearing, young man," Hooker Joe, said, moving closer to the boy. He reached out and rubbed the boy's ear. "No wonder you can't hear. Your ear is full of bread." He held a cold biscuit in his hand.

"How'd you do that?" Judge L. asked, shaking with fright. "I saw you do that over at Uncle Ferd's 'still one day. You must be a witch to be able to do that."

"No, I'm not a witch, son," Hooker Joe laughed. "I do a

few magic tricks once in a while. I work for a circus. I've learned a few tricks by watching the magicians with the show. That's all. I'm just bumming around right now. I was passing through and wanted to stay around and rest up a little. The circus I work for will be in Knoxville, Tennessee, next week. That will give me three days to get to Knoxville. I'll have to catch a ride going down that way and join back up with the circus once more. It's an interesting way to make a living. Nice meeting you fellows," he said, shaking hands with each person. "Have a good day." He then walked past the barn to the road that would take him to Big Onion Gap, where he could catch a ride—the bus maybe—to Knoxville, where he could join the circus once more.

"How does the doctor feel now?" Jake asked, laughing at Judge L. "You can't get rich if you don't have any witches around to practice doctoring on."

"Don't worry your pretty little head, Jake," Judge L. returned. "Uncle Corbitt's gonna teach me witch doctoring anyway."

Marn, Dalker, and Corbitt watched Hooker Joe walk down the Coaley Creek road, silently shaking their heads in disbelief.

Bulldoggin' Bart

"I'd like to be one of them rodeo stars—a bulldogger or something like that," Bart Cornfield told his brothers and friends as the boys left the Saturday matinee movie at the Big Onion Gap theater, after having sat through four runnings of the film. The theater manager had made them leave so other customers could have a seat.

"You'd get killed dead," his brother Clem told him. "You're too loggerheaded to have enough balance and control over a big animal like a horse or a big Brahma bull—one of them kinds of bulls with the big hump on its neck like a buffalo. Your legs are too short to reach around his belly and clasp together to hang onto him."

"Didn't you see the men ride 'em with a rope tied around the bull's belly to hold on to?" Bart asked. "Those fellers rake and gouge the bulls with spurs."

"It would take a lot of practice to be able to ride a bull or horse like that," Seldom Seedy said. "It would be a lot of fun to be able to do all that, but I'm sorta glad that I can't practice riding. I wouldn't want to get throwed, kicked, and stomped on by a big brute like a Brahma bull."

"You have to watch what you're doing when you ride a bull or bulldog a cow," Bart said. "You learn to go with the motions of the bull when you're doggin' him. You hang on with one hand or another, depending on which handed you are, left or right."

"We can dream about being in a rodeo, but we'll never be able to ride in one," Dump said, thinking of the excitement of bull riding.

"Did you boys notice how Johnny Buck rode, holding on with his left hand to that lasso rope that he tied around that

Brahma bull and swinging his hat in his right hand to give him good balance?" Bart asked. "Now," he went on, "that's the way I'm gonna do my riding."

"You can't bulldog and bull ride anything around here, Bart," Jake said, taking his eye off a pretty girl long enough to make his point. "We don't have a bull, and Ol' Heif ain't a fast runner. She's just a milk cow, and milk cows don't have a lot of pep in 'em. She wouldn't be any challenge to you, being so gentle and all. She wouldn't even run if you was to get on her back. She'd just lay down to rest."

"I can practice doggin' on her," Bart came back. "I can ride Ol' Jock and lasso Ol' Heif and get a little experience that way. After I get her used to being lassoed and roped up, I'll start going at a run and catch her running. I'll slide off of Ol' Jock's back and grab her by the horns and wring her neck like a chicken, throw her on the ground as pretty as you please."

"I want to see this," Seldom Seedy beamed, grinning from ear to ear, showing his buckteeth, pulling air through his teeth, into his lungs, and then forcing it back out with a wheezing sound as he snickered.

"I want to see it, too," Dump chuckled. "And then if anything goes wrong, I want to see how he acts when Dad tans his hide real good."

"Don't worry about that," Bart smiled. "Nothing's gonna go wrong."

"We'll see," Dump chuckled, shaking his head.

The boys crossed the big bridge spanning Bass Creek River at the edge of town and walked on toward the mouth of Coaley Creek. Everyone continued to talk about the rodeo scene in the movie that day, reliving the most exciting parts over and over again.

Bart continued to tell the boys that he was serious about practicing bulldogging and bareback riding with Old Jock and Old Heif. He knew that if other people could do that, he, after a little practice, could do it just as well, if not just a little better. A man had to have confidence to do anything, he realized. And he had confidence, even if not the ability. But ability came with practice and experience, he figured.

"Are you gonna practice any ropin' and doggin' this evening?" Seldom Seedy asked as the teenagers approached the hollow leading to the Seedy's house.

"I doubt if I'll have a chance to do any riding today," Bart told his friend. "Dad's home for the weekend, and he won't let me ride, rope, and throw the ol' cow down. He won't let me carry on with such foolishness. Horses are to work and cows are to be milked, and that's all they're for, the way he looks at it."

"He shouldn't ought to care for you having a little fun once in a while," Seldom argued. "You ain't gonna hurt them. You might get hurt yourself, but the cows and horses can take care of themselves okay."

"I'll have to wait till he goes back to Jenkins to work in the mines," Bart said. "You know?" he said, after thinking for a minute or two, "I could practice this evening, just to see what he might say. Maybe he has mellowed out just a little now that he don't get to see us young 'uns as often as he'd like to."

"We'll just go along and watch you," Shag Moss said, inviting himself to the big doings. "The rest of us could get in a little practice, too."

"That ain't too good of an idea, boys," Dump warned. "Dad might not be in much of a good mood. After working in the mines all week, he might be easy riled and thrash the whole kit and caboodle of us. We can't take that chance."

"Yeah, he needs his rest," Clem agreed.

"Well, if you ain't gonna practice, the rest of us may as well mosey on home," Shag Moss said, taking the right-hand fork of the Coaley Creek road. "I'll see you fellers later on in the season," he called over his shoulder.

"See you," the Cornfields called out in unison as they took the left-hand fork.

Soon Seldom Seedy left the Cornfields and went up Jestice Branch to his house.

"I'm gonna practice some this evening," Bart told his brothers, breaking a short period of silence—there was seldom any silence at all among that bunch of brothers.

"Are you really?" Dump asked, amazed that Bart was serious about trying to be a bulldogger and bareback rider.

"Sure," he replied. "I believe I ought to practice while it's fresh in my mind. If I put it off too long, I might forget how Johnny Buck did it in the show today. I saw it enough, though, to remember how to do it. Do any of you want to have a go at it with me?"

"Not me," Dump answered quickly.

"Me, neither," Clem replied, smiling.

"How about you, Judge L.?" Jake asked. "Are you gonna join him? I'm not."

"I'm not, either," Judge L. replied. "You'll have to go it alone, Bart, looks to me like."

"That's all right with me, fellers," Bart said. "You all can do what you want to. Me and Johnny Buck will be stars, and you all will be no-names in the world. You all can go to the theater at Big Onion Gap and pay your dime to see me on the big screen if you want to. I'll wave at the camera while I'm riding and doggin' them bulls and let you know that I'm thinking about you, and thanking you for paying a dime to see me. That'll be money in my bank account. Ever'time I go in the bank to make a deposit, the tellers and cashiers and presidents and vice presidents will look at me and gasp, 'Here comes Bulldoggin' Bart to make a big deposit of dimes that he got from moviegoers.' My name will be up on the marquee, in big letters:

BART CORNFIELD
THE RIDIN'EST AND ROPIN'EST AND
BULLDOGGIN'EST FOOL IN THE WORLD
ALL OF THE WAY FROM COALEY CREEK TO THE BIG TIMES

I can just see it now. People will point at the marquee and gasp for breath, they'll be so excited."

"They'll probably point to where the pigeons roost on the marquee at Big Onion Gap Theater and gasp," Dump laughed. "They'll point and say, 'Yeah, that looks like Bart

Cornfield up there on that marquee all right.'"

Everyone laughed, except Bart.

"Have your laughs now, 'cause I'm gonna be laughing at you, since you don't want to learn to be a dogger and become a celebrity like me."

* * * *

Chores were done and supper was over later on that afternoon.

"Where are you boys headed this time?" Marn asked his sons as they left the house and went through the paling-fence gate, letting the plow-point weight on a trace chain anchored to a walnut tree and to the gate pull the gate back with a bang.

"We're going 'round in Grandpaw's pasture field," Dump answered for all.

"What're you going to do around there?" Marn asked. "The milking is done for the day."

"We might ride our wagons off of the steep hill," Bart told him.

"Or ride Ol' Jock and lasso the cow," Clem mumbled, too low for Marn to understand.

"What was that you said, Clem?" Marn asked. "I didn't understand you."

"We might ride out trees, too," Clem came back quickly, speaking louder.

"Is that one of my good plow lines, Bart?" Marn asked, referring to a rope that the boy was swinging over his head as he walked through the gate.

"Yeah, it is, Dad," Bart admitted, knowing that it was better to tell his father the truth. He would be in a peck of trouble if he should tell an untruth and Marn found out the boy had lied to him. "We broke the old rope on our humongous wagon and now it's too short to use. I thought that maybe we could use this plow line and pull it to the top of the hill. I plan to put it back in the harness room when I finish using it."

"Be sure you do," Marn told him. "Just be careful," he warned, then returned to reading his King James Version of the Holy Bible.

"Clem, you almost got me in trouble," Bart complained. "I thought sure that you were gonna rat on me."

"No danger of that," Clem chuckled. "I want to see you lasso Ol' Heif while Ol' Jock's running at full speed."

"I believe I can do it," Bart boasted. "Will you help me catch Ol' Jock and saddle him up?"

"We'll all help," Dump volunteered. "I can't wait to see you in action."

"All five of us will chase that nag till we catch him, if he wants to be cantankerous and run from us," Clem offered. "We're like Dump. We want to watch you and see what you can do."

After about five minutes of chasing the hard-to-catch horse, the brothers succeeded in hemming him up in a corner of the rail fence.

Bart slipped the bridle over the horse's head and forced the bit against the clinched teeth, making Old Jock open his mouth so the bit would go in. He led the horse to the barn, where he saddled him, having to thump him in the belly to force the air out so he could tighten the cinch securely.

With his horse ready, the young cowboy tied a small loop in the end of the plow line and ran the end of the rope through the loop, making a lasso. He climbed into the saddle and twirled the rope above his head to get the feel of it.

"I think I'll practice on a stump first," Bart announced, thumping the horse in the ribs with his bare feet to make it move.

Old Jock went around the hill at a plow horse trot, moving a little faster each time the boy goaded him in the ribs with his heels. Soon he was at an awkward gallop, bouncing Bart around in the saddle.

Bart held the reins in his left hand and gripped the pommel of the saddle with the same hand to hold on, while he let out a length of the plow line to enlarge the loop of his lasso to rope a three-foot-tall stump by the edge of the uneven path. He whipped the rope awkwardly above his head, and when he was within about fifteen feet of the stump, he let the rope slip smoothly from his hand. It flew in a true line and encircled the stump, a perfect catch. A coil of the rope slipped out of his left hand and wrapped around his leg and the stirrup.

Old Jock continued his lumbering gallop, pulling the rope taut around Bart's leg, stripping the boy from the seat of the saddle, Bart hit the groud, knocking the breath out of him, and the horse came to a stop against the rail fence, unable to move, puffing like a freight train. Had the fence been another three or four feet further, the horse would've been yanked off his feet, probably landing on top of Bart. The boy lay there, his foot held up by the rope wrapped tightly around the foot and the stirrup leather, trussing him up like a roped calf.

"Ride 'em cowboy," Dump shouted, laughing so hard that he doubled over and fell to the ground, gasping for breath. The rest of the boys laughed at poor Bart, hung up in the rope, between the stump and the horse.

"Help me loose!" Bart yelled. "Try to control that wild horse!"

"If he gets any wilder, he'll just plain fall over dead," Clem laughed, trying to lift the taut noose from around the stump, but to no avail.

Finally, Dump was able to stand. He went to the gentle horse's head and talked to it soothingly. "Back up, ol' buddy," he said, pulling back on the bridle reins to encourage Ol' Jock to move. A couple of backward steps let Bart's suspended foot drop to the ground.

"Are you hurt?" Dump asked, unwinding the rope from around the stirrup and Bart's foot, freeing him.

"Naw, I'm all right," Bart reported, scrambling to his feet to see if he had an injury. "I feel okay." He limped around the stump a couple of times to loosen the tightness in his legs. "I'm all right," he repeated, walking with only a slight limp.

"I doubt if Bart would be in a holiday mood if that had happened," Judge L. grinned, looking at Bart, watching him still humping and gimping around on a stiff leg.

"I'll be all right," Bart said, winding his makeshift lasso into a neat coil. "I bet Johnny Buck had his scrapes, knocks, and bruises when he first started out to be a bulldogger. I ain't gonna let that little setback stop me. I'm gonna make it to the big time like Johnny Buck."

"The end might not be too far away if you continue the way you're headed," Dump chuckled.

"That wasn't nothing," Bart grinned, rubbing his leg gingerly, walking around to get the circulation back. "On to the next event," he said, reaching for the horse's reins to take him to the barn to be unsaddled and set free in the pasture field.

"You ain't perfected roping stumps yet," Judge L. called after the departing rider.

"I proved that I can lasso what I want to catch," Bart called over his shoulder.

"Yeah, if he can lasso a fast stump, he shouldn't have any trouble with a running cow," Clem laughed. "That sure was a fast stump."

"What's the next event, Bart?" Dump asked.

"Bull riding is next on the program," Bart told him. "Give me time to turn Ol' Jock loose in the field." He returned shortly, the plow-line lasso coiled around his neck, like he had seen Johnny Buck wear his in the movies.

"What are you gonna do with that rope—lasso the bull?" Dump asked.

"No! I'm gonna use the rope to tie around the bull's belly for me to hold on to," Bart explained. "That's the way Johnny Buck does it."

"Yeah, but you ain't Johnny Buck," Clem told him. "That man's a pro."

"I'll be a pro, too, just as soon as I get through riding Grandpaw's bull," Bart declared. "Come on. Let's get this show on the road. Bart then walked through the field toward the bull-lot.

The bull lay in the shade of a big oak tree, contentedly chewing his cud and chasing the flies out of his eyes and nose by shaking his enormous head. He was a mixture of several different breeds of cattle, crossbred due to the fact that there were no big cattle farms on Coaley Creek. People bred their cows to any available bull, resulting in a mixed breed.

"Hold this barbwire up so I can crawl through," Bart said.

Dump and Clem each placed a foot on one strand of barbed wire and lifted on the strand above it to the point that it squeaked as it moved in the staples holding it in place on the locust posts.

When Bart cleared the barbs on the wire, the brothers dropped that strand and took their feet off the bottom strand.

"Get up from there Ol' Bawler," Bart sang out, nudging the bull's belly with his bare foot. "You're gonna get rode like you ain't never been rode before," he threatened.

"Yeah. And you're gonna get throwed like you ain't never been throwed before," Dump laughed.

The bull reluctantly rose from his resting place, stretched the kinks out of his big body, and blew a sigh of relief through his moist nostrils, spraying bull snot into the air.

"You might as well stand up and take your medicine, boy, 'cause I'm going to ride you all over this lot—till you give up as a broke bull," Bart said, tying the rope around the gentle animal's huge body.

"It don't make sense to me for a bull to take medicine for your aches and pains, Bart," Judge L. said. "You're the one that's gonna be hurting, not the bull. You'll need the medicine, not him."

"That should be tight enough," Bart said, pulling on the rope and ignoring Judge L.'s barb.

The boy jumped upon the bull's broad back, settled himself in place, and took one of Marn's White Mule work gloves from his hip pocket and put it on his left hand. He gripped the rope with his gloved hand and swatted the gentle bull with his battered straw hat, startling the animal to moving.

Old Bawler lowered his head and trotted down the path toward an alder thicket at the edge of the slow-moving little stream that meandered through the swampy meadow.

The bull suddenly stopped at the edge of the creek, sending the boy sailing through the air. The boy landed smack-dab in the middle of the stream, leaving the big glove under the rope on the bull's back.

"Come back here, Ol' Bawler!" Bart yelled as the bull went into the thicket—out of sight. "I ain't through with you yet, big boy. You're gonna be rode before I'm through with you."

Dump and the rest couldn't say anything for laughing. The boys rolled on the ground hee-hawing so hard that they could hardly breathe.

Bart went into the thicket and drove the bull back to where he first began his ride. The second effort was almost identical to the first, without the big splash in the water. It was worse, though. The alder bushes tore at his clothes and the skin on his bare arms and face. The bull came out on the opposite side of the thicket, but Bart didn't. He had lost his seat somewhere in trees.

"Catch that bull, boys!" Bart shouted. "I'm gonna ride him yet."

There was no help in rounding up the bull. The rest of the boys were so weak from laughing that they just sat and watched while Bart rounded up the bull and drove him back.

"Will you help me just a minute, Dump?" Bart pleaded. "Will you tie the rest of this plow line, here," he said, handing the end of the rope to Dump, "to my right foot and run the rope under the bull's belly and tie the other end to my left foot? I ain't gonna fall off this time around."

"Bart, that bull will kill you if I tie your feet together," Dump said seriously.

"Tie me on. I'm gonna break this bull or he'll break me, one," Bart said, wiping mud out of his eyes with the heels of his dirty hands.

"It's your funeral, Bart," Dump said, shaking his head in disbelief. "I've seen you do some crazy things, but this wild caper caps the stack."

"Tie my feet, then stand back and watch," Bart said, jumping on the bull's back once more. "Hold him. Don't let him run."

Dump tied the boy's feet together, then stepped back, waiting for the bull to run.

The bull just stood there.

Dump picked up a piece of broken fence rail and swatted the bull on the rump.

Through the thicket the bull went, with Bart riding as low on its back as he could to keep from being torn off by the trees. A wooden gate in the barbed-wire fence on the other side of the thicket was no problem for the sixteen hundred-pound bull. He didn't try to jump it. He lowered his head and ran through it with no effort at all. The farther he ran, the faster he ran, with Bart screaming for someone to help stop the wild ride.

The rope tied around the boy's feet prevented his falling to the ground. Several times Bart had slid to one side, but by pulling on the rope he tightened it up enough to stop his fall. Tatters from his torn clothes were strewn from the alder thicket to the moving bull.

"Someone stop this crazy bull!" Bart continued to scream, but no one was around to help. How could anyone help, with the bull moving so fast.

The bull slowed only for a second, then sprang forward again at full speed. Slobber and snot were thown over the animal's back, striking Bart full in the face, blotting out his vision. He could not wipe the stuff out of his eyes. There was no way that he would turn that rope loose. He knew that if he did, off he would go to the ground and be drug along by the bull. He kept his eyes closed and let the slobber and snot either stay where they hit or be blown away by the wind.

Dump, Clem, Jake, and Judge L. ran far behind the racing bull.

"Hang on, Bart," Dump yelled. "You're doing about as good as Johnny Buck."

"Stop, you crazy bull!" Bart yelled, pulling desperately on the rope tied around the huge animal.

The bull finally came to a sliding stop in the hallway of Dalker Skinner's big barn, where he stood panting, his long tongue lolled out and his sides going in and out like a blacksmith's bellows. Slobber streamed from the tired bull's long tongue.

Dump and the rest of the brothers ran into the barn right after Dalker arrived. They heard him talking to Bart while trying to untie the wet rope to let the boy get off the bull's back.

"What are you plague-goned boys doing, riding Ol' Bawler like that?" the man asked. "You boys could get your brother killed dead by taking that kind of chance, tying Bart's feet together. You fellers know better than to pull a stunt like that. Dump, why did you boys do that?"

"Bart wants to be a rodeo star," Dump explained, taking a good look at the bedraggled boy on the bull's back. "You said that you'd ride him or die trying. You rode him, all right. And you almost got killed trying."

"I know," Bart groaned, sliding to the ground. He sat down on an upturned bucket. "Boys," he began, "Johnny Buck can be the star of the big time if he wants to. I don't want any part of it."

"You roped the stump and rode the bull, so I guess that makes you a rodeo star after all," Clem laughed.

"Yeah, it does, I guess," Bart groaned, rising. "Let's go home and get cleaned up. My bulldoggin' days are over."

"You plague-goned boys," Dalker growled, wiping the muddy bull with a seed sack. "I ought to chuck your heads right hard for mistreating my livestock."

Jungle Judge L.

Judge L. sneaked a peek over his shoulder as he entered the woods up above the milk-gap. He could hear the "dong, dong, dong" of Ol' Heif's bell as she chewed her cud while lying in a sinkhole under a big hickory tree. The cow's moving jaws shook the bell just enough to cause it to ring in rhythm with the chewing movements.

The cow lay there, without a care in the world, not even noticing Judge L. when he entered the dark, silent forest.

The boy walked cautiously from one tree to the next, stopping at each to look back down the path toward the house, hoping that no one was following him. If only he could get in enough practice before the county fair in the middle of October, he might land a job with one of the shows and travel all over the United States—maybe Canada—maybe the world. His practice sessions had been short during the last three weeks, with the farmwork to contend with. With Marn gone all week, the boys had to work harder to keep up with the weeds in the fields. The numerous rains had helped the weeds grow faster, almost to the point of smothering the late patches of corn and beans in the huge garden.

Judge L. had read an ad in the Big Onion Gap weekly newspaper that said the county fair would be arriving on Sunday evening, October 13. It would open Monday evening and run through the entire week, ending around midnight Saturday. An extra ad showed men and women dressed in tights, with the main attraction, a man dressed in jungle attire, swinging through the air on a trapeze. The main star was "Harry, the Jungle Man," dressed in a caveman-like suit, with a scruffy beard and long, flowing black hair.

Judge L. had never been to a county fair before. He didn't

even know what went on at the fair, but he was excited about it that year, the first year for him to attend, he hoped. Anyway, he was preparing for it, whether he got to go or not. It didn't hurt to be prepared for anything, he figured. He wanted to be a trapeze artist like the one shown in the newspaper ad. He could see it now. He would be billed as "Jungle Judge L."

The skinny boy took the bundle snuggled protectively under his right arm and unrolled it. A piece of very old tarpaulin wrapped around a brief-type swimsuit and a tattered piece of brown bed blanket made up the little package.

Judge L. shucked off his patched, bibbed overalls and faded blue chambray shirt to don the swimsuit and the ragged blanket, cut to make his upper body look like a caveman or a jungle inhabitant. When he had finished dressing in that outfit, he beat on his chest with his open palms. After the brief exercise, he suspended the tarpaulin between four trees spaced in a prefect square—to be used as a protective net in case he might fall—by tying a piece of blasting wire to each corner of the make-do net and then to a tree. There was a good supply of used blasting wire, brought home from the mines. Marn Cornfield was a saver, so he saved the used wire as he loaded the coal into cars to be hauled outside to market.

There was a chestnut stump and a big boulder beneath the canvas tarpaulin, Judge L.'s reason for hanging it there. The tarpaulin was so old that if a fly had lit on it, the insect would probably have fallen through to the ground, breaking its neck in the accident.

Everything done to his satisfaction, Judge L. took a grapevine—cut off at the ground and made into a swing—from a holly bush, where it appeared to be growing, and swung out over the suspended tarpaulin. When he was directly over the tarpaulin, he turned the vine swing loose and slapped his hands together and quickly grabbed the vine once more, swinging out as far as the vine would go. Then back he came to the uneven ground on the steep hillside, where he sat down to rest for a minute or two, still holding the grapevine swing with his right hand.

After he had rested for about three minutes, he stood up, gripped the vine with both hands, and swung out over the tarpaulin again, turning loose and slapping his hands together while suspended in the air. He grabbed the vine and floated back to earth once more.

After another short rest, the boy once again swung into the air on his crude trapeze-type swing. This time he did not release the vine and slap his hands together. Instead, he released the vine and grabbed for a limb on a nearby sturdy chestnut oak tree. He almost lost his grip on the limb, but he made it, grinning all over the hillside, satisfied with his feat—his first try. He slid down the slick-bark tree and climbed the hill to try the stunt again. He wanted to perfect his act to the point where it would be like clockwork—swing into the air, drop, catch the limb, slide down the tree, and back to the swing to try it again. With enough practice he was sure he could be perfect. "What's the old saying? 'Practice makes perfect?' Yeah, that's it," he spoke aloud.

After about thirty minutes of practice, Judge L. changed his clothes, wrapped them in the protective net, stashed the bundle under a fallen chestnut tree, and covered it with leaves so no one would find it. He then went back to the house, sneaking along, making sure no one was aware of his return.

"Here comes Judge L. out of the woods," Bart alerted his brothers. "Wonder where he went this time. He's been sneaking off up that way a lot here lately."

"Yeah, he's been acting real strange," Dump commented. "He's been slipping out into the woods, carrying a ragged bundle under his arm. I wonder what he has in that bundle, and what he's doing out there in the woods, all alone to boot."

"Yeah, I agree with you, Dump. He's acting sort of strange and mysterious," Clem said. "We ought to follow him and spy on him to see what he's got up his sleeve," he added.

"I saw where he keeps his mysterious bundle hid at," Bart said, getting into the discussion. "I saw him sneak it out from behind the quilt stack in the corner of Dad and Mom's bedroom. I acted like I didn't even notice that he was sneaking around in there when I walked in on him unannounced. I went in the room to get a piece of chalk out of Dad's jump jacket pocket in the closet. He jerked the bundle behind his back real quick and grinned like he always does when he's trying to pull something over on you. 'Is your back hurting?' I asked him, just to make conversation and not let him know that his actions looked sneaky to me. He told me that it was just itching a little was all, and he scratched real hard with his free hand to show that it was itching really bad."

"I hope he ain't sneaking out there to smoke by himself, to keep Dad from finding out about it," Dump said, pursing his lips thoughtfully. "We'll wait till he puts his bundle back in its safe hiding place, then we'll check it to see why he don't want us to know what's going on out in the woods. I hope he didn't suspect that you noticed anything fishy about the way he was acting."

"I went on in and got the chalk out of Dad's coat pocket like nothing had happed," Bart told him. "I'll watch him hide whatever he has when he comes back to the house. I'll hide in the closet and watch him put the bundle back in its place behind the quilt stack. You all stay here on the porch. Tell him that I had to go to the toilet if he asks my whereabouts."

"Judge L. should be allowed to be as secretive as he wants to be," Clem stated, defending the boy's right to have a secret and to keep it to himself if he wanted.

"Yeah, I guess you're right, Clem," Dump agreed. "Ol' Judge L. can't keep a secret long at a time. He'll end up telling us what he's doing. Maybe he's acting secretive just to keep us wondering."

"Well, let's just ignore him and see what he does," Jake suggested. "Maybe he'll tell us what's going on pretty quick if we p'like we ain't interested in his doings."

"You could be right, Jake, but let's follow him up on the hill after he gets in the woods the next time," Bart said. "We can sneak up on him and watch to see what he's up to and leave before he gets completely through so we can be back at the house when he comes home."

"What if he catches us snooping on him? Then what will we say?" Clem asked.

"We'll just have to tell him 'Howdy' is all that I know to do in a case like that," Bart laughed. "If we get caught, we'll just have to make the best of it is all that I can say."

"Let's do it. But remember, it's your idea, Bart," Dump said. "Here he comes up the hill from the chicken house. You'd better skedaddle if you're gonna spy on his hiding place."

"I'll take the blame for it all, but let's do it first and see how ever'thing turns out," Bart said, leaving the porch to go hide in the closet to await Judge L.'s arrival to hide his mysterious bundle.

"Where's Bart?" Judge L. asked as soon as he arrived at the porch where Dump, Clem, and Jake sat, each whittling contentedly on cedar sticks.

"He had to go to the toilet," Dump fibbed, continuing to whittle on the stick as if there was really nothing unusual going on and that Bart was really at the toilet.

"Has Mom about got supper ready?" he asked, going on into the house. "I'm tired and hungry," he called over his shoulder.

After a couple of minutes, Judge L. returned and sat down on the edge of the porch, his bare feet dangling. He drew circles in the dust of the bare spot under the eaves of the house, using his big toe.

Bart soon returned to the back porch and joined his brothers. He shook his head when Dump looked up, a question in his eyes.

"Where have you been, Judge L.?" Bart asked, taking a seat beside the younger boy. He rubbed his brother's head playfully.

"'Sangin'," Judge L. told him, continuing to draw circles in the dust with his big toe.

"Do any good?" Bart asked.

"Didn't find nary a bunch," Judge L. replied. "That hillside's plum' bare of ginseng. Else folks must've dug it all. I'll probably try it again tomorrow, though. I won't give up that easy. If I don't find any up there on that hill, I'll probably go on up to Isome Gap and Barn Holler and try them places. There's got to be some 'sang up there some'ers. Rough as them places are, I doubt if other people will try to crawl through the brash to look for 'sang, even though it brings a pretty price."

"You could be right," Bart agreed. "Are you going tomorrow?"

"S'pose so," Judge L. said, staring toward the mountain.

"Would you like for the rest of us to go with you?" Bart asked. "We can hunt for 'sang together and put it in one wad and sell it. We can then divide the money in equal shares."

"Naw, I can do all right huntin' and diggin' by myself," Judge L. came back, sighing contentedly.

* * * *

"What's he doing that for?" Jake asked, digging his heels into the soft dirt on the steep hillside to make his seat more comfortable.

"I don't know," Dump said. "Just sit still and watch. He might see us if you keep moving and thrashing around so much."

The four brothers watched Judge L. from their hiding place behind a rhododendron bush on the mountain.

Judge L. busied himself preparing his protective tarpaulin over the rock and stump, unaware that his brothers were spying on him. When he had everything to his liking, he dressed in his jungle garb and prepared to practice.

Snickers erupted from behind the rhododendron bush on the hill above him, too low to be heard though.

Judge L. took the swing from its resting place on the holly bush and slapped himself on the chest, imitating an ape. Holding the grapevine in both hands, he backed up the hill as far as he could, then lifted his feet off the ground and flew through the air. When he was over the tarpaulin, he turned loose of the swing and slapped his hands together and then grabbed the vine again.

"He'll fall and kill his crazy self!" Jake exclaimed. "Did you see what he did?"

"Sure did!" Dump said, slowly letting the air out of his lungs. "I thought he was a goner there. He'll kill himself if he misses that vine."

On his second swing, Judge L. went as far as the vine would go—toward the chestnut oak—then turned loose and tried a forward flip in the air. He made the flip, too late, though, and missed the limb—his target. Down he went, landing belly down on an uprooted tree. Jungle Judge L. lay draped across the log, not moving, the breath knocked out of his thin body.

Dump, followed by the rest, left their hiding place and ran to help the fallen boy.

"Are you all right, Judge L.?" he asked excitedly.

Judge L. looked up and motioned with his index finger for Dump to help him, his mouth opening and closing like a guppy in a tank, without any words coming out.

Dump and Clem picked the boy up and carried him to a pile of leaves near the chestnut tree where he had hidden his mysterious bundle. They laid him down, making him as comfortable as possible.

"What in the world were you trying to do? Dump asked as Judge L. began to breathe normally.

"I was practicing my trapeze act," Judge L. admitted, rubbing his sore ribs. "I want to join a circus and travel all over the world, doing a trapeze act. I read about in the Big Onion Gap paper," he explained, taking a paper clipping—the advertisement about the county fair—from his swimsuit pocket and handing it to Dump to read.

Dump looked at the piece of paper and smiled. "Which one were you going to be—one of the girls, or the jungle man?"

"I was gonna be Jungle Judge L.," the boy smiled sheepishly.

"It'll take a lot of practice to become a trapeze artist, Judge L.," Dump laughed. "And I know that you can't get in enough practice on that grapevine swing, the tree limb, and that log you landed on."

"I still want to join the circus," Judge L. groaned, continuing to rub his sore stomach and ribs.

"Jungle Judge L.," Bart laughed, pointing to his brother lying on the pile of leaves.

Judge L. smiled and said nothing. He knew he was licked but wouldn't admit it. He still wanted to join the circus.

Between the Wheel and the Rail

The five rambunctious boys planned to spend that Sunday afternoon riding a coal car—a part of the rolling stock—on a slightly inclined two hundred-foot section of the idle track at the Rob Road Coal Company—a safe place to play, they thought. The two-ton-capacity car was used to transport the mined fossil fuel from the interior of the colliery to the storage tipple on the side of the mountain.

During the previous night a thunderstorm had struck Coaley Creek with a fury, its torrential rain causing a mud slide near the tipple, partially covering the track. No one noticed the mud slide as the car was pushed along the track to gain enough speed to carry the boys on a ride to the end of the line, near the tipple.

As the boys approached the slide, Tester Seedy yelled, "Look out for the mud pile!" His warning was too late to stop their forward movement. As the car ran into the mud, Tester fell. His foot shot underneath the car, right in front of a wheel, just as the car came to an abrupt stop. The wheel pressing against his leg made it impossible for the boy to move. "Help me, fellers!" he yelled. "I can't pull my foot out of the mud. The body of the car is holding my leg down in the mud, and I can't move."

Judge L. Cornfield ran around the end of the car. "How did you manage to get your foot caught between the wheel and the rail like that?" he asked the entrapped boy.

"I don't know," Tester grunted, trying to pull his foot free. "I wanted to be the first one in the car when we got it to rolling real good. When we hit that mud pile, my foot shot underneath. The wheel ain't on my foot. It's just got my foot penned down in the mud."

We're gonna have to get you out of there as quick as we can, Tester," Judge L. said, studying the situation, hoping to come up with a plan to free Tester's foot before Derby Piddle might come along to check on his coal mine.

"Let's shove it into the drift-mouth of the mine," Esker Seedy suggested, pointing toward the mine enterance.

"Shucks, we can't do that, 'cause it's on Tester's foot!" Cousin Jubal Cornfield exclaimed.

"Let's all get in front and push back up the hill towards the supply building," Judge L. suggested. "When Tester gets free and we get over that little hump up there, it should be easy to handle. We can put it back where it belongs and get out of here."

They pushed in unison in an attempt to move the car backward a few inches to allow Tester Seedy to pull his foot free. But when Tester cried out in pain, the attempt to make that move was stopped immediately.

"What happened, Tester?" Judge L. asked. "Did the wheel get on you?"

"No. There are some rocks in that mud under there," Tester grunted. "There's not enough room for my leg and the rocks, too."

"Let's shove it back the other way, men," Judge L. said. "When the pressure goes off your foot, let us know and we'll scotch the car. Grab a sprag and shove it under the wheel when we move the car for'ards."

"That feels better right there," Tester announced as the car moved a few inches, lifted slightly on a hidden rock.

"Somebody get a sprag and chock it under the wheel!" Judge L. yelled, grunting loudly.

"Oh my gosh!" Tester screamed as everyone, except Judge L., released the heavy car to carry out the order to scotch the wheel.

"I didn't mean for everyone to let go!" Judge L. shouted. Then grunting under the weight of the heavy car, he tried to prevent it from moving backward against Tester's leg.

"I see what caused the car to move back after we pushed it forward and let go of it," Teed said, looking under the car.

"There is a round rock that moves when the car moves. We won't be able to shove the car off his leg."

"We'll have to do something to ease his pain," Judge L. said. "When we move it this time, Jubal, I want you to scotch it."

"Well, you didn't designate any particular person to carry out your command the other time!" Cousan Jubal retorted as everyone pushed to take the strain off the boy's leg.

"That's good right there," Tester sighed.

"Scotch it, Cousin Jubal," Judge L. ordered.

"Bust-take it, I can't reach the sprag," Cousin Jubal grunted, straining to reach the piece of wood four feet away.

"Are you all right, Tester?" Teed asked the boy held captive by the steel monster.

"I've been hurt worse in my days but can't rightly remember when," the skinny lad answered.

Cousin Jubal found a stick near the track and raked the chock close enough to grasp, then shoved it under the wheel. "You can turn it loose, boys," he said.

"Is that better, Tester?" Judge L. asked. "Will you be all right till we can figure out how to get you out?"

"Yeah, that's better," Tester replied. "I'm not in a lot of pain. My leg and foot are getting numb where the cirucula-tion is cut off. I still can't pull my foot out."

"Let's rest awhile, fellers," Judge L. said, lying down near the coal car. "Rest, then we'll try something else.

"Rest fast, boys," Tester begged. "This car don't have any sympathy on my leg."

"Is the pain very rough on you, Tester, ol' buddy?" Teed asked.

"I s'pose I'll live a little while longer if you boys'll hurry a tad faster and get me out of here," Tester said. "My foot and leg are plum' numb now. My sock has scrunched all the way down in my shoe towards my toes so far that it don't help much as a cushion. It don't feel like I've got any toes. I wouldn't mind to stomp toes with you right now, Teed." Tester managed a strained laugh.

"If your leg and ankle get numb enough, I can amputate

your foot," Teed snickered.

"Oh no you don't!" Tester blurted out. "I don't want to stump around on one foot the rest of my life. And, too, you ain't gonna get a chance to do any carving on my leg. It may not be shaped too pretty, but I'm satisfied with it. It takes me ever'where I want to go. So don't get knife-happy, boy."

"I was just joshing you, Tester," Teed laughed. "You know that I'd go after a rescue squad and doctor and nurses, the whole kit 'n' caboodle of them lifesavers, 'fore I'd practice my great skills as a surgeon and cut off your rusty foot."

"Just remember, no one carves on my foot," Tester stated flatly.

"Cousin Jubal," Judge L. said, "go look for a long pole and a header block. Let's try to lift the car off of his foot. Maybe we can put a cap wedge down at the end of the car and use a pole as a lever to lift it off the ground and get him out from under there," he said, pointing to the end of the car.

Cousin Jubal found a hickory pole that was used to punch coal through the doors of the tipple. Occasionally large lumps of coal would clog the sliding doors of the tipple, preventing it from flowing into the truck below. A pole was always kept by a support post of the tipple to punch the stubborn coal loose so it would flow freely. Cousin Jubal picked up a header block from a stack near the supply building to use as a fulcrum.

The pole and header block were too large to go under the extra-low car. There was no use in getting a smaller pole; a smaller one would bend if it were green, and a dead one would break and be of no use.

"If we had a chain, we could hook it onto the car and maybe lift the car straight up," Judge L. stated.

"How are we gonna lift it up when we hook a chain on it?" Teed asked. "We don't have a hoist of any kind," he explained.

"We're gonna have to have some help in getting Tester out from under that car," Judge L. said, gripping his chin, wondering where to get immediate help.

"Well," Teed began, "I guess we might as well go home. It's getting sort of late in the day. We can't hang around here all day doing nothing. I'd like to have a little fun for a change. We ain't done anything interesting at all. We've just been fooling with Tester under this car is all. What do you say about it, boys? Should we go look for something exciting to do?" Teed waited for a response from Tester, which was quick in coming.

"Boys, you wouldn't leave your buddy here, all hung up 'tween this car and the track, would you?" Tester whined pathetically.

"There's nothing else to do 'cept take off some place," Teed answered, grinning all over himself.

"Can't you think of anything else to do, and do it real quick?" Tester wondered.

"No, I sure can't think of a thing," Teed answered, continuing to tease his friend.

"Fellers, please don't leave me here," the whimpering boy pleaded. "I'll give you my belt and knife if you'll hurry up and get me out of here. If that ain't enough pay for you, I'll give you a little banty rooster that I have. My belt ain't the best, and my knife has some blades broke out and the rest are gapped some, but that little rooster is some chickey-diddle. He struts around like he is one of them big Red-eyed-Rolands. He struts around them big hens like he is the greatest thing since peanut butter come along."

Teed listened intently, then began to laugh, slapping his skinny legs, saying, "Tester, do you know what you said just then? You called that chickey-diddle a 'Red-eyed-Roland.' Don't you mean a 'Rhode Island Red'?"

"Yeah, I guess so," Tester replied, looking at his best friend. "I'm hurting so bad right now that I'm liable to say anything."

"Now, about that high-stepping rooster," Teed continued, showing interest in Tester's bargain. "I'd just like to see him around our flock of hens. That's a real bossy bunch of cacklers."

"Boys, get me out if you can," Tester begged plaintively. "Send for help, Teed. I'll give you my rooster if you'll go get somebody to help get me out of here."

"Don't listen to him, Teed," Cousin Jubal warned. "That rooster may have some kind of disease. You'd better watch Tester, I tell you. He's capable of some wild tricks. When he offers you something like that, there's always a catch to it. That's why he made the offer, I'd say."

"I'd give anything to get my foot out of this steel trap," Tester moaned. "But I don't think that I should have to pay my friends to get me out."

"You shouldn't have to, but I've got you right where I want you," Teed beamed. "And I'm gonna wrangle you out of ever' worthwhile thing that you own. Will you really and truly give me anything that you own if I set you free?" he asked, squatting beside Tester, looking him directly in the eyes. "If you don't tell me the truth about that rooster, I'll talk these boys into leaving you here until in the morning. The miners will help get you from under that car. There are enough men working here to lift that car plum' off the rails and over to that one there," he said, pointing toward the sidetrack.

"I promise you that my rooster is in the best health of any chicken in the world," Tester assured Teed.

"Tester, I'll go down to your house and check on that strutting chicken before I make any decision as to what to do about your predicament and let you loose. Let's go, boys," Teed said, turning to the rest of his friends.

"I'll allow that my rooster is in the best of health of any chicken in the whole world, Teed. Won't you please believe, Teed—me, your good buddy?" Tester begged.

"I sorta sense a little truth in him," Judge L. said. "I've been figuring," he went on. "Now, we can push one of these other cars up to the wye and throw the switch."

"Then we can push it down the track behind this one. Then what?" Teed asked.

"Let me talk. Don't butt in!" Judge L. retorted. "Now, let me finish. Let's push it down here like Teed mentioned. Then we can take a chain and a slate bar, if there's a bar to be found around here, and lift this car off the rail. Look for a chain and bar in the supply shack, Cousin Jubal. And Esker, you go up and throw the switch and have things ready,"

Judge L. ordered.

Cousin Jubal soon returned, carrying a short piece of heavy chain. He laid the chain in the bed of the first car on the sidetrack and ran back to look for a slate bar. After a thorough search he returned without any help from the tool shed. "Would a solid oak tie fit the bill? The slate bars must be in the mines, and without a light we can't find one in that dark pit."

"You're right, Cousin Jubal," Judge L. agreed. "Let's try the tie, but I'd rather have a slate bar."

Judge L. fastened the chain around the metal extension on the car hitch while Cousin Jubal selected a light but solid tie.

By using the end of the second car as a fulcrum, the boys hoped to be able to lift the car high enough for Tester to remove his foot from its cramped position. There was no reason why the idea would not work.

"All right, fellers," Judge L. said upon Cousin Jubal's return with a solid white oak tie, "let's move this empty car over on the main track. When we get to the switch, the track will be downhill. We'll have to be careful that it doesn't get away from us on the grade. We don't want to derail it. Get a sprag in case it gains speed on us." Judge L. directed the order to Teed, who jumped the track and ran to get a piece of wood to use as a scotch.

"All together now," Judge L. grunted, pushing against the car.

The rest of the fellows dug their toes into the dirt to get a good foothold, then pushed to get slack to remove the coupler pin holding the cars together.

Cousin Jubal removed the pin from the coupler bar.

"Easy does it now," Judge L. cautioned. "The track slopes toward the mines on the other side of the switch. We don't want it to get away from us."

The boys pushed the car through the switch, then dug their feet into the dirt to hold it back on the grade, grunting and groaning, trying to contain the speed of the heavy vehicle.

"Boy, if grunting helped any," Teed laughed, "Cousin Jubal could hold this car all by himself."

Don't get us tickled, Teed," Judge L. warned, laughing at the wise crack. Releasing his hold on the end of the car, he plopped down on the track with a thump. Everyone else lost hold of the car and fell down with Judge L. and watched the car go on down the track.

"That did it!" Tester cried. "That car will derail. Now I have to suffer a lot more on account of Teed. Bust take it, Teed! Why don't you act like a shut-up tarr'pin? It sure wouldn't stunt your growth any at all. My leg's gonna look just like a pokeweed that's been stomped around on by a big horse," he lamented, fearing further injury.

"Bust-take it, boys, I didn't go to cause you all to let go of that car!" Teed apologized, watching the car gain momentum as it sped over the descending grade toward the open entrance to the mine.

"He didn't mean any harm. He just wanted to joke a little to brighten up our predicament," Judge L. explained to the disgruntled boy lying on the ground by the coal car.

The car continued to gain speed, and everyone expected to see it jump the tracks. It, by some unknown chance, though, raced on toward the entrance to the dark mine. The boys watched as it was engulfed by the broad, dark mouth of the tunnel.

The track declined as the mine went deeper into the mountain. Where the car would finally stop, the boys had no idea. Maybe it would go to the heading, or veer at a break through and stop in one of the rooms which had been dug by the miners. Wherever it should stop, there would be a mix-up for the men on Monday morning when they reported for work.

"The men will be mad tomorrow when they come to work," Cousin Jubal chuckled. "I'd like to be around to hear them cuss and cut a shine when they find that things are all out of kilter."

"Talmage and Sadie Seedy ain't the only twosome that has a nasty-minded young 'un," Tester replied. "Cousin

Jubal, you're always saying that I have a filthy mouth when I say that you should listen to men talk and make jokes. Now you say it's all right for you to listen to cussing. Sturble and Bertie Cornfield have a nasty-minded boy, too."

"Quit your bickering, boys," Judge L. ordered. "Come on, you all," he went on, turning to the rest. "Let's get another car, and this time let's remain quiet—grunts and all."

The boys went through the same procedure of unfastening another car from the train of cars on the sidetrack. After having uncoupled the car, they began the tedious task of pushing it to the switch and then dropping it to Tester's car. Slowly and cautiously they moved forward. By selecting good footing on the oak ties, they were able to hold their own against the piece of equipment. Laboriously they inched the car forward, stopping often to stretch their cramped arms and legs.

Cousin Jubal had been designated the "spragger" and did a good job of holding the car while everyone took a breather every few feet.

A good mule driver can use a sprag effectively to slow the car on a grade to prevent it from running into his power source. A sprag is used like a type of portable brake, and an experienced driver can hold a car to a very slow speed with one, even when the car is heavily ladened.

The laborious task finally ended when the boys rammed the end of the car against the car holding Tester captive, bringing a scream of pain from the boy.

"Scotch it, Cousin Jubal! Then bring that oak tie here. Let's see what we can manage to do," Judge L. directed, continuing to give orders. "Boys, we put the chain on the wrong car. The one in the mine has the chain attached to it."

"And that was the only piece of chain there was to be found, too," Cousin Jubal exclaimed.

"Can you find a wire cable anywhere in the shack or around the mines?" Judge L. asked while surveying the situation, figuring a strategy for lifting the heavy car.

"I'll take a look-see," Cousin Jubal offered, running toward the tool shack. After a semi-thorough search, he returned with a yard or so of coarse cord. "No help?" he asked, holding the cord forward for Judge L.'s inspection.

"Ain't there anything else you can use to lift with?" Tester wailed, ready to cry.

"It ain't so bad," Teed soothed. "Just leave it up to ol' Teedy. He'll get you out, 'cause he wants that high-stepping rooster down at your farm. I'll get you loose if I have to gnaw the wheels off your car. We can get him loose somehow, can't we Judge L.?" He turned to his brother for assurance.

"We'll find a way if we have to go get Derby Piddle, the owner of this mine, to help us get Tester out," Judge L. promised. "You know that I don't want to do that. We would all be in a peck of trouble. Let's try to put the tie across the tailgate of this car and under the flange on the top of Tester's car."

"It ain't my car!" Tester protested.

"Well, under the car that's got you down," Judge L. replied, attempting to lay the tie in place.

"If you don't hurry a little, this cramped position that I'm in is gonna make me pass out," Tester complained. "I'm burning teetotally up, laying here in the hot sun."

"I wish you would pass out and hush crying and griping. Maybe then we could do something to help you," Teed told him.

Tester showed the others that he was as good as his word. He slumped over, a still, unmoving heap.

"You got your wish, Teed," Judge L. said.

"Come on! We have to do something. Try to bring him to life again!" Cousin Jubal exclaimed, jumping up and down excitedly.

Teed began to slap Tester's face. His hands' making contact with the boy's jaws brought color to the ashen cheeks.

"Boys," Teed laughed, "I can slap ol' Tester around now, and he can't do anything about it." Laughing and slapping, he attempted to revive his buddy.

The tie that Cousin Jubal had selected was too short. Another one would have to be found before they could make an attempt to free the unconscious lad.

"Ain't you gonna do something for Tester?" Cousin Jubal asked. "He might die, out cold like he is."

"He'll be okay," Judge L. laughed, watching Cousin Jubal hop around excitedly. "Quit you blathering around and go get another tie. Tester'll come to when he wants to. With him out cold, we won't have to listen to him cry and whine around. Go get the tie."

Cousin Jubal ran to the pile of ties to find a longer one.

The drone of an engine got the boys' attention as a truck sped up the steep grade to the coal mine, bouncing along over the rutted road.

"That's Derby Piddle coming to check on his mine and equipment," Cousin Jubal announced, sliding down the pile of slate near the tipple, where he had stood watching the oncoming truck.

"Take cover, men," Judge L. said, running behind the supply building.

The rest of the boys followed suit and huddled quietly behind the building.

Two grease barrels and some discarded brattice material partly obstructed the view of anyone who might chance to take a peek behind the supply shack.

The boys wedged themselves between the two barrels and the metal wall, pulled the dirty brattice material over themselves, and lay as still as a pile of saw logs.

"Hello, Brother Groundhog," Teed clowned, looking at Judge L. through the fogging dust particles.

"Don't start your funnin'," Judge L. said, trying to stifle a laugh.

Esker, Cousin Jubal, and Judge L. snickered, trying not to laugh out loud. It was hard to keep a straight face when Teed started his monkeyshines.

Derby Piddle stopped his four-wheel-drive pickup beside the mine's entrance track and got out, closed the door with a loud bang, stretched all over, cracked a couple of caps, and sighed contentedly.

The boys laughed hilariously, goading one another in the ribs to carry the laugh further.

Teed laughed so hard that he started to cough.

Judge L. put his big hand over Teed's mouth to muffle the sound, laughing as hard as the rest.

"He sure built up a head of steam as he pulled that steep grade," Teed said when he was finally able to pull Judge L.'s hand from over his mouth.

"Hush, Teed!" Judge L. warned. "Derby will hear you. I don't know what he'll do if he catches us. He may charge us with snooping."

"What about Tester? Do you s'pose that he's come to yet?" Esker asked.

"Let's hope and pray that he don't come to, and hope that Derby don't see something wrong with the two cars on the main line," Judge L. said. "If he don't notice the cars out of place, he won't see Tester, but if he happens to notice that things ain't just right, we'll have to reveal our hiding place and help Derby move the car."

"Now why did that mule driver leave these two cars on the main line?" Derby Piddle asked, talking to himself. "He knows," he continued, "that I want all the empty cars side tracked on Friday. Somebody could get hurt if they should happen to come around here. The car could get loose on this grade, and someone could get run over—get hurt bad. I'll have to have a talk with that driver tomorrow morning."

"We're sunk, boys," Judge L. groaned.

"What's this?" the mine operator exclaimed, spying Tester near the car. "That's Talmage Seedy's boy. I hope he's not hurt seriously. I'd better get some help. I wonder what he's doing here by himself, away from that pack of ragamuffins that he usually runs with. Son, are you dead?" he asked the unconscious boy. He shook Tester to see if there was any life in the limp body.

"Tell him, 'Yeah,' Tester!" Cousin Jubal yelled from behind the building. "Maybe he'll leave and not come back to bother us."

"Bust-take it, Cousin Jubal! Why did you have to go and yell loud enough for him to hear you?" Teed asked. "There's plenty room in your thick head for more sense than you've got."

"Well, if Derby thinks that Tester is dead, he'll go for help and we can get away," Cousin Jubal reasoned.

"Man, you're a nut!" Teed said, shaking his head.

"Come on out, boys," Derby Piddle called to the hiding youngsters.

The boys slowly emerged from their hiding place behind the building. Their clothes, faces, and hands were covered with coal dust from the used brattice material.

Derby Piddle bent over Tester, checking for a pulse. "Boys, what's the meaning of this?" he asked as he gave Tester a thorough examination.

"We were pushing the car up here to the top of this little grade and riding it back toward the tipple. We were just funning away the day," Judge L. said, apologizing. "We pushed the car plum' over the hump and then couldn't push it back across."

"How in the cat hair did he get caught in that position?" Derby Piddle asked.

"Tester was trying to be the first one in the car to ride it back down the hill when he stepped on a round rock and slid his foot between the wheels," Judge L. explained to the man. "How he got caught in the shape he's in, I just can't explain, other than that he stepped on that round rock and there he is caught between the wheels and the rail," Judge L. said. "Just leave it to Tester to mess up a good thing. We were planning on getting him out of there. We were gonna use a tie to lift the car up off of his foot when we heard you coming in your Jeep. We just panicked and ran and hid when we realized it was you coming up the hill."

"Get a chain out of the tool house," Mr. Piddle instructed.

"There ain't one in the tool shed," Judge L. reported despondently. "We looked but couldn't find one," he continued, fibbing about not being able to find an extra chain to replace the one that they had lost when the runaway car went into the mines, carrying their only hope for lifting the car off Tester's foot. "We looked for a piece of cable. We couldn't find any cable, either."

"The chain..." Teed began, but stopped when Judge L. looked at him, frowning, "...on our gate would help," he replied.

"That's no help to us," Derby Piddle said.

"I s'pose it ain't," Teed laughed. "But that's the only chain that I can think of right at the moment."

"What was your plan to free this boy?" Derby asked, directing the question to Judge L., who was acting as spokesman for the group of boys.

"Well, sir," Judge L. began, "we planned to use a tie as a lever. We were gonna put it under the top flange on the car that's on Tester, then push down on it, using this front car here to pry on. We figured that we could raise it high enough to get his foot out. He has just passed out from all the excitement. He's all right, though. We just need to free him and revive him up."

"Your plan sounds sensible to me. Let's try it and see if it works. I believe that you would make a good engineer," Derby said, eying Judge L. with a look of surprise on his friendly face.

"I hope to go to college someday and study to be an engineer," Judge L. replied.

"That's a good field to enter," Derby Piddle told the boy. "Industry needs engineers of all types."

Cousin Jubal returned with an oak tie.

One end of the tie was placed under the flange of the forward car, while the lever part rested on the rear car. As the boys pressed downward, Tester's car rose a few inches.

"I believe that will do just fine, boys, if you apply just a little more pressure," Derby Piddle beamed.

"All together. Careful now," Judge L. directed, pressing downward on the piece of lumber.

The car was raised high enough to permit the removal of Tester's numb foot, but before the foot cleared the rail completely, the car moved forward. The lever slipped from beneath the metal flange on the top of the forward car, letting the car drop, the wheels striking the rail with a metallic ring, catching Tester's toes, bringing the lad to life.

Tester looked around at everyone with a wide-eyed gaze, and the unexpected presence of Derby Piddle caused the boy to back away, like a scared crawdad.

"Don't be scared. It's okay. Derby Piddle helped to get you out from under the car," Judge L. said, trying to soothe the disturbed boy as he was suddenly brought back to reality.

"My toe's bound to be as flat as a beaver's tail!" Tester exclaimed, gripping his foot with both hands.

"It'll shape up in due time. Just be patient," Judge L. said. "Here, let's take off your shoe and check your foot."

The the boy's foot looked all right. There was only a little blood blister on his big toe, caused by the falling wheel as it caught a tiny bit of toe skin when it dropped back on the rail.

After having worked with the numb foot and leg for a while, Tester was able to rise and hobble over to the tool house, where he sat down in the shade.

The rest of the boys joined Tester, seeking a place in the shade of the building.

"Help me put these cars back on the sidetrack, boys," Derby Piddle said. "Then, I want you to go home. You boys can come around the mine anytime you want to, but don't mess with the equipment. This young man," he pointed to Tester, "could have got hurt bad. He's really lucky."

The boys, with the help of the mine operator, pushed the cars back to their resting places and coupled them to the cars already on the sidetrack.

Judge L. promised the mine operator that he and the other fellows had learned their lesson about mining equipment—there was more danger in it than there was fun. So, followed by his brother and pals, he sat down in the shade of the tool house to let Tester rest his sore foot awhile before leaving for home.

The Egg Man

Teed Cornfield sat in the living room, as close to the fire-place as he could get, one winter evening, listening to the burning chestnut wood pop and crack as it was devoured by the lapping flames dancing in the sooty throat of the field-rock chimney. The December wind blew harshly, whistling around the single-paned windows, causing little puffs of air to steal through the cracks where the rough construction lumber did not fit well. A thick layer of frost covered the glass where the moisture in the warm air froze as it condensed on the cold window panes.

The family lounged around, enjoying the warmth from the fireplace. As always, there was an interesting conversation just before bedtime. Gillis had just finished telling about an incident that had taken place during an afternoon class at Coaley Creek Elementary School that day.

As the story ended and a quietness settled over the room, Vann spoke to Teed:

"Did you gather the eggs up this evening, Teed?" she asked.

"Bust-take-it all to everything else. I sure didn't, Mom. I'm sorry about that," he apologized. "I'll do it in a shake or two," he promised, dreading leaving the warm room to go out into the cold night air to search for the eggs. He knew that he would have to gather the eggs to keep them from freezing and bursting in the frigid night temperature. The cold would probably knock the bottom out of the thermome-ter that night—knock on the zero mark, or close to it. Teed had the Toby dreads, but he would have to go ahead and do the forgotten chore.

"Yeah, hen granny, get your grannyin' done and get ready

for bed," Gillis joked.

"Don't worry about it Brud. I'll get my chore done," Teed said, rising from his chair to get his heavy winter Mackinaw coat and a toboggan for protection against the whipping wind.

Teed's mind went back to an earlier time—to a time when he and his family enjoyed life more, or they seemed to enjoy life more, he reflected. Slowly the boy's mind drifted back to when he was only about six years old.

Teed Cornfield grew up on Coaley Creek, near Big Onion Gap. He lived up a long hollow with his large family—about as far up the hollow as he could get. He often thought that he lived next to a foreign country.

During World War II, his parents often told the children that if they were to cross the big hill behind the house, the Japanese and Germans would catch them and take them away. They didn't dare to cross that mountain, afraid that they would be carried away as prisoners of war. They certainly didn't want that to happen. Teed found out many years later that one of his uncles had a moonshine 'still in one of the hollows leading up to that mountain. His parents didn't want the children to know that the 'still was there, afraid that they, in their innocence, might let the news slip out to the wrong people—the revenuers, the archenemy.

One day Marn and Teed walked the five or six long miles to Big Onion Gap—all the way from the head of Coaley Creek.

While in town, a friend of the Cornfields and Marn were talking in front of the Much-And-A-Plenty Foods Grocery, right at the end of the big bridge at the edge of town.

Olden Seedy, the friend, looked down at Teed. Olden was tall like Marn. The man smiled for a second or two, then asked, "Where do you live at, Teed?"

"Up on Coaley Creek," Teed responded immediately. He looked up and grinned at the man, his eyes squinting to shut out part of the sun's rays that were beating down upon the trio as they stood there talking. Teed thought that they should have found some shade somewhere and got out of the sunshine. Lower forms of animals, he realized, knew that much—enough to get out of the sweltering summer heat. The men didn't know much, evidently, for they just stood there in the sun and talked while Teed just stood around trying to look big, squinting up at tall Olden and and tall Marn, the sun striking him square in the eyes.

"What part of Coaley Creek do you live on, Teed?" Olden asked, continuing to smile.

Olden sure does grin a lot, Teed thought. "I live all the way at the head of the holler—right up against Japan and Germany," he said, continuing to squint up at Olden and hang onto Marn's overalls pocket, almost swinging on the permanent sag caused by Marn keeping his hands in his pockets so much.

"Near Japan and Germany?" Olden laughed, then looked at Marn, hoping for an explanation of Teed's statement.

Marn cupped his hand to one side of his mouth and leaned over to whisper something to Olden in a tone meant to be too low for Teed to hear, but sharp-eared Teed heard part of it, even though he didn't understand much of what was said at the time. A few years later he learned the meaning of what his father had cautiously whispered to Olden.

"'Still," he understood Marn to say.

But Teed thought that Marn had meant for Olden to hold still—maybe a biting fly or a gnat was on Olden, ready to bite him on the neck or somewhere.

"Oh, yeah. I see," Olden laughed, slapping his legs, an indication that he was really tickled.

Marn joined Olden, laughing loudly, slapping his legs like his friend was doing.

Teed just looked up and squinted at the sun. The little boy didn't see a biting fly on Olden's leg, where the man was slapping while laughing so hard. If a biting fly had been around anywhere, it would have buzzed and dabbed at Olden's and Marn's heads, trying to find a place to bite. It couldn't find Teed, though, down near the ground, in the shadows of the two tall men.

Teed returned to swinging on his father's sagging pocket while Marn laughed and talked awhile longer with Olden

Seedy.

After Marn had talked all he wanted to, he and Teed went into the store, where Marn bought some groceries and put them in a chop-sack and threw them over his broad shoulder. He told the man behind the counter, "Bye," and with Teed tagging along, left for home.

Trips to Big Onion Gap were few and far between for the smaller children in the family. The big boys and girls got to go to town more often than Teed did; they were big enough to go by themselves. Teed was big enough to go all the way to town by himself, he figured. But if and when he got there, he probably wouldn't know what to do or even remember why he was there.

Everybody was leery of strangers on Coaley Creek. When a stranger happened to walk up the hollow, he was spotted immediately. The Cornfield children were like a covey of hawk-shy quail, running from anything that moved. When they happened to see a stranger, they would scurry for shelter, afraid it might be a revenuer coming to look for 'stills in their holler.

Every time a stranger came up the road, the children would run behind the house to peep out and watch his approach. Little heads, stacked one over the other, would peep out to watch the stranger come on toward the house. It didn't take them long to recognize if someone was a friend or stranger.

If a person came on, walking straight, peering from side to side, searching for something, everyone knew immediately that he was someone to worry about—a revenuer, probably. But if he shuffled along, sniffing, spitting, picking his nose, and scratching, everyone knew that the stranger was one of their own. Out from behind the house the kids would bound and run to meet him, hoping that he might have some candy or some kind of treat to give them. Maybe he had eaten some candy and they could get up close enough to smell it on him. It didn't take much to satisfy the Cornfields.

There was a good old man who came up the hollow every week to buy eggs from Marn and Vann.

Teed liked to see Corb Morgan come to his house. He called Corb the "egg man." Well, the man bought eggs from his parents to take peddling over in Kentucky in the coal camps, so that was an appropriate name for him, Teed figured.

Immediately upon Corb's arrival, Teed would head for the henhouse to search for eggs, knowing that he would get a penny or two for his efforts to round up a few extra eggs. The hens couldn't hide their nests from ol' Eagle-eye Teed. The rest of the family called Teed the "hen granny" because he kept an eye on the hens and knew where they tried to hide their nests.

One day, while Teed and his sister Skatney and his brother Gillis were having a grand time playing stickball out in the chipyard, using a broom handle for a bat and a sock filled with rags for a ball, Corb came riding up on his horse, Ol' Smooth. As soon as Teed saw the horse racking along, giving Corb a ride like he was sitting in a rocking chair, he dropped his bat and raced to meet him, outdistancing the rest of his siblings. His little rusty feet slapped the ground like a beaver's tail on a still mountain pond as he ran to meet the egg man, ahead of the rest.

Skatney and Gillis remained with Corb and talked to him while Teed went in search of eggs. They weren't interested in hunting for eggs—Corb never gave them any money for finding extra eggs.

Teed crawled into hollow logs, peered into hollow trees and tree stumps, looked in the barn loft hay piles, and checked in the straw-filled nests in the henhouse. He found four eggs that day, a good two cents worth, he figured. He hurried back to the house, and to the waiting egg man, walking carefully to keep from breaking any of his precious cargo, for he needed money. There were several items in the Sears Roebuck Catalog that he had his heart set on. He didn't have money right then to buy the things he wanted. He was broke, but that wouldn't last forever. Corb the egg peddler, his good friend, had come to buy eggs. Money was on the horizon right then, he could tell.

Vann had already filled the big basket almost to the brim with clean, brown eggs when Teed arrived.

There were a couple of double-yolked eggs in the four that Teed gripped securely in his hands. He stood there waiting for a chance to put the four eggs with those already in the basket. A greedy grin covered his happy face while he waited impatiently for the chance to finish filling that big basket with eggs and then collect his reward—two pennies, he hoped. He had four eggs. Surely four eggs were worth two pennies.

"Well, I'll see you next week, Mrs. Cornfield," Corb said, putting his left foot in the saddle stirrup to mount Ol' Smooth for his trip back home. A smile played around the man's wrinkled mouth.

"Corb, I've got four eggs for you," Teed said, disappointment gripping his throat so hard that when he spoke his voice choked and trembled. He tried to act brave and grown-up about the situation, though. He gripped his lower lip between his teeth to stop his jaws from trembling.

"Well, I'll be dabbered! It's my good buddy, Teed Cornfield," Corb said, removing his foot from the stirrup and placing it back on the ground. "I didn't see you standing there," he teased. "What you got there in your rusties? Hey, looks like you got two double-busters there amongst them four eggs," he said, referring to the double-yolked eggs in Teed's hands.

"Yeah," Teed said, relieved that Corb had finally noticed him before riding off toward home. "How come you didn't see me? You always see me when you come to buy eggs. That sure did hurt—you not noticing me, and me and you being such good buddies and all."

"Aw, I saw you when you arrived with your eggs, Teed," Corb laughed, "but I felt like joshing you a little this morning. I got up feeling real good."

"You had me worried there for a minute or two, Corb," Teed said, breathing a sigh of relief. He wiped his brow to remove the sweat that had beaded up on it—like he had seen Marn do so often.

"Here, let me lay the eggs in the basket, then I'll pay you

for them," Corb said, chuckling. He placed the eggs on top of the almost-filled basket, then straightened up and took a bulging leather change purse from his front overalls pocket. He snapped the jaws open and dug through the purse's contents, causing the coins to sing out with a happy jingle, making the little boy gasp excitedly. Finally, after what seemed like an eternity to Teed, he selected a coin from the many there and handed it to his young friend.

Teed was disappointed. Corb had given him only one coin for four eggs! Gripping the piece of money tightly, he raced around the corner of the house to see what he had received for his efforts, followed closely by Skatney and Gillis, wanting to see what he had, hoping he might share the fruits of his labor with them.

Teed was almost afraid to look, afraid to find out what was gripped so tightly in his left hand. He turned his back to the rest. Very slowly, he used his right hand to force the fingers on his left hand open so he could peep in.

"Wow!" Teed shouted. "I got an Indian-head nickel!"

Well, that was all right with Teed. He had enough money then to buy something big, he figured.

"What're we gonna buy with it?" Skatney asked, almost drooling over the sight of the nickel.

"There ain't no *we* in this, Skatney," Teed snapped. He wasn't going to share his money with anyone, right then anyway. He had worked hard to round up those eggs to sell for that nickel. "I'm gonna save it for a while," he told her, pretending to put the money in his pocket.

"Be that way," Skatney said, showing disappointment. She turned and left. Gillis followed her around the corner of the house, just as disappointed as his sister.

When Skatney and Gillis were beyond the corner of the house, Teed slowly took his hand out of his pocket and looked at the Indian-head nickel for a while, wondering what he would buy with it. He thought about the possibilities of what he could buy with a whole nickel. With that much money on hand, he figured that he could be as choosy as he wanted to be. He wanted something that he had never had before—that could be almost anything, because he hadn't had very many new things in life.

* * * *

Marn let Teed keep his nickel in a change purse in the top drawer on the right-hand side of Vann's pedal-type Singer sewing machine. The change purse was really a fancy leather tobacco pouch. Marn had traded for it somewhere, of course. The man was constantly swapping for things, just to be swapping. Trading was in his blood, he often said.

No one in the family smoked, so Marn used the fancy tobacco pouch as a change purse.

Teed made several trips each day to the sewing machine drawer to check on his nickel. He often spent an hour or more at a time just sitting in the floor counting his nickel. He had the exact amount memorized by then. It didn't take him very long to finish counting it each time. He usually counted it several times just to make sure that he had the same amount each time he counted it. He wore the drawstrings almost in two from tying and untying them to get to the nickel nestled deep within the pouch's protective lining.

* * * *

One day Teed finally figured that he had saved the nickel long enough. It wasn't going to earn any interest by just lying there in that tobacco pouch.

Teed approached Skatney about three days after Corb gave him the Indian-head nickel. Teed figured that it had been that long. He was just a shaver and couldn't keep up with the days. He knew the days of the week by heart and could recite them in order, but he wasn't much interested in how often they came around.

"Skatney," Teed said, coming up to where his sister was playing with a rag doll, "will you fill out an order from the Sears and Roebuck Catalog for me?"

Skatney was a good scribe. That was what Vann often said

about Teed's sister. Maybe she was, but you couldn't prove it by Teed. He wasn't old enough to be a scribe, he figured.

Teed hadn't learned much since he started school. Learning didn't jump out and grab him and hang on to him. It seemed to just slide over him. If he wanted to keep a little learning, he had to grab it and hold on tightly. He tried in earnest to learn and remember.

Skatney could do cursive writing already. Well, she should; she was in the third grade.

Teed was just in the primer. He was sneaking up on printing fairly well, but he couldn't make sentences or fill out orders from the Sears Roebuck Catalog.

"Go and get the catalog while I get a pencil," Skatney said, laying her rag doll on the table. She went into the next room and got a short, stubby pencil that needed sharpening.

Teed ran and got the catalog and returned. He handed the book to his sister and waited for her to pull a chair up to the table.

Skatney sat down and opened the catalog, turning to the order blank section. "What do you want me to order, Teed?" she asked. She held the index finger of her left hand at the order blank section and began thumbing through the book, stopping at the dolls and doll carriages.

"I sure don't want no doll!" Teed blurted out.

"Well, what do you want?" she asked, continuing to look at the dolls, a sadness gripping her young face. She realized that she could never have a doll like the beautiful ones for sale on the catalog page.

"Turn to the bicycles," Teed suggested, almost bursting with happiness, realizing that he would at last get a bicycle, the one thing he had always wanted, as far back in time as he could remember, ever since Judge L. had wanted one.

Skatney searched through the catalog till she came to the contents section. She then ran her finger up and down the column under *B* until she found what she was looking for.

"It's on page 1036," Skatney read. She flipped through the pages until she came to the right page.

"Boy, you're smart!" Teed marveled.

There they were—bicycles galore! Teed's eyes bugged out, and he almost drooled on the page. "I'll take that 'un," he said, pointing to a beautiful bicycle large enough for a giant. He didn't care how big it was or how much it cost. He wanted it!

Skatney wrote "bicycle" on the first line of the order blank. "What else do you want?" she asked.

"Do I have enough for a scout knife?" Teed asked happily.

"S'pose so," she replied, then waited for Teed to make up his mind.

"I'll take it," Teed beamed, jumping around, unable to stand still. He was so excited that he could hardly control himself.

"Hold your horses, Teed," Skatney said, fingering through the pages to the contents list. She looked under column K.

Teed wondered why she looked under K when she should look under N. He was only in the primer, but he was educated well enough to know that knife didn't start with a K. She didn't look under N as Teed thought she should have, but soon she found the knives.

Teed couldn't understand how Skatney did that—find knives under K. He wasn't smart like she was, though. He thought maybe that she used some kind of code that he had never heard about to figure out that catalog.

There was a scout knife on that page, with a hundred blades in it Teed thought. "I'll take that 'un," he said. "And if I have any money left, I'd like to have a suit of underwear. I've always wanted a suit of that little brief-type underwear. Will there be enough money left to get me some of that kind of underwear?" Teed wanted to know.

"Most likely will," Skatney said, smiling. She wrote "knife" on a line, using a K instead of an N, then wrote "underwear" on another line, without first looking it up in the back of the catalog.

Teed thought that was strange, not looking up the underwear. She had looked up everything else.

"You didn't look up the underwear," Teed told her.

"They'll send it anyway," she replied. She tore the order

blank out of the catalog. "Give me your nickel," she told Teed. "Judge L. is going to the show Saturday. We'll let him take it to Big Onion Gap and mail it for you."

"Good!" Teed shouted. He grabbed the order blank and put his nickel with it, then ran to find Judge L. He found his brother out in the chipyard whittling on a cedar stick.

"Where're you going in such a dither, Teed?" Judge L. asked. "There ain't a fire anywhere, is there? I don't see any smoke anywhere."

"No, there ain't any fires anywhere. I want you to take my Sears and Roebuck order and mail it for me when you go to see the show at Big Onion Gap Saturday," Teed told him.

"What did you order?" Judge L. asked, then smiled, continuing to whittle on that stick.

"Skatney filled out an order blank for me a bicycle, a scout knife, and a suit of that little brief-type underwear," Teed replied, a silly grin trying to tear his lips up and rip his face apart.

"That'll cost you a fortune, Teed," Judge L. chuckled, stopping his whittling for a moment.

"It don't matter if it does. That'll be all right with me, 'cause I've got a big fortune—my Indian-head nickel that Corb Morgan gave me the other day," Teed said happily.

Judge L. laughed till he cried, slapping his legs to show how tickled he really was. "Give it here," he said after he had taken control of his laughing box. He folded the order blank and placed it in his front pocket, along with the Indian-head nickel.

Teed hoped that Judge L. took his order blank and nickel with him to Big Onion Gap when he went to the show that Saturday and mailed it like he said he would.

Anyway, that order was never delivered, even though Judge L. mailed it. Teed was sure that Judge L. mailed it, for he told Teed he did, and Judge L. was as honest as ol' Abe himself. But Teed knew how slow the post office was when it came to delivering the mail.

Teed's mind was snapped back to the present by a blast of cold air hitting him full in the face as he reached for the door to the henhouse. He shined a flashlight on the first nest he came to, the weak beam winking feebly at the darkness. There lay an egg, already burst by the chill of the night. He picked it up. Several hay straws clung to the lump of egg white that had oozed out before the egg froze solid. Teed hurried through his chore, finding several eggs in the same frozen condition as the first one.

The weather was just a tad colder than it was that day when the egg man came to Coaley Creek to buy eggs from the Cornfields, Teed remembered, shivering as he made his way back to the warm house. "Those were the good ol' days," he reminisced.

Maybe that package would still come, someday—after all that time—but the waiting was about to wear Teed's patience a little thin about then....

Soapy-dope

Teed Cornfield hurried back to his seat after evening recess with great anticipation of relating a story to his friends and classmates. He sat down and waited for the rest of the students to take their seats and get settled in for the last part of the school day. Teed hoped that the recess break had not interfered with his concentration and that he could tell another story.

The young storyteller had a good one that he wanted to share with his friends. He hoped to be the first student called on by Mr. Gallmathy to go to the front of the room and tell one that everyone would remember for a long time, maybe the rest of his or her life. He got his wish—the chance to be first. He stood there, grinning happily. With his wide-spaced front teeth he looked like a happy beaver hunting for a tree to gnaw on.

"My story today is called Soapy-dope. This story took place not too long ago, and not very far from here. It so happened that ol' Soapy-dope lived in a chug-hole by the side of the road on the south fork of Bass Creek River one time," Teed began.

Everyone sat as quiet as mummies, knowing well that they were in for a treat. Teed was good at making up stories, they knew.

"Each evening," Teed continued, "just before nightfall, Soapy-dope came out of his chug-hole in the road to sit around and watch the world go by, and oftentimes he enjoyed scaring things and making them run away crying and whimpering, wanting someone to console them in their fright.

"One evening Soapy-dope sat by his chug-hole home, waiting for an unsuspecting victim to come bounding, hopping, prancing, moping, or moseying by his place of residence. The evening was cool, just the right type of weather to make scaring exciting.

"A little rabbit came hippity-hopping along, happy and content with the world and ever'thing in it," Teed went on. "As the furry little feller approached the ogreish Soapy-dope's chug-hole, the mean old varmint set himself to pounce on the timid little bunny.

"'Squeakity-squeak. Squeakity-squeak,' Rabbit sang happily—not a care in the world to bother him, he thought. He hopped along, the happiest little fur ball in the world."

Teed hopped a couple of times, then skipped in front of the class, the way he thought a rabbit would act.

"'Wam-biff-ah!' Soapy-dope shouted, hopping into the middle of the road to block the forward movement of the rabbit."

Teed jumped toward the first graders on the front seats, causing the little fellows to shriek in fear of the mean old Soapy-dope.

Mr. Gallmathy smiled. The little fellows were really scared, he could see. He didn't say anything to Teed, afraid that he might break the boy's concentration in his effort to tell the story.

"Rabbit turned in fright and scampered back up the road toward home," Teed continued. "The little feller was screaming in panic, never looking back until he reached his house. He didn't even look back then, when he got there. He just ran on inside and hid under the bed, shivering and shaking so bad that he almost shook the whole room around him.

"Soapy-dope fell on the ground and laughed, almost falling into his chug-hole. He didn't, though. He gained a good foothold on the solid edge of the hole and held on. With a little extra effort, he pulled himself upright and sat there, impatiently waiting for another victim to come by so that he could scare it and get another good laugh to store in his laughing box. He could store his laughs in his laughing box when he was tickled. Then he could replay them later, maybe when he had more time, like in the winter when the snow was on the ground and his chug-hole was froze over solid.

"Finally, after he had thought that no one else would be coming by, he heard a happy little sound.

"A little fluffy-tailed squirrel came along the road, in search of nuts, most likely. His little squeaky voice belted out a song that only a squirrel could sing. 'Squeakity-squeak. Squeakity-squack,' he sang happily, unaware that there was something nasty nearby that wanted to stop that happy sound and put fear in its place. The little squirrel's tail flitted back'ards and for'ards above its head, forming an umbrella, shading its whole body against the late evening sun."

Teed ran across the room in a skip-jump motion, flipping his shirttail, like the movement of a squirrel's tail. That got a big laugh from the students, setting them up for Soapy-dope's yell, to come later, of course.

"As Squirrel approached Soapy-dope's chug-hole," Teed said, "the troll-faced monster prepared to pounce on the fluffy-tailed critter to give it the scare of its little, short life. It was only one year old—just a baby squirrel—the right age to scare easily, Soapy-dope figured.

"Soapy-dope grinned a big ten-yard smile—almost out loud—as he scrunched around, getting ready to jump.

"'Wam-biff-ah!' he shouted, hopping awk'ardly into the middle of the road."

Again the little ones screamed, startled by Teed's jumping toward them, causing his shoes to strike the floor with a slap.

"Now, let me tell you!" Teed laughed, "Squirrel stopped his happy singing. His tail went straight out like a fuzzy arrow as he changed course in midair, turning around like a weather vane on a barn roof when the wind blows real hard. The little feller scampered back in the direction from which he had come. He didn't stop till he got to his house, where he ran inside. He saw a trapdoor in the ceiling, and right through that trapdoor he went—into the loft of his house. He trembled and shook real bad for a long time before his nerves settled down.

"During all of that, Soapy-dope laughed until he fell over into the chug-hole in the road, hiccuping so hard that he almost choked. Gaining control of his ugly self, he climbed out of that chug-hole and sat on its edge once more, waiting for his next victim. He didn't have to sit and wait very long, I tell you.

"Possum came lumbering along the road, grocery shopping, searching for a road-killed rabbit or something for a quick snack. It was now almost dark—about snack time for Possum. He was happy. So happy that he was trying to sing to show just how happy and excited he was to be alive and kicking around.

"'Lumpity-dum. Lumpity-dum,' he sang, as happy as a possum in his own pokeberry patch." Teed hopped across the front of the room in a lumbering movement, imitating the slow movements of an opossum, which caused the students to laugh, which was what Teed was trying to get them to do.

"And just as Possum approached the chug-hole in the road..." Teed had to stop and laugh a little at what he was going to say next... "he was still singing and hopping along in his slow, deliberate way, still real happy. Right about then, Soapy-dope lunged out in the road in front of Possum and yelled, 'Wam-biff-ah!' causing Possum to put it in an extra-fast gear and skedaddle out of there in a big hurry. He ran all the way home. He went through the door, shaking with fear from what he had seen down there next to that chug-hole by the side of the road. He didn't stop at all. He ran right up the chimney. When he got rid of his fright, he came out with black streaks in his fur. And today possums have black hairs mixed in with white. That's how possums got to be gray 'stead of white."

After the screaming and laughter ceased, Teed continued.

"Soapy-dope just laughed and rolled in the road. He was so tickled that he couldn't get up. Soon his laughing box went dry, causing him to quit laughing. He just hiccuped and heaved like a sick dog.

"Pretty soon, though, he gained his composure and sat up by his chug-hole," Teed said, chuckling. "All at once he saw two lights coming toward him. It was almost completely dark by then. Ol' Soapy-dope was having so much fun scaring things that he didn't realize that it was getting late—almost dark.

"'Aha!' he said excitedly. 'Looks like the animals are gonna be out all night tonight. I should have some real good fun throughout the night. They're even coming out in twos, with lights to see by. That'll make it easy for me to scare 'em real bad.'

"Ol' Soapy-dope didn't know that what he saw coming down the road was a Jeep.

"Maybe the man driving the Jeep was late for work and was in a big hurry to get to his job, or something like that, for he was really pouring the gas to that four-wheel-drive truck."

Teed stopped a few seconds to get his breath, then went on.

"Ol' Soapy-dope was so excited he just couldn't stay still.

"The Jeep came on, bouncing over a bunch of smaller bumps in the rough road. They weren't as big as Soapy-dope's chug-hole. If they had been as big, or bigger, Soapy-dope would've moved into one of them. He was content in the hole he lived in.

"Just as the Jeep got right at Soapy-dope's home, mean ol' Soapy-dope jumped right in front of the Jeep and said, 'Wam....'

"There was a 'thump, thump,' and then all was quiet as the Jeep went on down the road in a hurry. Soapy-dope was as flat as a board, just lying there in the middle of the road next to his chug-hole.

"The next day," Teed went on, after he saw the pleased smiles on the smaller students' faces, "Farmer Joe came down the road in his two-horse wagon, pulled by his pair of high-stepping, dapple-gray horses. They were moving along at a fast clip when Farmer Joe saw flat Soapy-dope lying in the middle of the road.

"'Whoa,' Farmer Joe told his horses, pulling back on the check lines to make them stop. 'There's a good board laying there in the road. Wonder where that thing come from. I can use it on my barn, b'drabbs. The wind blew one off the barn the other night, and now I need a new one. Ain't I the lucky one! B'drabbs! Ain't it a real caution that I've found just what I need?'

"Farmer Joe talked to himself as he got out of the wagon, picked up the Soapy-dope board, and threw it in the wagon. He took the board home and nailed it on the barn. It fit the hole left by the missing board perfectly. And that was the last of Soapy-dope."

"Why did you make up a tale like that 'un?" Tester Seedy asked, breaking the silence. "I know that you're the windiest boy in the world. You could blow up a onion sack and bust it without even straining your lungs."

"That really happened," Teed smiled, almost laughing out loud.

"I know better'n that," Tester continued to argue. "You can't make me believe something as farfetched as that, Teed."

"That's up to you," Teed told his friend. "I can show you the very board that used to be Soapy-dope."

Teed sat down in front of Tester, showing no further interest in the conversation. "Have somebody else tell one, Teacher," Teed suggested, addressing Mr. Gallmathy. "But if no one else wants to tell one, I'm willing to tell you another one."

"Where's that barn that's got a Soapy-dope board in it?" Tester asked, his curiosity not yet sated. "Me and ol' Esker and Satch would like to see it for ourselves. We sorta doubt you on that 'un, my good buddy. I still say that you're lying through your teeth about that. You don't know how to tell the truth."

"Let's listen to another story, Tester," Teed said, trying to stifle a laugh. "I'll take you to see it some Saturday. And I'll take you to see the chug-hole that Soapy-dope lived in, too," he promised.

"That's a deal, ain't it, Esker? But I still don't believe you," Tester replied, settling into his seat to listen to another story, shaking his head in disbelief.

Teed could not keep from laughing.

The Great Debate

It was storytelling time again at Coaley Creek Elementary School that Friday afternoon many years ago. Satch Hood had just finished telling an exciting, action-packed story to his avid listeners.

"Who's next?" Mr. Gallmathy asked after Satch had taken a seat next to his buddy, Teed Cornfield

Everyone looked at everyone else, but no one volunteered.

"Well, if there are no more stories for today, we will get back to our regular classes," Mr. Gallmathy announced, taking a seventh-grade history book from a desk drawer.

"Wait a minute, Teacher," Teed Cornfield sang out, rising from his seat. He walked to the front of the room, grinning all the way. "If no one else has a story to tell, I have a real good 'un if you have time to listen to it. I hope that I'm not jumping the gun and getting in front of someone else—hope I ain't going out of turn. It's storytelling time, so we should tell some stories. We don't want to quit now."

"Now that's more like it," Mr. Gallmathy said, replacing the history book in its resting place in the desk drawer. "Does anyone else have a story? I want to give each of you the chance to tell a story today. Surely Satch and Teed aren't the only ones who want to entertain us. They're good storytellers, but someone else could participate and help them out. It seems that we have only a few students who are willing to tell a story, while the rest of you only sit and listen. Everyone wants to have storytelling time, but only a few tell the stories."

"That's all right, Teacher," Teed said, continuing to grin happily. "I enjoy storytelling hour. And I've got enough stories to last all day and into the night if you want to listen to me tell 'em. I really like to get up here and entertain people. I can talk all night if I have to."

"You don't have to," Mr. Gallmathy told him. "Is there anyone else who wishes to tell a story? Teed needs a little rest."

Blank faces stared back at the teacher sitting in his chair behind the scarred oak desk. No one wanted to interrupt Teed, that is if he ever got started telling a story. Everyone knew that Teed had a storehouse of material to select from.

"Well, Teed, I guess it's up to you. Go ahead with your story if you're ready," Mr. Gallmathy said.

"Okay, Mr. Gallmathy. Thanks for letting me take an extra turn," Teed said, clearing his throat and scuffing his foot on the floor. "Ever'body," he went on, "I've got a real good 'un for you. This story is titled *The Great Debate*."

Everyone sat on the edge of his or her seat, looking toward Teed at the front of the room.

"It so happened," Teed began, "that a real long, long time ago—when animals could talk like people—a rabbit and a possum (the same rabbit and possum that Soapy-dope scared so bad) were looking for a place to sleep after a long night of shopping for groceries and eating their fill. They had just hunted up their food and eaten it right there on the spot—didn't save anything for later when they might need it. I guess that's the way with most all animals, except maybe birds and squirrels and chipmunks.

"The possum," Teed said, "came up to a big holler log deep in this beautiful forest, way back in the mountains, and the rabbit came up to the opposite end of that same log at the very same time. Both of the tired, sleepy animals peered inside the log to see if it was empty, looking each other smack-dab in the eye.

"There was this big, nice, dry pile of leaves right in the very middle of that holler log." Teed stopped and waited for an excited reaction from his audience.

When no one moved or made a sound, Teed went on.

"'It's my log,' Possum decided immediately, letting Rabbit know that he was setting up squatter's rights in the holler log. He hurried as fast as he could to the pile of leaves in the middle of the log. He just ambled along 'cause possums are real slow.

"Rabbit rushed in and sat down near the pile of leaves, ahead of Possum.

"'It's my log, I tell you,' Possum argued. 'I saw it first. I know I was here before you was, Rabbit.'

"'No you was not, and I know that for a fact. You wasn't anywhere near here when I arrived,' Rabbit declared. 'I could see all the way through the log, and you wasn't at the the other end of it, as you say you was.'

"'Oh yes I was,' Possum continued to argue. 'I was here and you wasn't there,' he said, pointing to the opposite end of the log. 'Now,' he went on, 'this is my log 'cause I was here first. You'll have to go out and hunt for another 'un if you want to sleep in a holler log. I tell you, this 'un's mine and I ain't giving it up.'

"'No it ain't, Possum,' Rabbit snapped.

"The two little fellers continued to argue back'ards and for'ards for a while. Then the rabbit had a good idea.

"'Let's settle this thing once and for all times,' Rabbit suggested. 'What I propose is that we settle this debate by seeing who can talk the fastest. The one that talks the fastest will get to sleep in this holler log. What do you say to that?' he asked the slow-thinking possum.

"'All right. I'm real easy to get along with. I'm willing to do that,' Possum said, agreeing.

"Now," Teed went on, "Rabbit smiled right big and reared back to think of what he could say real fast, while Possum rested his chin on his left front paw and grinned. Possums grin all the time, you know," Teed laughed, watching the rest of the students as they sat spellbound by the exciting story.

"Possum and Rabbit sat and thought for the longest while, their minds busy trying to think of something unique to say—that would be real fast—faster then the other one could say something.

"After about five minutes of deep, deep, silent thought, thinking hard enough to stop Possum from grinnin', Rabbit said, 'Well, Mr. Possum, have you thought of what you're gonna say?'

"'Yeah, I sure have, Mr. Rabbit,' Possum answered, stirring from his thinking posture, moving his front left paw from under his chin. 'I've got a good 'un. What about you? Have you thought of what you want to say yet?'

"'Yep, I sure have,' came the quick answer from Rabbit. 'I've got a good 'un, too, but you'll have to go on and say yours first off.'

"'No, Mr. Rabbit, you'll have to go and say first,' Possum came back.

"'You'll have to say first,' Rabbit argued.

"'No, you'll have to say first,' Possum said.

"They argued that way for a while longer. Then Possum got tired of arguing and agreed to go first.

"'All right, I'll say first,' Possum said, real slow like. Then he went on, slower than usual, trying to remember what he wanted to say. 'Great-t-t, gro-o-o-ow, gro-o-o-o-wed-up-p-p ra-b-bit,' he said. He then looked at Rabbit and said, 'Try to cap that 'un, Rabbit.'

"The possum smiled, blew on his paw, and held up a toe, indicating that he was number one.

"'Not bad, Possum,' Rabbit said. 'Now, listen to this,' he went on, talking real fast. 'Whoopie Tom to me laddie,' he sang out, sure that he had won the contest.

"Rabbit looked at Possum, grinning a little rabbit grin. 'Ain't that a whole lot faster than you can talk, Possum?' he said.

"'I guess so,' Possum admitted. 'You won fair and square, Rabbit.'

"'I told you that I could talk faster than you could,' Rabbit reminded Possum.

"Rabbit won the holler log," Teed said, "and Possum had to go look for another place to sleep. As Possum left, Rabbit curled up in the leaves and was sound asleep immediately."

"Where did you hear a story like that 'un?" Esker Seedy asked Teed, breaking the silence after the sudden end to the tale. "I know that you ain't never read something like that in a book. They ain't no such story as that in a book that I've ever read before."

"It's in the beans," Teed answered, touching his temple with an index finger. "My grandpaw, Forrest Cornfield, was a great storyteller. They called my grandpaw "Tree" Cornfield. I guess I got my gift for telling stories after him. It's in the beans," he repeated.

"It's in the genes, Teed," Mr. Gallmathy corrected, smiling at the boy.

"Whatever," Teed replied, taking a seat in front of his good buddy, Satch Hood.

Grandpaw and Ugly

The summer passed quickly—quicker than the Cornfield children could imagine—for Teed and Gillis especially. It seemed only yesterday that school had ended, and it would start again the third Monday in August.

The Sunday before the beginning of the new school year, Teed and Gillis were talking about facing that dreaded first day of school.

"Teed," Gillis said, stacking stove wood in a neat pile and placing it on his arm to carry into the house. The wood-box behind the cast-iron cookstove was empty and the boys' chore was to fill it to the brim. "It's sure gonna be odd without you, Satch Hood, and Esker Seedy in Coaley Creek School with the rest of us this year."

"I dread going over there," Teed replied, striking the chop-block with the sharp axe, sinking the blade into the wooden block, where it would rest until the wood-cutting chore came around once more—the next day. "I hope," he continued, squatting to pick up an armload of stove wood, "that Dad and Mom will let me wait until we move to Blue Domer Creek to start school. That's only about two months. They ought to let me wait. I'm going to talk to them about it."

"I don't think they will," Gillis said. "You'll just be wasting your breath talking to them about laying out of school."

"I'm going to ask them anyway," Teed came back. "I don't want to go over to Lick Fork School for two months and then have to leave for another school. I'll have to make new friends and everything. I know that I'll meet new people and become good friends with them, but I'll miss being with you and my friends at Coaley Creek Elementary."

"You'll have to make new friends when we move to Blue

Domer Creek and go to that big school at Big Onion Gap," Gillis said.

"I know that, Gillis, but I don't want to make new friends and then have to move off and leave them," Teed complained.

"I'd like to be going over to Lick Fork with you, Teed," Gillis sighed. "But I'll have to face that same ol' crowd—no new faces for me."

"But you'll have Tester Seedy and that bunch that you already know to shag around with," Teed grunted, trying to stand up with a big armful of wood that caused him to stumble while trying to keep from falling back on his rear end.

"Esker Seedy and Satch Hood will be there to shag around with over on Lick Fork," Gillis said, waiting for Teed to get straightened up to walk with him to the house.

"You're right, Gillis," Teed said. "But I'm going to ask Dad if I can wait till we move to start school."

"You'll be wasting your breath, Teed," Gillis warned.

Teed had passed from the seventh grade—the highest grade taught in Coaley Creek Elementary School—to the eighth grade. He would have to go across the mountain to Lick Fork Junior High School—for two months—or persuade his parents to let him wait until they moved to start school. He thought the situation over and decided that it would be useless to try to argue his case with his stern parents. Reluctantly, he decided to go across the mountain to Lick Fork School.

* * * *

Teed Cornfield and Esker Seedy headed up the road, on their way to school. They walked briskly along the narrow path that ran across the mountain to Lick Fork School, and talked continuously about numerous subjects. Dogs, hunting, and fishing were their major topics. Had they been tested on those subjects, they would have passed with outstanding marks.

They reached the top of the ridge, where they were joined by Satch Hood, and looked down on the pleasant little valley below. The schoolhouse sat on the side of the hill, above the stream that was Lick Creek. They watched students running playfully about the little structure.

The three boys ambled slowly down the steep hill, talking incessantly and watching the youngsters run helter- skelter in their unorganized games of play.

The schoolhouse showed signs of age and wear. The paint had cracked and peeled in many places, and the rough surface of the peeled paint held the grime from many dirty little hands that had made contact with it over the years of its existence.

Dust, caused by the many coal-hauling trucks which made numerous trips past the edifice, gave it a grayish tint. There was little chance of repairs to the building, since the county school system was consolidating many of the smaller schools to create a better learning atmosphere, or a more convenient implementation of the educational system in the county. The rumor was that one more year would be the life of the school. The parents in the community had fought the very idea of closing such a convenient school, but progress had won the battle of attrition between the parents' organizations and the county school system.

Horseweeds grew at least six feet tall in the turfy sections of the schoolyard, while the hard-packed, grassless spots had a few sand briars in their centers and along their outer edges.

A game of tag was in progress as girls and boys ran about the playground. The larger boys were into a rough game of touch football, playing with a stuffed sock for a ball. There were several small, adventurous lads who were brave enough to enter the game. An occasional scream of pain was a clear indication that some of the kids weren't too sure that they had made a smart decision by entering into the scuffle.

Teed, Satch, and Esker watched as the little children had a grand time playing their games.

"You're it," could be heard as a small boy was able to catch a little girl and touch her, making her the one to chase the other scrambling youngsters.

Teed cut a ragweed with his stub-bladed barlow knife. As he cut the leaves from the stem, a little boy walked up to him and looked on with a puzzled squint.

After the little fellow had stared at the knife and weed for a while, he moved closer to watch Teed cut the leaves from the stem of the plant with smooth, even strokes of the broken knife.

"Hello, little girl," Teed teasingly addressed the curious little boy.

"I'm not a girl, I'll have you know!" the child answered, responding spontaneously to Teed's insolent remark.

"Well, I do see that you're wearing a pair of britches and a shirt. Your hair's clipped short, too," Teed replied, smiling, amused at the disdain the little fellow showed. "I must have overlooked your masculine appearance. You do look somewhat like a boy, after a second glance."

"Don't call me a girl again. If you do that one more time, you will get a thrashing," the tyke threatened, bowing his back and clinching his tiny fists, ready to tear into Teed with a vengeance.

"I'll have to remember that," Teed said, smiling. "I didn't know I was riling a wildcat. Did you, Esker? What about you, Satch? What do you think of this little wildcat?"

"No, I didn't," Esker said, giving the little boy a friendly smile.

"He's sure something else," Satch chuckled.

"How old are you, big boy?" the little one asked, continuing to squint up at the boys. He had already forgotten about Teed's wisecrack.

"Well, I'm sorta old for my age and big for my size," Teed replied.

"What's your name, big boy?" the child asked before Teed could half answer his first question. He seemed to be chock-full of questions.

"My name's Teed Cornfield," was the ready reply. "By the way, who's daddy are you, little feller?"

"Brady Bentley's," the child answered quickly.

"So, you're Brady Bentley's daddy?" Teed laughed.

"No, not that! He's my daddy. You got me all mixed up. My name's Byron Bentley," he replied with a silly laugh.

"I just said that for a joke," Teed said, cutting more leaves from the ragweed.

"What grade are you in, big boy?" Byron asked.

"I'm in the eighth grade," Teed informed the inquisitive little boy.

"How old are you, big boy?" Byron asked a second time.

"I'm thirteen, going on fourteen," Teed answered proudly. "I suppose that I'm a little old for my age. I'll be old enough pretty soon to quit school and wipe the schoolyard dust off my shoes. Then I can bid this place good-bye forever."

"How come you're just in the eighth grade at thirteen, going on fourteen?" Byron asked childishly. He was at that question-asking age. "My sister's in the tenth grade. She's just thirteen, and you're thirteen and just in the eighth grade. Why?"

"Well, I went through school once. I got through too quick the first time. I got through 'fore I was sixteen, so they made me start back over to keep me busy till I get sixteen and get old enough to quit for good," Teed answered. His reply was so convincing that the little boy believed him.

"Did you really?" Byron asked, continuing to squint up at Teed.

"Sure did, little shaver," Teed replied, a thistle-eating grin threatening to rip his face apart.

"I'm in the first grade. I'm just starting for the first time," Byron said seriously. "Who's that ugly boy with you?" he asked.

"You sure have a long way to go to get to the eighth grade like me," Teed told the kid.

"Who's that ugly boy there?" Byron asked again, pointing a little finger at Esker Seedy. "He doesn't look very bright to me. Is he retarded or a slow learner?"

"That's my buddy Esker Seedy. He's all right. Maybe he isn't the smartest friend a person could have, but he's a pretty good pal to shag around with."

"I may be a slow learner, little boy, but when I get it all

learned up, I know it just right," Esker replied. "I don't go around asking silly question and squinting my eyes like a little white rat with red eyes. Why don't you go play with the other little girls and leave us men alone?"

"The little feller is all right, Esker," Teed smiled, patting his friend on the back. "He's little and has to ask questions. All children have to go through that. Don't be too hard on him."

"He looks like a slow learner to me," Byron said, still squinting in his obnoxious way. "My sister says that there are a lot of slow learners in the high school in Big Onion Gap. She doesn't understand why boys and girls can't learn fast like her. You see, she makes the honest roll. That's 'cause she's an *A* student. She's the smartest girl in the school, and smarter than the boys, too. I know that she is, 'cause she told me and Mother and Daddy that she is. That's why I know it for a fact. She gets a dollar for ever' *A* that she brings home on her 'port card. She makes a lot of money that way. I'm just starting to school, and I'm going to make the honest roll, too. My mother said that she will give me a dime for ever' *A* that I bring home on my 'port card this year."

"Why don't she give you a dollar, too?" Esker asked, showing more interest in the conversation between Teed and the little kid.

"Mother says that high school is much harder than the first grade," Byron replied. "My sister has to study about all the time to make those good grades."

"High school may be hard for her, but the first grade is going to be real hard for you," Teed said. "I believe," he continued, "that you ought to hold out for a dollar for each *A* that you get."

"I don't think that I will have to study very hard to make good grades. I'm real smart already," Byron bragged. "I'll get dimes for my *A's*. Mother says that a bunch of dimes will make a dollar, and I can change my dimes for dollars at the bank. My big sister puts her dollars in a savings account at the bank. It draws interest for her. I'm going to put my money in the bank, too, when I turn it into dollars. I want some of that interest." He finally slowed down enough to catch his breath.

"I would like to meet your sister," Teed said. "Since she's thirteen years old like me, I'd write her a love letter, but I don't know her name. What's her name?"

"Her name's Leota Bentley. Me and her have the same last name, since we are brother and sister," Byron said. "Did you know that Buck Skyler and his sister don't have the same last name?"

"Is his sister married?" Teed asked.

"Yes. She married some man with a different name," Byron said.

"That's the reason why she has a different last name. She's married. She changed her last name," Teed told the little boy. "Now, if your sister, what's-her-name, married me, she would be a Cornfield."

"Boy, you sure have a long way to go," Esker said, grinning slyly. "Don't call me a slow learner, 'cause I already knew that, little boy. I already knew that a girl changes her last name when she gets all hitched up in marriage."

"Now, what did you say that your sister's name is?" Teed asked. "I forgot while you were burning the mold off your tongue talking so fast."

"If you had been listening while I was talking, you would have heard me say that it's Leota Bentley," Byron said. "But, we call her 'Lota.'"

"Leota Bentley. That's a beautiful name," Teed said, repeating the name several times just to get the feel of it as he rolled it off his tongue. "Does she like to court? Does she have a sweetheart?"

"I don't know if she courts or not. She has does have a sweetheart, though. She likes a boy named Jack," Byron replied. "She calls him on the phone, and he calls her on the phone, too. Seems like they talk forever when the phone rings. Daddy has to get after her all the time for tying up the line so much. My sister talks about Jack all the time."

"I'll write her a love letter tomorrow," Teed said enthusiastically. "I would write her one today and let you take it to her, but I don't have a pencil and paper. I'll get some this evening when Dad and I go to the school board office to get my books. I'll tell her in my letter that I don't have a phone, but I can write her letters and come to see her and court her in person. I'm sure that she will like that more than talking on a phone to that stupid Jack feller. And your daddy will like it a lot better, too, 'cause the phone will be idle for him and your mother to get calls on. I can see that we'll hit it off just right at the beginning—me and your daddy. You can tell Leota to expect a sweet love letter from a charmer. You can put in a good word for me, since you and I are such close buddies."

"Wait till you see her 'fore you spread on the 'lasses too thick," Esker said, teasing Teed. "She could be a real dog."

"Yeah, she could be as ugly as a mangy hound," Satch Hood chimed in.

"No, she's a girl," Byron replied. "I would know the difference between a dog and my sister. Lota's ears are shorter than a dog's ears is about all the difference that I can see."

"I want her to know just what to expect when I go up to her house to court her. I can explain to her in my letters what a catch she's getting," Teed said, ignoring Byron's reply to Esker. "But I still want to see her up close in person."

"I don't see why you want to court my sister, 'cause she's such a hateful thing and all. She thinks that she knows everything," Byron said. "Why do boys and girls want to court?"

"Well, I see that you are lost on that subject, Byron," Teed laughed. "He's lost ain't he, Esker?"

"He sure is," Esker agreed. "Maybe we have a slow learner in our midst."

"What did you say that that ugly boy's name is?" Byron asked again. "I forgot what you said it was."

"That's Esker Seedy," Teed told the kid.

"Teed and Esker. Teed and Esker, and Satch, too. You boys have the funniest names. They sound like dogs' names," Byron laughed. "Can't your parents afford a dog? I bet they named you dogs' names so they can p'like they have a dog for a pet."

"Why don't you run and play with those little tykes over there and leave us men here to talk alone?" Teed suggested to his new friend. He didn't want to shake the little fellow for downgrading his name. He had fought several battles with other boys to prove that he was just as proud as could be of his unusual monicker.

"Well, I'll leave Grandpaw and his ugly buddies alone," Byron Bentley said, dashing away across the playground. "Look at the grandpaw and his buddies over yonder," he said, stopping near some playing children. He pointed his finger, indicating the three friends standing near the building.

Teed heard the children join Byron, elated, looking in the direction that he was pointing.

All eyes were on the big boys as the children began to yell, "Grandpaw! Everybody look at Grandpaw and his ugly friends." The chorus carried over the entire schoolyard, and soon more kids ran to Byron and chanted with the other little antagonists.

Teed looked at his friends and grinned. "Let them have their fun," he said, chuckling.

A little girl ran up to Teed and asked, "Where is your straw hat, Grandpaw? Why do they call you Grandpaw? You aren't old enough to be a real grandpaw. You aren't even old enough to be a daddy. That little boy that you were talking to is cute."

"Well, I'm not old at all, and I'm not a daddy, or a grand-paw, either. Those kids just thought that I stood out like a grown-up, I suppose," Teed said, smiling at the pretty little girl. "And as for my straw hat, I dropped it where a cow had been and I couldn't wear it this morning," he joked. "Why don't you go and tell Byron that he's cute?"

The little girl blushed, giggled shrilly, and ran to join a group of girls jumping rope.

Teed and Esker sighed in relief as they walked around the school building in search of a secluded spot to sit and talk, while Satch went to talk to a boy he knew.

Teed's mind was filled with ideas which would help him to do well in class. He expressed his built-up hopes to Esker, but his friend wasn't as excited about the school year as

Teed. Teed led the way in a nonchalant walk toward an old horse-apple tree that spread its gnarled limbs over the fence, which kept the cattle in an adjoining field from tramping in the schoolyard. The boys sat down in the coolness of the dew-covered grass beneath the tree.

A little girl rang a bell, ending the children's pre-class play.

"That sounds like Ol' Dancer's come in to be milked," Teed said, rising from the comfort of the shaded grass. "Let's shake a leg and get in there and face the facts, my good buddy," he suggested.

Esker Seedy stretched his skinny body and brushed his tangled hair out of his eyes with dirty fingers without speaking.

The two buddies sauntered slowly to the front of the building, where the rest of the students were lined up to march inside.

The girls stood politely in one line, their nervous minds excited with the very idea of getting a start toward learning something new. The other line was made up of boys, slouched at ease, looking over the nervous girls.

Teed and Esker took a position at the end of the column of boys, behind Satch Hood.

"Who do we have here?" the teacher, Miss Potter, asked, looking at the three boys at the end of the long row of students, a happy smile spreading over her pleasant face.

"That's Grandpaw and his ugly buddies," Byron Bentley commented, giggling.

The rest of the students joined him, the girls giggling, the boys laughing uproariously.

"Aren't you ashamed of yourself, young man?" Miss Potter asked politely, frowning down at the little boy standing in front of her, scuffing his shoe in the dust.

"Not really, ma'am, but I guess that I'll have to say that I am, though, 'cause I don't want a good thumping on my first day of school," Byron said, continuing to scuff the toe of his shoe in the dust in front of the steps.

"You should apologize to the young gentlemen, don't you think?" the teacher asked, smiling—the type of smile that was such a great help in persuading the students to do her bidding.

"What does that big word mean, Teacher?" Byron asked. "This is my first day of school, you see, and I've not had time to learn big words like that yet."

"You must tell the boys that you are sorry for offending them," Miss Potter told him.

"I didn't do that...that word that you said I did," Byron said, continuing to kick up the dust in little puffs as his shoe made contact with the ground. "I just said that they look like a grandpaw and his buddies 'cause they are really old people. I said that Esker Seedy is ugly 'cause he is about as ugly as anybody that I have ever seen before in my whole life."

Miss Potter restored order.

"But you must tell them that you are sorry, and quickly, because we must go inside and begin our schoolwork," Miss Potter ordered. "The rest of you students are making matters worse by laughing at him. Apologize to the boys right now. Tell them that you are sorry for making those unkind remarks."

"Aw, shucks, Teacher, that's all right," Teed said, his face turning red due to the fact that so many kids were staring at him. "You didn't have to make him tromp on his dignity just to apologize to us. We're big fellers—big enough to take care of ourselves without anyone else butting into our affairs. Now, if some big boy had insulted us that way, he would've got a good thrashing, and it wouldn't have been necessary for you to help us out."

"Young man, I try to teach manners and respect along with the school subjects," Miss Potter replied. "I feel that manners and respect are part of the school curriculum, and I expect you fellows to remember that."

"We will, ma'am," Teed promised.

"That's wonderful! Now, let's march into the building and take our seats," she said, pointing a finger at the line of little girls. "We need to get our records prepared. Go to my room; it's the largest one. After I make a few announcements, you will report to your homerooms."

Teed felt that he would like studying this year—in the eighth grade. He especially liked the pleasant teacher. She seemed to be extremely nice. Some of the other students had told him that the previous year she had been very crabby at times. Maybe she was nice because it was the first day of school, and, too, she could have found herself a boyfriend to keep her company and teach her how to be nice. Things could change back to normal, though, and she could become the same old Miss Potter of last year. He would have to wait and see. He figured that he would give studying at the new school an honest stab in an effort to make things work out well.

Miss Potter counted to three, and as she said, "Three," the students marched into the building, beginning with the girls, who walked quietly up the steps, followed by the raunchy boys, who were as noisy as a herd of yearling calves racing for the feed troughs.

When everyone was situated in a temporary seating arrangement, Miss Potter introduced herself.

"I'm Miss Potter, your principal and eighth-grade teacher for this school year. I am sure that we will have a very interesting first semester. I hope that I can be your friend, as well as your principal. If you have problems, I want you to feel free to come to me for help in solving those problems. We have two new teachers with us this year—Miss Baker, seventh grade—Miss Shuller, sixth grade. Let's welcome our new teachers to Lick Fork School."

The two ladies stood as they were introduced, smiling appreciatively upon receiving a round of applause.

After the introductions, Miss Potter quieted the energetic students by snapping her fingers to get attention.

"After I make a few announcements, we will get down to business. We will have a short session today—no lessons. I suppose you will like that."

"Yes, ma'am!" everyone screamed.

Everyone was excited—all except Teed and Esker Seedy. Teed wanted the day to last so that he wouldn't have to work in the cornfield that afternoon, and Esker did not care one way or the other.

Miss Potter sat down at her desk at the front of the room and began to sort a stack of papers and forms.

The students looked the room over in a very apprehensive manner. Some of the eager beginners whispered the letters of the alphabet with which they had already become acquainted. The large letters were attached to the wall above the sectional blackboard. A few partially erased words were on the blocks of slate. Those words were part of the final examinations given at the end of the previous school term.

Teed Cornfield remembered well the examinations which he had taken the previous year at Coaley Creek Elementary School, but there was some eighth-grade subject matter on this board with which he wasn't familiar. He felt that he would become acquainted with the new material soon. He looked around the poorly furnished room.

A large globe sat on the badly scarred oak desk positioned at the front of the room. Names and initials were carved into the desks' tops, giving the rest of the furniture a rugged, worn appearance. A big cast-iron heating stove sat in the corner, its smoky pipes showing their age. Soot had fallen on the top of the already-dusty stove and onto the oil-treated floor. The windows were covered by a heavy layer of dust stirred up by the big coal-hauling trucks as they sped past the structure in a constant convoy. A thorough cleaning of the entire building wouldn't hurt its appearance, and Teed felt for certain that he would be a part of the cleanup detail involved in scrubbing away the dust to see what the original layer of paint looked like.

The morning hours passed slowly and uneventfully. A recess bell, rung by one of the older girls, announced dismissal for a break.

The children filed out the door in an orderly manner.

Teed and Esker were the last ones outside. They went back to the horse-apple tree and sat down on the grass to enjoy a chat.

After about fifteen short minutes of rest, the bell rang once more and the students marched back into the building.

"I should have joined the Army, since I'm gonna have to do so much marching," Esker Seedy complained.

Each student went to his or her designated homeroom after the recess break.

Miss Potter weighed each student. She checked for tooth defects, skin ailments, and body lice. Teed watched her gag when she looked into Esker Seedy's tobacco-stained mouth to check his teeth and tonsils. When she finished her health examinations, she gave each student a list of the required textbooks and wrote the homework assignments on the blackboard, then dismissed the class early, saying, "You may go home, but be sure that you are here by nine o'clock tomorrow morning. If anyone is late for our first class tomorrow, I will take a paddle and dust that person's britches. I expect everyone to have his teeth brushed to a shiny-clean when you return in the morning." She looked at Esker Seedy as she spoke. "Good-bye, students—till the morrow."

Teed, Satch, and Esker walked along the narrow road that crossed the mountain to Coaley Creek.

At the top of that beautiful mountain, Teed looked down at Coaley Creek Elementary School, wishing that he could once more study in that little building and play and have fun with his younger brothers and sister and the friends he had left behind when he passed to the eighth grade.

Mumble-peg

Teed was having a wonderful time at Lick Fork School. He had made new friends, and Miss Potter, he had learned by talking to her, was a very nice, well-informed teacher. The students were different from those at Coaley Creek Elementary School—only a short distance over the mountain—but they were good people to shag around with.

One day Teed, Esker, and Satch were at the horse-apple tree in the corner of the fence surrounding the schoolyard, playing mumble-peg. Teed could hardly keep his mind on the game and keep up with what Esker and Satch were doing for having to drive the pesky little girls away. He had first used threatening words, but that had done nothing to discourage the little ladies. He had just recently resorted to throwing clods of dirt at the innocent little females to try to deter their advances. He wanted them to go pester boys their own ages.

Teed was still waiting for an answer from Leota Bentley, but he had not received even a tiny note, nor had he received an oral message carried by her brother, Byron. He had not reached the point of panic yet, but he was treading on the verge of it.

During one of Satch's turns at trying to flip the dull-bladed Case knife into the ground, Teed was approached by three rough-looking characters.

"Are you Teed Cornfield?" the apparent leader of the group asked as he leaned on the web-wire fence, sucking on a lump bulging his lower lip. Apparently the lump was some type of tobacco.

"I'm Teed Cornfield, if it's any of your business," Teed replied, giving the trio a good scrutiny. He did not like the tone of the leader's voice.

"It's my business, and I'll give you a good lesson to show that it is my business," the stranger replied, threatening to cross the fence by placing a foot in the webbing of the wire, but he did not carry out the outward threat.

"I think I would stay on that side of the fence if I were you, or if you have good sense," Teed warned, his eyes narrowing, looking as mean as he could, expecting and hoping to have a good scuffle. He slowly slid his right hand into his empty pocket as an indication that no one was going to thrash him in the advent that an altercation should happen to erupt.

"What do you have hid in that pocket?" the leader of the trio asked, taking his foot out of the webbing in the fence, almost tripping in his haste to get both feet back on solid ground.

"It could be almost anything in here," Teed replied, moving his hand around in his empty pocket, hoping to worry the stranger.

"I doubt if he has anything in it, 'cause his pants fit too tight to have anything very big," one of the companions replied.

"He don't have anything in there," Esker said. "He's like me," he continued. "He can't afford much to put in his pocket."

"Esker!" Teed yelled at his friend. "I had him worried there for a few minutes, and then you had to go and open your big mouth. Why can't you keep that trap shut once in a while?"

"Who's the ugly guy?" the group leader asked.

"You should know your own name," Teed replied emphatically.

"I was asking about that excuse standing there beside you. My name's Jack Long," he replied with a sneer of contempt, trying to look menacing. "I'm sure that you've heard of me. About everybody knows me around in this neck of the woods."

"You climb over that fence and you'll be Mr. Jack *Short*," Teed threatened. "I'll take you down a notch or two. Then we'll see just how long you are."

Teed planted his feet in preparation for the onslaught that never materialized. "And for your information," he declared, "this young lad by my side is Esker Seedy, my good friend."

In a less intimidating tone, Jack Long said, "Are you the guy who wrote that silly love letter to my girl, Leota Bentley?"

"I wrote a letter to Leota Bentley. I didn't know that she was your girl," Teed replied as coolly as could be. "I don't think you own her, my friend. You might claim her as your sweetheart, but I know you don't own her. I have just as much right to write letters to her and court her as you have. You can't stop me from writing letters to her if I want to write 'em."

"We'll see about that, boy," Jack said, a dash of sarcasm in his voice as he pronounced the word "boy." "If Leota happens to receive another silly letter from you, I'll be back and take this matter up where I'm leaving it today. Come on, fellers," he said, addressing his two cohorts. "We ain't going to find any action around here with this bunch of dudes."

"I'd watch who I called 'dudes' if I were you," Teed shot back.

The three strangers left the fence and walked away, with an occasional backward glance as if they expected to be followed by Teed, Esker, and Satch.

"Don't hurry back," Teed called after the departing boys. "We can do without your smiling faces."

"Yeah!" Esker shouted after the retreating trio. That one word was all that he had to say.

"What do you think of that bunch of curs?" Teed asked, kicking the ground with his sneakers, digging a hole in the soft sod. "That Jack Long will have to grow a little if he thinks he can tell me what to do, where my courting is concerned. I'm more determined now than ever to get to know that little girl. She ain't answered my love letters yet, but there is one thing for certain: she's gonna get a letter from me ever' day of the week, that is if her brother will carry it to her for me."

"I wouldn't worry about that Jack guy," Esker said. "He

ain't nothing to worry about. We can take that citified bunch any time we want to. I want you to know that we are on your side. Dan Cupid has stirred up your heart by causing you to write love letters to a strange girl, someone that you ain't even met yet. Jack Long has stirred up a bunch of boys that he has just met, and I'm sure he'll regret that he ever met us, after we finish thrashing him and his wimpy followers. Did you see that little skinny one with that humpbacked cigarette clamped in his mouth there when they got ready to leave. I hadn't seen him puffing on anything while he stood there grinning like a skinned groundhog—while you and Jack Long went at each other with all that arguing and threatening."

"Yeah, that is a bunch of barrel bottoms," Teed laughed. "Imagine someone trying to tell me that I can't write letters to anyone that I want to. This is America, and in America a person can do anything, as long as it don't hurt somebody else when you're doing it. And I don't think that I'm hurting Jack Long by writing love letters to the love of my life."

"You sure told him off," Esker laughed. "I don't think that he'll ever come around here again, making threats, after the way you put him to going down the road with his tail tucked between his legs."

"That kid with the humpbacked cigarette was a skinny little scuzzer," Teed laughed. "I believe that he is smaller than you are, Esker. I believe you could have given him a good thrashing by yourself. I guess he stunted his growth by sucking on his humpbacked poke rolls. He had to've rolled that one himself, 'cause the factory rolls are real smooth and even."

"I could have whipped him if he hadn't been half that big," Esker joked, grinning, showing his tobacco-stained buckteeth.

"He was a little squirt," Teed laughed. "I believe that cigarette made him almost top-heavy. Did you notice how wormy he looked with that little rumpled smoke in his dirty mouth? I'd say that he's been sucking on cigarettes ever since he got big enough to roll one. He's a good example of what smoking cigarettes will do for a person."

"He could have been carrying it around in his pocket for a few days, waiting for the chance to look mean and tough by smoking it while instigating an argument," Esker said. "You know, we should have chose up sides and whipped them three cowards by ourselves. I would have thwacked that little cigarette sucker while you and Satch took care of them other two wimps. I believe you could have mowed the grass with them. Anyhow, I regret not giving it a try."

"I noticed that you didn't say anything until they had their backs turned, going down the road at almost a trot," Teed said. "How many words did you say to them anyhow?"

"I don't quite know what I said to 'em 'cause I was so mad and het up that my tongue just rattled on, throwing words right and left without me knowing what I was saying. That's one of my weaknesses, and I know that I'm gonna let my mouth running off all the time get me into trouble someday. I'm gonna have to control myself at times like that."

"Yeah, your tongue flaps like a loose-leaf notebook in the wind when you stand up to riffraff like that and tell them off," Teed laughed. "I'm going to take some lessons from you. Maybe then I can stand up to strangers like you do."

"I'm glad that I could set a good example for you and Satch to go by," Esker said as the bell rang, ending the recess period.

"Do you think we should mention this to Judge L. and Cousin Jubal?" Teed asked, thinking about the threats made by the strangers.

"I doubt if we will ever see them again, after the word scuzzing you gave them," Satch Hood said. "But it could be this mumble-peg knife I'm holding."

"Yeah, I guess it could," Teed said, ascending the steps to the classroom. "I believe I'll write Leota Bentley two letters this evening, just for spite."

"Good idea," Esker agreed.

Here's Fly In Your Eye

The morning dawned sunny and calm, a good day for fishing, Teed Cornfield reflected, but he was stuck with having to help with preparations for the family reunion.

Teed's older brothers and sisters had moved away from Coaley Creek when they became old enough to find employment—far from the old home place. And when the big coal company came into the area and bought the Cornfield's farm, Marn, Vann, and the younger children moved to Blue Domer Creek to live. Teed, Clem, and Koodank were the only ones who stayed in the area after they grew up.

Teed looked forward to spending time with his brothers and sisters, and the reunion was about the only time that he got to see them. He was really looking forward to the get-together that day, but the desire to fish was lurking back in his mind, occasionally poking a naughty finger just to tantalize his thoughts.

Teed had done all that he could to help in the reunion preparations, for one day. He had hurried through each chore that his wife had given him, those that she felt that he could do by himself.

"Why don't you look for something else to do?" Zel, his wife, suggested. Teed had married Zel Seedy, who turned out to be a raving beauty, after he outgrew that hate-little-girls age.

Zel assigned Teed to small, easy-to-do chores, knowing well that to get the job done right and on time she would have to jump in and help finish it so she could tackle another one. At least it kept Teed busy and out of the way.

"I think I'm doing rather well—just about as well as everyone else," Teed replied, bustling about the room, doing a rather good job of almost nothing. "I don't think you could do without me."

"That's your opinion," Zel quipped.

Teed and Zel were helping host the Cornfield reunion at their son, Teed Jr., and daughter-in-law, Josie's house down on Bass Creek River, not far from Big Onion Gap.

"Dad, I have several rods and reels in the basement. Try your luck down at the pond," Teed Jr. suggested in a manner pleasant enough for Teed to deduce that his son really wished that he would take his suggestion seriously and leave Zel, Josie, and himself alone long enough for them to finish their work.

They knew that they would never finish reunion preparations if Teed were continuously underfoot, strewing things as soon as they picked them up and put them in neat order.

The pond was down below the house. No matter how anyone looked at it, that body of muddy, murky liquid was still a mere pond. It was an acre or less—probably a lot less than an acre—of a fisherman's paradise. Within its depths swam bluegill, crappie, and bass. And it was said that there were a few very nice lunkers in there somewhere, but Teed had never seen one that size. Teed was a realist, though, and would believe anyone who informed him of the location of a bunch of lunkers until they proved to be unworthy of his believing them.

The pond belonged to a neighbor who lived next-field to Teed Jr. The neighbor granted fishing privileges to the Cornfields for the duration of the reunion festivities, lasting the full three-day Memorial Day weekend.

Teed wanted to see if there were any fish in that pond to brag about, to prepare the visiting members of the family for the moment of truth. So he, being the great outdoorsman, but still referred to by Zel as the greatest couch potato of the decade, took a glancing inventory of the numerous rods and reels that covered one entire wall of the full-sized basement. Teed was really amazed with the number of rods and reels that his son owned. How could the man possibly use all of that fishing paraphernalia? Teed had no idea as to how many rods graced that big wall. He didn't take time to count them. He wanted to get down to that pond in a hurry. The thought of one person owning that many rods, when no one could possibly use all of them at the same time, kept running through his head.

Teed had only one rod and reel combination, and that one was all that he could fish with at a time. He couldn't afford to spend hard-earned money on fishing gear that he would never use. But that didn't mean there was anything wrong with having more, if one could afford it.

Teed Jr. usually bought a new rod or reel each time the moon changed, but that was all right since it was his money he spent.

"Maybe I'm not very good at organizing family reunions, but I'll show that bunch of know-it-alls that I am a good fisherman," Teed mumbled aloud as he bustled about, preparing to leave.

"Get your skillets heated up and greased. I'll be returning *soon*. And I'll be hooked into one of the biggest fish that you have yet to pop your peepers on."

"Yeah, I've heard you say that before, with no evidence of your prowess as an angler. Put your hook where your mouth is," Zel said as Teed prepared to depart company from the bunch of smart alecks.

"I'll make believers out of you all—just wait and see," Teed called out.

With that prediction, he picked up his fishing paraphernalia and stamped toward the door. He stopped to check his tackle box to see what was in it and to see if he might need something else.

"Doesn't that just grab you where it hurts the worst? Zel wants proof of my catch!" he spoke aloud, looking over the contents of the tackle box. *Why do anglers always have to have proof of their fishing reports?* he wondered.

Teed always released his catches to let the small ones grow into big ones and the big ones grow into *bigger* ones. He usually caught numerous small fish. If he were to keep all of those little fellows, other anglers would never be able to catch a fish. He was a true fish conservationist.

Teed had selected from that bunch of great brand-named rods and reels a Zebco 33, his favorite. The Zebco 33, a closed-face reel, won't backlash, and Teed was an expert when it came to backlashing a cast. That was the reason for his selecting the Zebco 33. He also selected a fly rod.

The fly rod that he chose was one with a very limber consistency, the type that he was very partial to. On a limber rod, like the one he had picked out, a set of fish eyeballs feels like a big lunker. Maybe that's why Teed was told there were so many big lunkers lurking about in that murky pond.

"What kind of fly is this one on your line, and is it a good, lucky one?" Teed asked his son.

"It's a little brown one," came a smart-aleck reply from Teed Jr.

"I can see that it's brown," Teed snapped as he stamped out of the house and headed for the pond, bent on proving something that he had committed himself to. He hadn't even checked the fly rod and reel to see if he could compare brand names with the others on the wall.

A butterfly lit on the end of the fly rod and bent it almost double as Teed made his way through the armpit-high grass in the field that bordered the pond. As he fought his way through the tall grass, the fly caught on a blackberry briar. Thinking maybe he had tied into a huge fish—one of those lunkers that Teed Jr. had told him about—he felt the clear line leave the reel with a singing scream.

Teed's forward motion was stymied, and with labored efforts he reeled in the line as he retraced his steps to the point of the entanglement.

As he approached the blackberry briar, Old Dink, Teed Jr.'s English setter, decided that he was needed to help with the snarled line. Suddenly, under Teed's efforts to pull the hook loose, the fly released its hold on the briar and attached itself to the dog's collar.

The line began to play out further as the dog spied a meadowlark and gave chase, dragging Teed through the jungle of grass and briars.

Old Dink should have pointed the bird, but instead he chased after it, his hind feet digging into the soft sod as he tried to narrow the distance between the fleeing meadowlark and himself.

If that dog had been trained to obey on command, Teed would never have been able to get him to sit, but, with a dunderhead like him, the man's first command of "Sit, Dink!" caused the dog to plop down on his behind as if he had made straight *A*'s at obedience school. It looked to Teed like that dog's tongue had run out about three feet of drool-dripping pink ribbon. Dink's eyes were slanted back toward his ears so much that he was just peeping through slits in his forehead.

"Good dog," Teed soothed. "Hold, Dink. Hold, boy." Teed commanded the dog in an almost inaudible voice, in the same tone he had heard his son use while training that setter to point. A grouse's wing tied to a fishing line was how the dog learned to point so well. That was the reason for the twenty-pound test line in the reel, Teed assumed. He had selected the wrong rod and reel. But he would go ahead and use it if he had to. He didn't want to go back up to the house—through that jungle of grass, vines, and briars—just to swap it for a lighter line. Twenty-pound test line would hold any lunker that might tie into it in that pond. It would hold a small one, too—the size that Teed usually caught.

"You surely have learned your lessons well, Dink," Teed said as he continued to commend the big setter while making his way toward the obedient canine. As Teed drew nearer, he could hear the dog breathing hard—in and out with short, whistling sounds—like a wind-broke horse.

Teed knew that Old Dink was so dedicated to his inherited desire to point game that he would sit there and point without breathing, if necessary. But he had never seen a dog with a tongue that long. And, too, he had never seen so much drool come from a dog's mouth. He figured that the dog could almost taste that meadowlark that he had pointed out there somewhere in the grass.

Cautiously, Teed approached the petrified dog. He certainly looked petrified to Teed; now he wasn't breathing at all, and his eyes were completely closed.

Teed stumbled on, trying to keep the line of the other rod and reel from grabbing something and stopping him dead in his tracks, for he had the line from the fly rod wrapped around his left foot. How it got there, he couldn't figure out. He figured that the least pressure from the dog would pull the line tight enough around his leg to throw him for a loop into the briars and grass, and by the way Teed was all trussed up, he would have to call for help. He certainly didn't want Zel to know that he was that inept.

Suddenly Old Dink surged forward. Maybe he fell forward, for he didn't bound away. He staggered on for a few feet, like a drunk man trying to stifle a fall. Finally his eyes opened and his tongue ran back into his mouth—like the cord ran back into Zel's Electrolux when she unpluged it after vacuuming the house, Teed thought.

The hook in that brown fly had straightened out under the pressure of the dog's pulling against it, and the twenty-pound test line had snapped like a banjo string as the hook pulled out of the dog's collar and shot into the tall grass.

Teed hadn't controlled that dog by word command. The line had jerked him to attention when it snarled on a hidden stump.

The grass rippled as Old Dink continued his quest to catch the meadowlark, which by that time was out of the county, headed for the Kentucky border, probably, with a checkered flag flying from its tail feathers, an indication that it had won the race with the big setter.

Teed finally made his way out of the tall grass with a sigh of relief. He envisioned himself as Dr. Livingston returning to his base camp while searching for the source of the Nile. He brushed the grass and flower pollen from his clothes and hair and sneezed several times in an effort to remove the little pollen grains tickling the mucus membranes in his nose.

Old Dink had long since vacated the area, still on the strong scent of that elusive meadowlark.

Teed wondered just how the dog would have reacted had

he come across the spoor of a covey of quail or a ruffed grouse. Teed had seen quail in the yard earlier in the day. They could have been looking for Old Dink.

With the battle of the south forty behind him, and the dog from under his feet, Teed settled down to do some serious fishing. He was in a great quandary, though. He couldn't decide whether to fish with plastic worms and the Zebco, or to try his luck at fly-fishing with the recovered and repaired fly. He made his decision after a series of pauses and looking undecided—first at one rod, and then the other. Finally, he flipped a quarter to decide which rod to use, but to no avail. He missed the quarter on its way back down and watched helplessly as it plopped into the water and sank out of sight in a zigzag descent. So much for that method for making an important decision. He would have to do it scientifically. So, he saved up a good sluice of spittle, spat it into the palm of his left hand, slapped it with his index finger and middle finger, and watched as the larger portion flew in the direction of the fly rod. The big decision was made. How simple! If he had thought of that method first, he would not have lost his quarter. Fishing could be very expensive, he realized.

Teed gently laid the Zebco reel and rod in a safe place to protect it from any danger as he made room to dash about the pond in preparation to cast that brown fly to the serene surface of the murky water.

He gave the rod a few flicks to get the feel of it and to see if the line would feed through the line guards. He then let out a good four feet of line to see if it would work well. He gave the rod another wrist flick, resembling someone beating a rug on a clothesline. The rod made a loud whistling noise as he waved it back and forth above his head. He then released the reel catch and pulled out two or three more feet of line. He prepared to cast to the point where he had seen a big gulp by a lunker as it came to the surface and devoured a mosquito that had fallen into the pond while laying its eggs in the tepid water.

Teed's adrenaline began to flow like the waters of a rushing trout stream back home on Blue Domer Creek when he saw the size of that fish's mouth. He started another whipping session, imitating a lion tamer with his whip snapping to control the animals in their cages. In his excitement he let the line whip as far out into the pond as he could. It plopped on the calm water about eighteen inches from the bank—almost at his feet. Well, he would have to try again. He let out more line and whipped it through the air a few times. That cast wasn't much better than the first. The fly landed in the top of a maple tree behind him. He had the distance down pat, but the direction was off just a tad.

After about twenty minutes of casting and cutting the tops out of the bushes around the pond, Teed could see a little daylight, since he had cleared away about a half acre of brush and trees.

That brown fly surely was a tough one. Its feather and hairs weren't even ruffled. Teed could tell that he would have some good luck as soon as he could get the fly in the water.

Finally, after many, many trials at flipping the line toward the pond, Teed placed it about thirty feet behind him, in a tree that he thought he had already cleared out of the way. On the next effort, though, that confounded fly landed in the water, about three yards from the bank. Teed had improved way over one hundred percent. Things were looking up, and he wasn't looking up into those trees where that brown fly wished to perch.

Teed gave the line a little jerk to imitate a fly trying to escape from the water after having fallen in. Something hit it and gave a tremendous jerk.

Teed began to reel in his quarry. The rod bent almost double as he frantically fought the fish. He couldn't crank the reel very fast, afraid that he might strip the gears out of the sucker. With a lot of grunting and puffing, he got his fish near the top of the water.

There it was—a pair of eyeballs and a streak of dark substance inside a transparent body—about two inches of fighting terror—looking up at the angler. The fish had put up a valiant struggle. Teed released the baby bluegill back into the pond. Maybe it swam away. He couldn't see anything where it was released, only a faint ripple.

The avid angler clipped a few more bushes off about eyeball high to a short goat. He caught two more bluegill and one nice crappie. "Enough for the little ones. Lunkers, look out!" Teed threatened.

The next cast caught in a tree behind Teed. Where did all those trees come from? He couldn't reach the fly from his position on the ground, so he began to jerk on the line, like someone in a tug of war with himself, knowing well that one should never jerk on a hung line. The fly held fast to the limb. Teed figured that the fly would hold a lunker if he could finally tie into one. He had a feeling that time was about to run out for the one he had seen catching mosquitos out near a brush pile in the center of the pond.

If only he could get the tree to give up possession of the brown fly, he would accommodate that big fish with a meal much larger than a mosquito.

The maple tree seemed to be just as hungry as that lunker patiently awaiting Teed's cast.

One final hard tug on the line brought the fly whistling toward Teed. The fly struck him in the face, about an inch and a half below the right eye.

Teed calmly reached up—with shaking hands—and tried to free the barb from his jaw, but to no avail. He was unable to see the point of its penetration, so he sat down to ponder his dilemma. He just had to get that barb out of his jaw before Zel saw it. He was afraid that she might find out that her husband was just a tad inept.

Teed looked into the pond to see if it would reflect his problem. It didn't. The water was too murky.

He began to reel in the line in preparation to make his exit from the old fishing hole. The filament end of the line was hard to see, thereby allowing the angler to reel it in sooner than he expected. As the slack went out of the line, it pulled his jaw up to the side about three inches, giving him a one-sided grin.

Right about then Old Dink bounded out of the brush with

an expression of disappointment on his face. Teed thought maybe the dog wanted to ask a question, although he was still after that meadowlark, still running helter-skelter about the meadow.

Teed was afraid that the big setter might get tangled in the fly line and rip the fly out of his jaw, taking his punctured face with it, so he jumped behind a bush just in case Old Dink might want to be friendly and jump upon him.

The dog didn't even notice Teed cringing behind that bush. He passed on by, sniffing the wind.

Teed retrieved the Zebco and stole toward the house, hoping that the family was still hard at work in their reunion preparations.

"Come here a minute," Teed called to his son as he scaled the stairway from the basement to the main floor of the house.

"Did you land a lunker?" Teed Jr. asked, looking over his shoulder at his father. Then noticing that something wasn't quite kosher, he asked, "Is that a tick on your jaw? They're thick down there by the pond."

"No, it's not a tick, I'm afraid," Teed replied, an embarrassed grin cracking his face wide open.

"You hooked yourself!" Teed Jr. exclaimed. "Hey, Mom, Dad hooked a big 'un!" he called out, laughing hilariously.

"I want to see it," Zel called back. "Make him bring it in for show and tell."

"I hooked myself," Teed said, beginning a lame explanation for his act of awkwardness. He hoped the reporting of his negligence would be a good lesson for others, especially for his sons.

"You didn't!" Zel said, her joviality changing to sincerity.

"I'm afraid I did," Teed replied, looking at himself in the mirror in the bathroom, trying to pull the barbed hook from his jaw. "Son, you'll have to strip that stuff off the hook and run the barb through the skin to the outside and clip it off," Teed instructed, turning to let Teed Jr. check the problem while Josie searched in a cabinet drawer for a pair of side-cutting pliers.

"And, Dad, you used my favorite fly, the *brown* one," Teed Jr. complained, showing signs of regret for letting his dad use it. He continued to strip tyings from the hook.

"I'll buy you another one to replace it," Teed replied, patting his son on the back, trying to console him.

"That's all right, I'll find another one, but that was my *lucky* fly. I should have known that you would lose it, since I'm so partial to it," he said, a hint of a smile playing around his genial face. He turned away momentarily.

When his son turned back, Teed could see a lingering trace of a thistle-eating grin and a twinkle of semi-controlled amusement in his eyes.

"You'll have to have a tetanus shot," Zel informed Teed, looking closely at the mess clinging to her husband's white face. "If you pull that stuff through the skin, you'll have a nasty puncture in your cheek."

"I'll take you to the emergency room at the Big Onion Gap Clinic," Teed Jr. said, taking his Swiss Army knife from his pocket and clipping the line from the hook.

"Why didn't I think of cutting that line?" Teed wondered. "I could have left the rod at the pond until later, and there I had to fight the tall grass while I held the line in my hand to keep it from snagging on something and ripping my face off," he told Teed Jr.

"Well, why didn't you?" Teed Jr. wanted to know.

"Just didn't think of it is all I know," Teed replied. "I guess I've got a whole lot less brains than I should have."

"Well, jump in the car, Dad. Let's get to the hospital as quickly as we can, if you aren't going to let me yank that fly out," Teed Jr. said, hurrying his father. "Mom, if you and Josie are going you'd better shake a leg. Dad and I are on our way to Big Onion Gap."

* * * *

The hour-long trip to the medical clinic was made with as much joviality as possible. Everyone joked about Teed's catch.

Teed Jr. said that his dad had caught a six-foot sucker, and Zel said that he had caught a "largemouth," and she didn't mean a bass.

The doctor and nurses at the emergency room were so nice and caring while they tended to Teed's needs. The doctor removed the fly from the punctured jaw without inflicting the least bit of pain, after having given the angler a shot of novocaine. He asked if Teed wanted the fly for a souvenir.

"No, sir!" Teed replied. "I don't need anything as a reminder of my accident. I have a number of tongue-waggers out in the waiting room to keep the memory alive for a long time without a bedraggled fly to remind me of it."

The nurses joked with Teed about his plight. One asked him when the fish fry would be. His answer to that question was just a bit slow in coming. "As soon as I catch a bigger sucker," he finally responded.

The expiration date hadn't run out on Teed's last tetanus shot. It was still under warranty. He was glad of that, for he had been punctured enough for one day.

* * * *

"I believe I can get in another hour of fishing before it gets too dark to see," Teed said, crawling out of the car upon the return to the house.

"Fishing is over for today, Hon," Zel sternly replied, placing herself in front of the door, barring her husband's entry to the house to get his rod and reel, the Zebco 33.

"That's a fine how-de-do!" Teed said, facing his sweet, precious, easygoing wife. He was just a bit baffled by her behavior. Heretofore, she had never said anything about his fishing trips.

"You could have said, 'Here's fly in your eye,' and it wouldn't have hurt any worse," Teed said, searching her face for a hint that would tell him that she was only joshing. There was no change in that beautiful frown.

Teed wanted to go fishing several times after that most memorable day, but he couldn't find his rod and reel. Anywhere! His face healed up and haired over very quickly, and he hoped he wouldn't have to wait very long before getting his rod and reel back. Surely he'd get them back someday, he figured—then he would take his Zebco 33 and go get that lunker.